shannon stacey

falling for Max

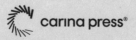

carına press®

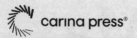

carina press®

ISBN-13: 978-0-373-00229-0

FALLING FOR MAX

For Megan, whose love for a certain 1964 musical
will remain forever inexplicable to me.
Don't ever let anybody try to change you
because you're perfect just the way you are.

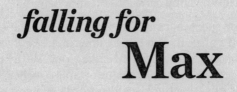

falling for
Max

Dear Reader,

Sometimes a character is meant to have a walk-on role and then exit stage left. Sometimes, though, those characters refuse to stay behind the curtain and keep sneaking back into the limelight.

With no sports bars in Whitford, Josh and Katie needed a place to watch the games in *All He Ever Dreamed,* so Max Crawford came along. With his big-screen television and comfortable couches, Max's house was the place Whitford's sports fans loved to cheer on their favorite teams. But Max intrigued me, and I knew from his first appearance I wanted to see Max fall in love. Tori Burns refused to stay behind the curtain, as well. She came to Whitford to escape her parents' acrimonious divorce and works part-time in the diner just to get out and meet people.

Tori meeting Max and sparks flying came as a surprise to me, and I hope you enjoy reading their story as much as I enjoyed writing it.

Happy reading!

Shannon

New York Times and *USA TODAY* bestselling author Shannon Stacey lives with her husband and two sons in New England, where her two favorite activities are writing stories of happily ever after and riding her four-wheeler. From May to November, the Stacey family spends their weekends on their ATVs, making loads of muddy laundry to keep Shannon busy when she's not at her computer. She prefers writing to laundry, however, and considers herself lucky she got to be an author when she grew up.

You can contact Shannon
through her website, shannonstacey.com,
where she maintains an almost daily blog,
or visit her on Twitter, at twitter.com/shannonstacey;
her Facebook page, facebook.com/ShannonStacey.AuthorPage;
or email her at shannon@shannonstacey.com.

ONE

ON THE FIRST day of each month, Max Crawford made it a habit to compile a list of everything he wanted or needed to accomplish that month. Without a list, he tended to immerse himself in work and then wonder why he was out of mouthwash and the car payment was overdue.

As the calendar ticked over to October, he catalogued which projects he was working on and their due dates. He noted there were two birthdays on his calendar, which meant shopping for and sending gifts to his mother and niece. The furnace needed its annual checkup. And he wanted to find a wife.

After a moment of deliberation, he drew a line through the last item. Then he wrote *find a girlfriend*.

On a separate sheet of paper, he jotted down a list of work supplies he needed to replenish. It took a while, as he had a tendency to jot down the items running low on any scrap of paper near his workstation, including the occasional napkin. Another sheet of paper for the monthly grocery order he'd place online.

Flipping back to the original paper, he amended his list again. Marking out *find a girlfriend,* he replaced it with four simple words. *Go on a date.*

He should probably start small.

Once he was satisfied he wouldn't forget anything

in October, he pinned the pages to the bulletin board attached to the side of his fridge with magnets.

Already on the bulletin board was a calendar sheet he'd printed out so he could write in the sporting events for the month. Post-season baseball. Football. Hockey. Then he'd highlighted the games he'd probably have a crowd for. With no wife and a big TV, his home was the closest thing Whitford had to a sports bar.

Making friends after moving to Whitford, Maine, seven or so years ago had started with his car breaking down. He'd called the only tow truck in town and, when Butch Benoit had shown up, the man had been listening to football on the radio. When Max had apologized for taking him away from the game, Butch had grumbled about his wife rarely giving up control of their ancient nineteen-inch television, so he was used to listening to them on the radio in his shop.

Max told Butch he had a big-screen TV, a living room full of leather furniture and no wife, and the implied invitation had spread through Whitford. Now Max had friends, and those friends had a hassle-free place to watch sports.

It was a system that had always worked well for Max in the past.

A knock drew him to the door and he opened it to let Josh Kowalski in. He was a game day regular and a good friend, so Max had been pleased when he'd called about dropping by. He was holding something wrapped in crumpled newspaper.

"Thanks for letting me stop by," Josh said, walking to the island to deposit the package. "Trying to get away from the lodge on a secret mission isn't easy."

"Sounds intriguing."

"I know you paint model trains, but I'm wondering if it's possible to paint this." Josh unwrapped the layers of newspaper as he spoke. "You know we've done a lot of work on the property, right?"

Max nodded. The Kowalskis owned the Northern Star Lodge, which had catered to snowmobilers for decades, but had recently gone year-round with the opening of the ATV trails into Whitford. Over the last couple of years, the family had done a great deal of renovating and rehabbing around the place.

"I found this half-buried in the back of the barn," Josh continued, peeling away the last layer to reveal an old die-cast Farmall tractor. It was in rough shape, with flaked off paint in some places and years of crud built up in others. "I have really fuzzy memories of Mitch playing with this when we were kids, and it was our dad's when he was a boy."

Max leaned in to get a closer look at the toy. The tractor had definitely seen better days, but it wasn't beyond salvaging. The paint was no big deal, most of the corrosion was on the surface and the tires were still in decent shape. He was used to working with brass, not die-cast metal, but it wouldn't be the first.

"I can do it," he said.

He barely noticed Josh grabbing the paper as he examined the toy, but he heard the crunch as he shoved it into the trash and then the thump of the lid.

"Get a date?"

Max realized too late his garbage can was next to the fridge, where his bulletin board was hung. He winced as Josh leaned closer, squinting. He knew his friend was trying to read the words he'd struck out.

"Probably a good idea, breaking it into smaller

steps," Josh said, and Max couldn't miss the amusement in his voice.

"Finding a date seemed less ambitious than finding a wife."

"Any particular reason why this October is a good time to date?"

Max shrugged, staring at the metal Farmall on the counter. There were still flakes of the original red paint, which would make it a lot easier to match than working from photographs. "Thirty-five seems like an average age for a man to start thinking about starting a family."

"Did you read that in a book?" When he glanced at Josh, his friend held up his hands in an apologetic gesture, but he was smiling. "Sorry. It just seems a little... logical?"

Max was very familiar with people saying *logical* in a tone that suggested the word had negative connotations to it. "I just think it's time to move on to the next stage of my life."

"I get that. But I'm not sure love is something that lends itself to organizational structure." Josh helped himself to a soda from the fridge. "I know it hasn't for any of us."

"It's simply a directive to get out and start meeting people, I guess. I'm not going to meet women here in my house."

"Since the only woman I've ever seen in your house is engaged to me, you're probably right."

Josh's fiancée, Katie, was a huge sports fan and had been Josh's best friend until the guy finally got smart and realized there was a lot more than friendship between them.

"Working from home doesn't give me a lot of opportunity to meet people."

"You should go to the Trailside Diner a few times a week," Josh suggested. "You can meet people, eat good food, and pad my sister-in-law's pocketbook all at the same time."

Max laughed. "That sounds very logical."

"You're rubbing off on me." Josh pointed to the toy. "So you really think you can save that?"

"Absolutely. Do you want it to look like it just came out of the box, or do you want it weathered a little?"

Josh shrugged. "You're the expert."

"I'd recommend restoring it to like-new condition, and I'll research the original decals and everything. Then I'd give it a light weathering so it looks like it was enjoyed by two generations, if you know what I mean."

"Sounds perfect. I'd like to give it to Mitch. As thanks, you know."

Max didn't get out much, but he knew Josh's oldest brother had been the first to return to Whitford when Josh broke his leg and was laid up. When he'd seen what rough shape the Northern Star Lodge was in, both physically and financially, Mitch had rallied the family. Now the lodge was restored to its former glory physically and both the family's business and the town had seen the financial benefit of their work to bring four-wheelers into town.

Reviewing his schedule in his head, Max calculated how long the restoration would take. "I can definitely have it done by Christmas."

"This must be a busy time for you and it's kind of last-minute. I can give it to him anytime."

"This isn't my busiest time and you're a friend," Max

said, and they were words he didn't take lightly. "It's not a problem."

Josh extended his hand and Max shook it. "I appreciate it. I know it'll mean a lot to him. To all of us, actually. I don't want to cut into your dating time, though."

Max recognized the teasing tone and smiled. "I think that's going to be a slow process."

"I'm telling you, you should go to the diner. It's the social center of Whitford. And they make a mean meat loaf."

"Maybe I'll stop in there tomorrow. I need to go into town, anyway." It was a start, at least. Maybe he'd get lucky and meet the perfect future Mrs. Crawford at the town diner.

THE ALARM ON her phone made Tori Burns jump, and she cursed under her breath as she silenced it. Time to wrap up the digital design—mostly of science fiction, urban fantasy and horror book covers—that was her primary income and head to her part-time job. She hadn't been on the schedule at the diner, but Liz, who worked the morning shift, had asked Tori if she could cover for her for a couple of hours.

She changed her faded flannel shirt for a Trailside Diner T-shirt and brushed her hair into a ponytail before walking up the street.

As soon as she saw Tori walk through the door, Liz untied her apron and folded it neatly. She'd been Liz Kowalski until she married Drew Miller, the Whitford police chief, who was sitting at the counter in civilian clothes. Interesting.

"Thanks so much for covering for me," she said.

"Not a problem." Tori took her apron from where

she'd stashed it under the counter and took the order pad from Liz. "Got a hot date?"

Liz looked at her husband, a light blush coloring her cheeks. "Just something we have to take care of. It's been quiet today, so there's nothing to catch you up on."

"Go." It was obvious she was anxious to leave. "Enjoy the time off."

Tori watched the couple leave, hoping her suspicions were right and they were off to the city for a doctor appointment. It seemed as if the entire population of Whitford had been anxiously awaiting pregnancy news from the Millers—to the point Fran at the Whitford General Store was offering bribes in the form of discounts to anybody who could confirm Liz was in the family way.

Liz hadn't been exaggerating when she said it was a quiet morning at the diner. It was more like *dead*. Even though the ATV trail system that had revived Whitford's economy was still open, four-wheeler traffic cut down considerably once school was back in session and families stopped taking weekend trips. And it would be at least a couple of months before the snowmobilers started filling the tables.

But at this time of year, there tended to be what passed for a breakfast rush and then a crowd for lunch. The in-between was very, very slow.

Tori didn't mind, though. She hadn't taken the part-time job at the diner for the money. It had been her way of getting out of her apartment so she didn't turn into a total hermit, and a way to get to know people in her new town. Now, a couple of years later, she was still working there. It was good exercise, she enjoyed the work, and she not only had family in Whitford, but now good friends, as well.

Today, she was restless. Even if she wasn't worried about missing out on tips, being busy made the time go by. Not being busy made it seem like the hands on the clock were moving in slow motion. Working that morning had thrown her off a little, too. She usually did her computer work during hours that aligned more with a second shift, but a lot of authors were trying to get books ready to release for the rush of readers who'd get new devices and gift cards for Christmas. While she was choosy when it came to taking on new customers, just keeping up with her existing clients meant working extra hours. Her hours at the diner were usually a nice break, but standing around straightening sugar packets just so her hands had something to do seemed more like a waste of time than anything.

Her mood perked up when a tall, blond and very hot guy walked through the door. He was dressed in jeans that were just the right amount of faded and a cream cable-knit sweater, and he was alone.

Max Crawford, Whitford's very own man of mystery.

She watched him pause, scanning the empty restaurant, before taking a seat at the counter.

"Are you looking for somebody?" she asked, setting a napkin and silverware in front of him. Maybe he was meeting somebody for lunch. Somebody who hadn't shown up yet.

"No. I was just expecting it to be busier. There isn't anybody here."

"People will start coming in for lunch soon. And, in the meantime, you get all of my attention."

His eyes widened a little and she noticed they were a soft green color. "I…don't know what I want yet."

"Here's the menu." She pulled it from the rack and

set it in front of him. "Do you know what you want to drink? Coffee?"

"A chocolate frappe?"

"Coming right up."

While she made the frappe, Tori watched him study the menu. She'd seen Max Crawford before, but always in passing. Walking by each other on the sidewalk didn't give a girl a chance to really appreciate looks like his.

While the blender whirred, blending milk and ice cream and syrup, she watched him unwrap the silverware rolled in the napkin she'd set on the counter. He folded the napkin precisely in half and then lined up the knife, fork and spoon, fiddling with them until they were just so.

She'd heard a lot of gossip about Max Crawford, but nothing of substance. The whole rumor about him being a serial killer because nobody knew what he did in his basement that required its own security system was more a joke than anything—a crazy story that probably started because people didn't know anything about him.

What she did know was that he hadn't been in the diner during any of her shifts before, so she wondered what brought him in today. And, since she wasn't shy, maybe she'd find out.

After pouring half the frappe into a glass, she set it and the frosty, metal mixing cup in front of her customer. Then she pulled a straw from her apron pocket and handed it to him.

"Thank you. I think I'm going to have a salad with grilled chicken and Italian dressing, please."

"That's not very adventurous."

"I'm not an adventurous sort. Especially when it comes to food."

He said it so seriously, she almost laughed at him. "I'll give your order to Carl. Luckily, he's a great cook, but not very adventurous, either. My cousin Gavin cooks for the afternoon and evening crowd and he's the adventurous one."

She pinned the order slip in the carousel and yelled for Carl, who was probably sitting at the break table doing word searches, then went back to her customer. "So what brings you in today?"

"I was hungry."

If there was any hint of sarcasm or hostility in his tone, she would have taken the hint and walked away. But he had simply answered the question asked of him, and she was nosy. "You came to the right place."

"Made more sense than going to the post office." She laughed and his expression relaxed a little. "It's early yet, but the Patriots are looking pretty good this year."

"I've heard that rumor, but I don't really follow sports at all."

"Oh." He actually looked disappointed.

"Sorry."

"No, *I'm* sorry. I'm not very good at small talk."

Despite her curiosity, she decided to let him off the hook. "Somebody left this week's paper by the register if you'd rather read."

"No." He smiled, and she was struck by how it transformed his face. He had a great smile. "I'd rather talk to you."

She leaned back against the island where the coffeemaker sat. "What do you like to talk about, Max Crawford?"

MAX WASN'T SURPRISED the waitress—Tori, according to her name tag—knew his name. Of course she did.

That was the way of a small town like Whitford. It also meant she was half-convinced he did mysterious things in his basement. The most popular theory, of course, being that he was a serial killer. The few people he'd talked to about it had yet to explain how they thought he made money from such an endeavor.

"With sports off the table," he said, "I don't suppose you're into trains?"

"Trains?" He wasn't surprised when she gave him an odd look. He got those a lot. "I don't really know a lot about trains."

Of course she didn't. Not many people did. "It's a nice day today."

"Wow, we regressed to the weather pretty quickly."

He liked the way her eyes crinkled up when she smiled at him. They were a warm brown color, like hot cocoa, and a little lighter than her hair. She wasn't very tall, but she was nicely curvy and he might have considered asking her if she was in a relationship, but she was also younger than him. He couldn't guess by how much, exactly, but the difference was noticeable to the eye, so therefore probably significant.

"How about the basics?" she asked, and he braced himself for the probing personal questions. First up would be his job, as always. "So, what do you do for a living?"

"I don't kill people in my basement."

She laughed, the sound loud and happy in the empty diner. "I hope you don't take that personally. It's just people being silly and bored and, to be honest, it drives everybody crazy not knowing what you do. I think they spread that story hoping you'll be horrified and feel a need to spill the truth."

"The story amuses me. Especially the holes in it, such as how I'd pay my mortgage with body parts from my basement freezer." He lifted an eyebrow. "So why would I tell people what I do and ruin all the fun?"

"You're my kind of guy, Max."

Even though he knew it was just an expression and meant she appreciated his sense of humor about the issue, satisfaction that this woman liked him flooded through him and made him sit up a little straighter.

The cook called her name and she went to get his salad. Sucking chocolate frappe through his straw, he watched her walk away. Rather than a seductive sway of the hips, there was a happy, positive bounce to her step that he liked.

Maybe Tori the waitress would be a new friend, even if she didn't like sports.

A few people came in while he was eating his salad, which made it hard to have further conversation with Tori. There was a married couple in one booth and two guys having lunch at another table, so it didn't look as if he was going to meet a dateable woman this time.

He left a tip on the counter before going to the cash register to pay his bill. She gave him another smile as she made change. "I hope we'll see you in here again soon."

"I'm sure you will. I've decided I'd like to get out of the house more often." He didn't think it would be a good idea to go around advertising he was looking to meet women with the long-term goal of marriage. The gossip mill would have a field day with that.

"I totally understand," she said. "That's why I started working here, actually. To get out of my apartment and meet people. And I'm still here because I enjoy it."

He'd assumed she worked there because jobs were fairly scarce in Whitford, but she made it sound as if it was something she did for the enjoyment of it rather than financial necessity. Before he could ask her about it, the cook called her name and, after wishing him a good day, she walked away.

Making a mental note to ask her about it next time he was in, which would be soon, he stepped outside. It was time for a haircut, so he left his car where it was and walked up the street to the barbershop. He usually went later in the day, but before most workdays ended, so the wait wasn't too bad. He hoped, with it being closer to lunch hours, it wouldn't be too full.

Katie Davis, Josh Kowalski's fiancée, looked up from the head of hair she was trimming to smile at him when he walked in. "Hey, Max."

"Hi." It looked as if she was almost done with the customer in her barber chair and there was one fellow waiting, which wasn't too bad. He sat in one of the chairs along the big window and looked at the magazines fanned across the table.

None of them interested him, so he leaned back into the curve of hard plastic and watched Katie work. He knew, from all the times she'd been in his home to watch sports, that her father had been the only barber in Whitford. After his death, Rose Davis had hired a man to run her late husband's business, but he'd almost run it into the ground instead. Katie had worked hard to get the education and licensing she needed and then had taken it back. She'd been cutting Whitford's hair ever since.

He wondered what would happen when she married Josh and they decided to start a family. Even if Max liked change, which he didn't, there wasn't another barber to get used to without burning the better part of a tank of gas. Katie was the only one in town.

When it was his turn, he sat in the chair and let her snap the cape around his neck.

"You're earlier than usual," she said.

"I went to the diner for an early lunch. The food's very good there."

She laughed, looking at him in the mirror. Her blond hair was pulled through the loop of a Boston Bruins ball cap and she was wearing a Patriots sweatshirt. Some combination of New England sportswear had been her work uniform as long as he'd been in town. "You sound surprised."

"It's been a while since I was in there. A long while, actually. I like to cook, so I don't eat in restaurants a lot."

"Liz must have been surprised to see you."

"She wasn't there. It was..." He concentrated for a few seconds, but he didn't even have to picture the name tag pinned to the waitress's shirt. It just popped into his head. "Tori. Her name was Tori."

"Huh. I could have sworn Liz had said she'd be working today. I'll have to call her later. So, Max, going to do something wild and crazy today? Want a mohawk? Maybe some colored gel?"

The question would have startled him if he didn't know she was teasing him. She asked him the same thing every five weeks, and he always walked out with the same cut, just a neater version. Not too short, but off his ears and neck.

As he relaxed and let Katie do her thing, he thought about the waitress at the Trailside Diner and how quickly her name had come to him. He wasn't very good at names, as a rule, and he'd just started being able to get the librarian's name right on the first try and without hesitation.

He'd liked talking to Tori and it was good that the diner would, assuming it usually attracted more customers as she'd claimed, become part of his routine for the foreseeable future. He could enjoy her company while trying to meet a woman he'd like to date. Or, more importantly, who would like to date him.

TWO

THE NEXT DAY, Tori slept in until ten, but she woke up feeling antsy and not as well rested as she should have, considering she'd been in bed before two. Maybe it was the dream.

It hadn't been a sex dream—unfortunately—but it had been sensual, nonetheless. She'd woken while it was still dark with a lingering sense of touching and intimacy and just being held. Left with a vague yearning for affection and emotion rather than steamy sex, she'd been unsettled and dozed restlessly, off and on, until her alarm went off.

She couldn't picture the man in her dream, which ticked her off even more. If she was going to ache for a guy's touch, she should at least get to know what the guy looked like. And she didn't want intimacy and emotion. She wanted sex—hot, sweaty and with the least emotional involvement possible.

Shuffling to her coffeemaker without turning on the lights or opening blinds to let the sun in, she hit the button to start the brew cycle. Then, after a quick detour to the bathroom, she powered up her computer and took her cell phone off the charger.

Two missed calls from her mother. Great. The fact they were spaced two hours apart and her mom had chosen not to leave a voice mail told Tori it wasn't an emergency, so she made a mental note to call her back later. Maybe.

She took the phone off the setting that only allowed calls from a few people through, including the diner, Gavin's cell, her aunt's house and Hailey Genest. She used the setting at night and when she was up against a work deadline, but also when she wasn't in the mood to be caught in the center of her parents' drama. Their divorce was final, but their mind games raged on and her affections were the prize. Even the fact she'd packed up and moved to Whitford to stop being their tug-of-war toy hadn't sent a strong enough signal for them to grow the hell up and move on with their lives. So she was moving on with hers.

Once she'd filled her oversize mug with strong, black coffee, she pulled up her email and lost herself in the morning routine of deleting, sorting and flagging some to deal with later. No emergency fires to put out or drama this morning.

When her phone rang, she assumed it was her mother again and almost ignored it. But habit made her glance over and she saw the diner's name on the screen.

It was Liz. "I hate to do this to you, but can you come in for a few hours today?"

She took a few seconds to mentally scroll through her to-do list for the day, but she knew she wouldn't say no. Even though she was always happy to fill in, they didn't take advantage of her and when they asked her to come in outside of her scheduled hours, it was usually for a good reason. But it was odd for Liz to need unexpected time off two days in a row. "I need to jump in the shower first."

"Oh, not for my shift. Ava's not feeling so hot. Paige

is going to come in, but we've been getting a decent crowd for Friday evenings so she could probably use a hand. So if you came in about four, you could help with the dinner crowd and then you and Paige can flip for who goes home when it starts winding down."

Paige would win. Not because she owned the diner, but because she had the most adorable baby girl on the planet waiting at home for her. Sarah Rose was six and a half months old, with the Kowalski blue eyes she got from her daddy, Mitch, and dark hair sticking out all over because it refused to be tamed by one of those palm tree ponytails on the top of her head. Attempts at cute headbands had resulted in them being flung around like slingshots, so Sarah's hair was left alone to be a wild and crazy cloud around her face. Tori really loved that kid.

"I can come in for four o'clock," she told Liz. "Not a problem."

Once she'd finished her coffee, Tori hopped in the shower and rummaged through the clean clothes basket for a Trailside Diner T-shirt. After smoothing most of the wrinkles out—she needed to set an alarm to remind her to fold her clothes, dammit—she pulled it over her head and set an alarm for three. She got some work done, but decided to head to the library before her shift.

Hailey Genest was the town's only librarian and Tori's best friend in town. Thanks to a little misadventure in the woods back in the spring, Hailey had fallen in love with and was engaged to Matt Barnett, the hot game warden in town.

"Oh, thank God," Hailey said when Tori put the books she'd finished on the counter for her to check in. "Millie's next on the waiting list for that book and she calls me twice a day."

"It's not even due for another week."

"Which I tell her twice a day. So what's new?"

"Max Crawford came in the diner yesterday."

"No way! Why was he there?"

She shrugged. "When I asked him that, he said he was hungry."

Hailey laughed. "Katie's at his house a lot to watch sports and she said he's a really nice, funny guy. Paige said he never goes in the diner, though. Weird. If he comes in again, try to find out what he does in the basement."

"Maybe it's a studio where he makes porn videos."

"Alone?" Hailey looked skeptical.

"What? That makes less sense than him being a serial killer?" She tried to picture the shy guy with the slightly awkward conversational style who'd sat at the counter yesterday making porn. Maybe he was shy and awkward when it came to talking because he expressed himself in other ways. Alone. With a camera.

"Have you tried running a Google search on him?"

"Why would I do that? I've seen him around, but yesterday's the first day I've ever spoken to him. Have *you* run a Google search on him?"

"I haven't." When Tori just looked at her, eyebrow raised, Hailey rolled her eyes. "Because Rose said she did and nothing came up. But, now that I think about it, she's not the most computer savvy person in town."

"I have to go to work now. But I'll see you Saturday night, right?"

"Yeah. I already picked the movie and everything.

Hey, can you bring those cookies you made last time? They were *amazing*."

If she could find time to get the refrigerated cookie dough out of the tube and onto the cookie sheet. Not that she'd ever admit it. "Sure."

The diner was quiet at four o'clock and Paige was talking to a couple of customers toward the back, so Tori went out back to the kitchen in search of her cousin, Gavin. He'd been working at the diner for several years, before Tori had moved to town. It had started out as an after-school job, but he was a great cook and Paige had given him the freedom—and ingredients—to hone his craft. The citizens of Whitford were generally okay with being his guinea pigs, but they were suspicious of any foods they couldn't pronounce and had almost boycotted over a tofu incident. It was a meat-and-potatoes kind of town, except for the traditional all-you-can-eat fish fry on Fridays.

"Hey, Tori," he said when he spotted her. He was several years younger than her, with the same dark hair and eyes, and had a younger brother still in high school. "You working tonight?"

"No, I thought it would be fun to roam around the place in a Trailside T-shirt on a Friday night." She laughed and dodged the towel he snapped in her direction. "What's the special tonight?"

"Pork tenderloin with a brown sugar and balsamic vinegar glaze."

She winced. "I wonder how many times I'll be asked what balsamic means."

"I'm appeasing the masses by serving it with garlic mashed potatoes and a choice of creamed corn or the spiced, chunky applesauce they loved last time I made it."

"They did like that applesauce. I ate more of it than I should have myself."

Paige kept a tally sheet next to the register and they made a checkmark on it whenever somebody ordered Gavin's special. Over the years, there were more and more checkmarks, and fewer wasted ingredients. He was saving for culinary school, or at least for a move to a city with more restaurant opportunities, and Paige's support of him over the years was one of the reasons Tori rarely hesitated when the diner needed her, even if it set her back on her graphic design work a little.

Speaking of the boss, Paige walked through the swinging door. "Tori, thanks so much for coming in. I hope it picks up a little or I'm going to feel like an idiot."

"It's fine either way. I swear."

Tori loved her boss. Paige had been passing through Whitford, her car broke down and—long story short—she'd bought the closed-up diner, reopened it and made it her own. When Mitch Kowalski had returned to town to help his brother with the lodge, Paige had made *him* her own, too.

At five, just enough people started rolling in for dinner so neither of them had to stand around doing nothing, although Tori wouldn't call it busy. It would be a long night, but at least Gavin's pork tenderloin was going over well.

Then, at exactly six o'clock, Max Crawford walked through the door. From behind the big coffee machine, she watched him look around the restaurant as he had yesterday.

For some reason, seeing him caused a low hum of anticipation through her body, which she scoffed at. Must have been the porn studio discussion and her dream. It had been a while since she'd treated herself to a fling with a guy, so maybe it was time to dress herself up and drive into the city for a night out.

When he took a seat at the counter, Tori shoved sex out of her mind and went to greet her customer.

MAX HAD OFTEN heard Laundromats were a good place to meet women. He wasn't sure why, since he wasn't one to speak to strangers while folding his underwear, so he didn't imagine women would be any more comfortable doing so. But he'd tried it anyway, using a comforter that didn't fit in his washing machine as an excuse to spend time in the town's only Laundromat.

After spending ninety minutes listening to the life story of a man who was newly divorced, Max had decided the rumor of Laundromats being a good place to meet women was probably started by a Laundromat owner.

So he was back at the diner, perusing the menu and working up the courage to talk to the woman sitting farther down the counter. She looked vaguely familiar to him, and he'd finally placed her as the woman who owned the secondhand store near the bank. He'd seen her on the sidewalk sometimes, setting up sale racks, but he'd never spoken to her. And even if he'd ever known her name, he wouldn't have remembered it.

She wasn't wearing a wedding ring. Granted, that didn't mean much, but it's not as if he was going to open with *your place or mine?* Casual conversation would give him plenty of opportunity to clarify her relationship status before it came time to make a decision on asking her out or not.

He'd left two empty stools between them. It seemed enough to respect her personal space, but not so far away they couldn't have a conversation if she was so inclined. Assuming he worked up the nerve to speak to her.

"Do you know what you want, Max?"

He looked up at Tori, who had her order pad and pen at the ready. Just seeing her friendly smile relaxed him. "What do you recommend?"

"Gavin made pork tenderloin for the special tonight, with a brown sugar and balsamic vinegar glaze. Served with garlic mashed potatoes and your choice of creamed corn or a spiced, chunky applesauce."

He noticed she hadn't actually answered the question he asked. "He made it, but do you recommend it?"

"Absolutely. I taste-tested it myself when I got here so I could give my honest opinion. It's delicious."

"Then I'll try it. With the applesauce, please. And decaf to drink, if it's fresh."

"Paige just started brewing a fresh pot, so I'll grab you a cup as soon as it's done."

When Tori walked away, Max snuck a look down the counter. The secondhand store woman had dark hair cut into one of those smooth cuts that ended just below her chin. She was around his age and she was reading. It was a magazine, but that still counted. He also took note that her bill was on the edge of the counter, along with some cash, which meant she'd probably be leaving very soon.

He cleared his throat and turned his head, making

sure his voice would project to her. "The weather's nice today."

She glanced sideways at him and then, apparently realizing he was talking to her, gave him a brief smile. "Yes, it is."

"It'll start getting cold soon."

"Every year."

She turned her attention back to the magazine she'd been reading, but he wasn't ready to give up. "Do you follow any sports?"

"No, I don't. Sorry," she said, glancing at him again, this time without the smile. Then she turned the page of the magazine and lifted it so there could be no missing the fact she was reading.

Even Max could take that hint. Stifling a sigh, he tried to not think about how quickly he'd been shot down. He wasn't sure what the average time was, but he felt like a guy should get more than three lines.

Tori set a mug of decaf in front of him and he could tell by the kindness on her face, she'd witnessed his lame attempt to talk to the woman. He felt his cheeks heat, so he focused his attention on unwrapping his silverware and setting it on his napkin. "Here you go, Max. It shouldn't take too long for your supper to come up."

"Thank you."

He took his time fixing his coffee because it gave him something to occupy his attention until the secondhand shop lady left. As he sipped it, he heard two female voices coming from a booth behind him, talking in the kind of hushed voices that meant they didn't want to be overheard.

"Muriel says his car is always in the driveway. He doesn't go to work anywhere."

"Maybe he does one of those work-from-home things I saw on the internet."

"It's just weird if you ask me."

Max purposely tuned them out, taking the menu out of the holder to read the dessert offerings printed on the back. He probably wouldn't have anything, but it gave him something to focus on.

It seemed like forever before Tori brought him his meal. It looked delicious, and he told her so while she refilled his coffee cup.

"Gavin's a great cook," she said. "I'm not sure where he gets it from, but I hope he gets to work in a fancy restaurant someday."

"Does that mean you can't cook?"

She laughed. "I can keep myself fed well enough, but I don't have the skill or patience to put together meals like Gavin does. Seems like a lot of time investment for something you're just going to eat."

"I like to cook. Especially after sitting all day, working. It's good to move around the kitchen."

"I know all about wanting to move around after sitting all day."

He remembered meaning to ask her about her employment next time he was in. "Is this a second job for you?"

"Yeah. My primary job is graphic design. Mostly I do book covers. Actually, though I'll design promotional materials for my clients."

That surprised and intrigued him. "Really? So you're an artist, too."

"Too?" She grinned and he realized he'd given her a very big clue.

"I meant in addition to being a waitress here."

"Sure you did."

She went away then to take care of her other customers, and Max dug into his meal. She hadn't been exaggerating about the cook's ability, and Max's reason for being in the diner slipped to the back of his mind as he enjoyed the food.

Since he had nobody to talk to, he pulled out his phone and scrolled through the news apps while he ate. It was part of his usual routine, so he felt less awkward sitting at the counter, eating alone.

When he pushed his empty plate away, Tori showed up with the pot of decaf and he accepted another cup.

"You want dessert tonight?"

"I don't think so."

"I saw you reading the back of the menu earlier," she said. "You know you want some pie. Or the chocolate cake. It's downright sinful."

He didn't bother telling her he'd been reading the menu earlier only to distract himself from being the subject of gossip just by being in the restaurant. "That applesauce was almost like a dessert itself. Like apple pie without the crust."

"I told you so."

He fixed his coffee, aware that the restaurant had emptied out considerably since he'd first gone in. The diner had been a disappointment as far as his plans for the future, but the food was good and he'd possibly made a new friend. It wasn't a total loss.

"Okay, Max," Tori said. "The curiosity's killing me.

You never come in here but, all of a sudden, you've been here two days in a row. What's up with that?"

He probably shouldn't say anything, since it would probably become grist for the gossip mill, but he was probably going to scrap the plan, anyway. "I was trying to find a date."

THAT WAS PROBABLY the last thing Tori would have expected Max to say. Even after witnessing his awkward attempt to strike up a conversation at the counter, she'd assumed he had some other reason for being in town two days in a row and was just trying to be sociable.

He was actually trying to find a date at the Trailside Diner? "Is that why you were talking to Jeanette?"

"Who?"

"The woman reading the magazine."

"Oh. We never got as far as introductions."

Because he'd run through his sports and weather routine and struck out. He really needed to broaden his conversational horizons. "You need help."

"You mean like a matchmaker?"

She snorted. A matchmaker was just one of the many things Whitford didn't have, though there were plenty of women who'd probably claim to have a gift for it. "No. Like somebody to help you be more...dateable."

He thought about it and, judging by his expression, those thoughts weren't good. "I don't think pretending to be somebody I'm not is a good way to start a relationship."

"That's not what I said." She tilted her head. "You think you're not dateable at all?"

"You said I need to be more dateable. Which means I'm less than dateable."

Tori sighed, hoping she hadn't hurt his feelings. He was quite possibly the most literal person she'd ever spoken to. "Do you own a mirror?"

"There's one over the bathroom sink. It came with the house."

It wasn't until the corners of his mouth twitched that Tori realized that, while he might be very literal, Max was also aware of that trait and wasn't above having some fun with it.

"Then you must know you're pretty hot."

That made him smile, and she liked the way his cheeks turned a light shade of pink. "I've been told I'm attractive…until I open my mouth."

Anger pushed through her amusement and for a few seconds she wished she could slap whoever had said that to him upside the head. "You just need to find a woman who'll appreciate you."

"I'd hoped getting out of the house was a step in that direction, but it doesn't matter if I can't make conversation."

"I'll help you." His skeptical look made her laugh. "We can practice different scenarios until you're comfortable approaching a woman and asking her out."

"So you're saying you'll help me find a wife?"

Tori frowned, leaning her hip against the counter. "I thought you wanted to go on a date."

"A date which will, hopefully, lead to a relationship, followed by marriage and kids. Isn't that the point of dating?"

"Some people date to find people compatible for… hooking up."

"That's hooking up. Dating is dating."

It was an unusual conversation to be having. "That seems very narrow."

He shrugged one shoulder. "I see a distinction, I guess. Don't you?"

"I've never really analyzed it, especially since the last thing in the world I want is to get married."

"Ever?"

"Ever. But I'll still help *you*."

"Why?"

She supposed that was a valid question. "Because you seem like a nice guy. I know Katie likes you. I don't like seeing you bummed out just because one woman shut you down. And I like a challenge."

He took a sip of his coffee, probably giving himself some time to think. "How do you think you're going to make me more dateable?"

"We'll spend some time together and I'll get to know you a little better so I can help you play up your better qualities. And, like I said, we can have practice conversations. It'll be fun, like one of those dating makeover shows."

"So that makes you Professor Higgins and me Eliza Doolittle?"

"Huh?"

"From *My Fair Lady*."

"Isn't that some old musical? Like from the black-and-white days?"

"It's not black-and-white. And, no, I'm not old enough to have seen it the first time around, either."

"How old *are* you?"

"How come women can ask men how old they are, but it's poor manners for a man to ask a woman the same question?"

"I'm twenty-seven."

"Now I feel old." He sighed. "I'm thirty-five."

"Prime of your life, Max. The perfect time to find yourself a woman. What do you say?"

"I don't think I'm going to get far sitting at this counter, so why not?"

"I'm busy tomorrow and, from what I've heard, Sundays you've always got a game on. How's Monday evening sound? We can get together at your house, where it's more private."

"That sounds good. I'd be happy to make dinner." He picked up his cell phone. "We should exchange numbers. Do you prefer talking or texting?"

"I guess texting, but talking's easier for longer conversations." He tapped at his phone, then looked up at her expectantly, so she gave him her cell number. She was pulling her phone out of her back pocket when she heard a telltale shutter sound. "What are you doing?"

"I'm horrible with names, so I like to attach a photo to each contact."

"Wouldn't it be better to ask? Then you'd get a nice picture instead of the side of my head while I'm trying to get my phone out of my pocket."

"I'll take another. You can say cheese."

"Smart-ass." When he pointed the phone at her, she was tempted to flip him the bird, but she settled for a saucy smile. Then, just because she'd had to go through it, she took a picture of him with her phone and saved it with his number. "So Monday, about six?"

"It's a date." He grinned. "Not the kind of date I was looking for, but it's a good start."

She definitely wasn't the kind of date he was looking

for, since she liked her relationships to end after a few hours and he was looking for until death did they part.

But he was a nice guy and she had a soft spot for underdogs, so she was going to do whatever she could to make sure Max found his Mrs. Crawford.

THREE

MAX WAS IN his basement by eight o'clock the next morning, ready to get some work done. It had taken him longer than usual to fall asleep but, once he had, he'd slept soundly and he was well rested enough so his hands would be steady.

Sometimes, if he'd had a rough night or drank too much caffeine, his hands would shake and that wasn't good when you were painting HO scale models. It was as though a full-size steam locomotive was zapped by a shrink ray until it fit in the palm of his hand while maintaining meticulous detail, right down to hoses and rivets.

As he looked at the shelf labeled Chesapeake and Ohio Railway, looking for a particular shade of yellow paint, he found himself whistling. It wasn't something he did often, but as he ran the tune through his mind, he realized it was a song from *My Fair Lady*. Obviously, even if he wasn't consciously thinking about it, his conversation with Tori was on his mind.

It was encouraging, having a plan. If not for Tori, he would probably have given up after his failed discussion with the woman at the diner and gone back to his usual routine. Now he was not only going to push forward, but he had the support of a friend.

Because it was a Saturday, Max only worked half a day. He was fairly rigid with his schedule because he'd, in the past, gotten so involved with his work, he'd all but lived in the basement. It hadn't been healthy, so he made himself a schedule that included spending some time aboveground.

He was watching a really bad horror movie while paying bills when his phone rang. Hitting Mute on the remote instead of Pause, because he didn't think he'd miss much, he answered the call. "Hello?"

"Hi, honey," his mom said. "Are you working?"

"Nope. Just doing some bills and stuff." He'd long ago stopped explaining to her he didn't answer the phone while he was working because, no matter how often he did, she still asked him. "How's everybody?"

"Great. The grandkids had a sleepover last night, so we're enjoying the quiet this afternoon." Max's two older brothers had five kids between them, all as rowdy as their dads. "You wouldn't believe how big they're getting. You're coming home for Thanksgiving, right?"

He thought about it for a few seconds. It was the beginning of October so, even if he did find himself in a relationship, it would be too soon for them to spend family holidays together. "I'm planning to be there. How's Grams?"

"She's doing really well, though I think we've finally managed to convince her to give up driving. Her reflexes aren't what they used to be."

That wasn't news. The last time Max had gone back to Connecticut, back in July, Grams had driven up onto the curb and taken out a row of trash cans to avoid a small pothole.

He listened to his mom talk about the family for a while, while watching the horror movie play out silently on the television. His mom usually held up more

than her share of the conversation because Max didn't
really care for phones and his mother didn't care for
long silences. They texted quite often, but she always
called him at least once a month because she wanted
to hear his voice.

"Are you seeing anybody?"

He frowned at the guy with the axe on-screen while
debating on his answer. He wasn't seeing anybody, but
that could change in the near future. "I'm not dating
anybody, but I have a new friend."

"Really?" She drew the word out, sounding pleased,
and he smiled. Since the day Max started kindergar-
ten, his mom had worried about his inability to make
friends. Thirty years later, it was still a big deal.

"Her name is Tori. She's a waitress at the diner where
I went for lunch, but she also works from home doing
graphic design."

"Oh, so she's an artist, like you. How old is she? Is
she smart?"

Max realized she might be getting the wrong idea.
"She's twenty-seven and she seems smart. But she's
only a friend, Mom."

"Mmm-hmm. Is she pretty?"

"She's attractive, yes. And easy to talk to. I like her,
but we're not going to date."

"We'll see," she said, and that was the end of that.

Once she'd rung off with the promise of calling him
again soon, Max unmuted the television, but he didn't
go back to the bills right away. Since the phone was still
in his hand, he pulled up the photo album and tapped
on the picture of Tori he'd taken last night.

Yes, she was definitely pretty. Her smile was one his
mother would have described as cheeky, and it made

her brown eyes crinkle just a little. The picture captured her personality, including her friendliness, and it made him smile.

Max didn't usually take to new people in his life so easily, but he was glad he'd taken Josh's advice to go to the diner. Tori was the perfect person to help him find a wife.

MOVIE NIGHT WAS a long-standing tradition among some of the women in Whitford. The first Saturday night of each month, they'd gather to watch a movie, eat snacks that weren't very good for them and, sometimes, have a drink or two. This month it was Hailey's turn to host, which worked well for Tori. Since they were friends, she'd managed to harass Hailey into grabbing a copy of *My Fair Lady* from the library and substituting it for the Sandra Bullock movie she'd had planned.

She got there early and met Hailey's fiancé on his way out. Matt Barnett was a game warden who, back in the spring, had rescued Tori and Hailey when they got lost in the woods. He'd been on vacation at the time and his scruffiness had gone beyond manly and straight to backwoods hermit. But when he'd moved to Whitford—right next door to Hailey, actually—he'd been transformed into the *hot game warden* and eventually, despite her attempts not to, Hailey had fallen in love with him. They'd been engaged about a month now, and the house next door was once again empty.

Tori crouched to give some love to their black Lab, Bear, looking up at Matt. "Did she throw you out?"

He looked over his shoulder, then shook his head. "This house will be full of women in about a half hour.

I didn't need throwing. Since Liz is coming here, I'm heading to Drew's."

"Beer and baseball?"

"There might be beer, but we're catching up on some paperwork and deciding if we have enough interest in a snowmobile safety course next month."

She wrinkled her nose. "Have fun."

As she neared the open front door, Tori could hear a vacuum running, so she didn't bother knocking. When the screen door closed behind her, she kicked off her shoes and set them on the mat next to Hailey's before heading to the kitchen.

She set the plate of cookies on the counter and snuck a few M&M's out of the trail mix Hailey had made. Then she ate a few more.

"I'm here," she called when the vacuum shut off, so she wouldn't scare Hailey.

A minute later, her friend stepped into the kitchen. "How can a dog leave that much hair all over my house and not be bald?"

Hailey's house was bright and cheery and, before she fell in love with an outdoorsy guy and his dog, it had always been immaculate. Now it was just *really* clean. "How's the addition going? I saw it's all sided now and blends right in with the garage."

"It's almost done. *Finally.*"

Tori had thought it was crazy to extend the garage to add a shower room until she was over one day when Matt got home after a work day that had ended with a long struggle to get a deer out of a bad patch of swampy mud. Then she understood why, even if he stripped in the garage, Hailey wouldn't want him walking through the house and up the stairs to the shower.

Hailey peeled the plastic wrap off the plate of cookies so she could take one. "So tell me, why are we watching an old musical? I've heard that Sandra Bullock movie is funny and I've been waiting all month to watch it."

"Somebody was talking about some professor and Eliza somebody and a makeover, and I was curious. That's all."

"Who was talking about that?"

"Max Crawford."

Hailey's eyebrows shot up. "That's the second time you've mentioned Max Crawford."

"I didn't realize we were keeping track."

"Why was he talking about *My Fair Lady?*"

Tori knew she shouldn't say anything, but Hailey was her best friend. "You can't tell anybody."

She nicked another cookie. "Promise."

"I'm going to help him find a date. You know, help him be more comfortable talking to women."

"This might be a dumb question, but who do you think he's going to date?"

Tori tried to come up with a name, but none popped into her head under pressure. "There are plenty of single women in Whitford. I think."

"Women who'll date Max Crawford?"

Tori frowned at her friend. "What's that supposed to mean? Max is a nice guy."

"Half the town thinks he's a serial killer."

"Oh, come on. Everybody knows that's just a joke."

Hailey shrugged. "Even so, it's kind of weird that nobody knows how he makes his money."

"Probably because it's nobody's business."

"Maybe *you* should date him."

Tori gave her an *are you serious* look. "Really? He's

looking for a wife and you know how I feel about marriage. And if you say I just haven't met the right man yet, I'm leaving. Right after I tell Fran you're the one who keeps rearranging the canned vegetables on the shelf so they're not in alphabetical order."

"You wouldn't."

They heard a knock on the screen door, and then the slight squeak of its hinges. "Hailey?"

"In the kitchen!"

Rose Davis walked in with her daughter, Katie, and a big basket of what Tori knew would be amazing baked goods. It didn't even matter what was under the towel. It would be so delicious, Tori would be hard-pressed not to make herself sick.

"I've been crazy-busy, so I'm claiming credit for half of Rosie's basket," Katie said. "I didn't have time to make or buy anything. What are we watching tonight, anyway?"

"My Fair Lady."

Both women paused, but it was Rose who spoke. "What made you pick that movie?"

Tori tensed, giving Hailey a look she hoped would remind her she'd promised not to tell anybody about her Max makeover.

"I thought it would be fun to have a sing-along." Hailey smiled. "And Audrey Hepburn never goes out of style."

Tori's aunt Jilly showed up next, with Gavin's buffalo chicken dip, followed closely by Liz and Paige, who'd left Sarah home with Mitch. Nola Kendrick brought homemade soft pretzel rods with a sinful cheese dip, and Fran brought a bag of chips and the makings for margaritas.

As the movie went on, Tori realized several things. One, they'd all made fun of the movie choice but, strangely enough, they all seemed to know all the words to the songs.

Two, Liz Kowalski Miller did not have a single margarita. Since she knew Liz usually had a couple of drinks during movie nights and, combined with the mysterious daytime errand Drew had accompanied her on, Tori suspected the town's gossip mill was going to have some good news to chew on very soon. But, since she wasn't sure if Liz and Drew had told their families yet, Tori kept her mouth shut.

And, third—and most importantly—it occurred to her that Nola Kendrick was single. She was in her early thirties and worked at the town hall. Her honey-blonde hair was cut into a soft bob, she dressed somewhat conservatively, and she was a very nice lady. A little on the quiet side, but Tori had only really crossed paths with her when she was at work or at movie nights.

She just might be the perfect woman for Max.

AT FIVE-FIFTY on Monday evening, Max sat at the kitchen island, his hands folded in front of him. As a child, he'd coped with anxious waiting by pacing the floor. When his parents had tried to break the habit by making him sit, he'd drummed his fingers on the table. He didn't particularly like driving his parents crazy, though, so over time he'd learned to sit quietly with his fingers intertwined so he couldn't drum them.

This was the first time he was having a visitor to his home who wasn't a sports buddy. They weren't going to watch a game and munch on potluck snacks. Instead, they were going to have conversations and eat a meal together.

Even though he liked Tori and was already considering her a friend, he wasn't accustomed to playing the attentive host role. And he'd grown up in a family of social extroverts, so he'd always been able to fade into the background and let them do all the talking.

When he heard her car pull into the driveway five minutes later, he walked to the door and went out to meet her, so she'd know to come into the kitchen. Nobody ever used the front door.

"Did you have any trouble finding the house?" he asked, because people always seemed to ask that the first time they had visitors over.

"It's Whitford. Believe it or not, I already knew where your house was. I didn't know it was so cute, though."

"Oh, good. I always dreamed of having a cute house," he said, smiling when she rolled her eyes at his sarcasm.

While he'd made some changes to the interior—notably to the basement—he'd left the outside primarily as it was when he bought it, including the window boxes that had started their lives as cranberry, but had faded to a dark shade of pink. Miniature white-picket fencing lined the walkway and surrounded the shrubbery along the front of the ranch-style home. He assumed it was the flower boxes that led her to use the word *cute*.

"Let me guess," she said. "It all came with the house."

"Actually, yes." He led her into the kitchen, and she looked around in a casual way, as if she was trying not to be too nosy.

"We had movie night on Saturday," she said. "I talked Hailey into showing *My Fair Lady*."

"Ah. So now you get the Professor Higgins and Eliza Doolittle reference."

"Yes, but at the cost of watching one of the worst movies I've ever seen."

Her vehemence surprised him. "While it's not my favorite musical—which admittedly is not my favorite kind of movie to begin with—I don't think it was *that* bad. And I can't be alone or it wouldn't be a classic."

"I don't care if the whole world loved it. The movie sucked, Max. He finally realizes he loves her and wants her to stay and, instead of pushing her up against the wall, kissing her until she couldn't breathe and then banging her right there on the floor, he tells her she can fetch his slippers?"

Something about the way she said *banging her right there on the floor* made it hot in the room all of a sudden, and Max moved to stand on the opposite side of the kitchen island, just in case that wasn't the only physical reaction her words would invoke. It had obviously been too long since his last relationship, which had ended shortly before he left Connecticut.

"I don't think banging a woman on the floor was allowed on the big screen in the sixties," he said.

"But fetching his slippers? She's not a Labrador retriever."

"From the sound of it, I should cross a willingness to bring me my slippers off of my list of desirable qualities in a wife, then?" She simply stared at him for so long, he finally gave in and smiled. "That was a joke."

"I thought it might be. But now I'm wondering if you actually do have a list."

"Of course I do." He paused. "But not in writing because that would be weird."

When she laughed, some of the tension that had gripped him before her arrival eased and he felt like himself again as he led her into the living room, pointing out the bathroom door down the hall in case she should need it later.

"Ah, the infamous couches," she said when she saw the two oversize leather sofas, one a sectional, and the matching recliner. "And that big TV screen."

"They're comfortable. I like a living room that feels lived in, you know?"

"It suits you." Tori flopped in the corner of the sectional couch, which was Katie's favorite seat when she was over for a game. Maybe women liked corners. Something to keep in mind, anyway.

"Thank you."

"So tell me about this list of desirable wifely qualities you have in your head. What kind of woman do you want to date?"

"I'd like to date a woman who's intelligent, friendly and wants to get married and have children. It would be nice if she likes trains, but that's probably asking too much."

She gave him a funny look. "You mentioned trains at the diner, too. Are you one of those guys who chases after trains to take pictures of them?"

"Sometimes. I like trains."

"Okay. What else?"

"That's it."

"Smart, friendly and wants a family? Come on, Max. Brunette? Blonde? Redhead?"

"My previous relationships were with blonde women."

Tori rolled her eyes. "There's a shocker."

"I don't have a preference as far as hair and eye color. Or height or weight." He paused, and gave a little shrug. "I'm just looking for a woman who'll love me enough to marry me and risk having little *odd duck* kids. That's pretty much my list."

FOUR

THE WAY MAX said those words hit Tori, almost like a physical blow. Somebody had sure done a job on this guy in the past and, once again, she wished she could find that person and slap her—or maybe him—upside the head.

She'd heard the phrase used about him, of course. He was a little different from most of the other guys, and it was a shorthanded way of saying so. But the idea of Max believing a woman wouldn't want kids like him made her realize that phrase had burrowed under his skin in a bad way.

"What woman wouldn't want kids with your looks and sense of humor?"

He smiled, and it chased the sadness in his eyes away. "I just need to find her. So where should we start?"

"Well…" It was worth a shot. "It would help if I knew what your job is."

"It would, huh?"

"What people choose to do for a living says a lot about them." Maybe if she kept a straight face, he'd believe she had a logical reason for needing the information.

"It's hard to explain."

"What's your job title?"

"It's complicated."

She crossed her arms and gave him a stern look,

which probably lost some of its effect because she was nestled into the corner of the couch. "Not really. I'm a book cover designer-slash-waitress."

"I guess it would be easier if I just show you."

There was no holding back the victory grin as she, somewhat reluctantly, got off the couch. That corner seat was too comfortable for her own good. "I agree."

She followed him down the hallway to the basement door. When he just looked at her expectantly, she rolled her eyes and then turned her back so she couldn't see the number he punched into the security panel. "Way to show trust, Max."

"There's not much sense in having a security code if everybody knows it."

"I'm not really everybody." When she heard the door open, she turned back to him. "Should I call somebody and let them know you're taking me into your basement?"

"If I say no, will you think it's because you don't need to or because, as a serial killer, I wouldn't want you to do that?"

She laughed. "Good point."

"Also, you'll need to sign a waiver to be on camera. Standard porn-studio rules."

Her mouth dropped open and there wasn't a damn thing she could do about it. "You heard about that?"

"People have a tendency to forget I'm around. For example, if I'm wandering the aisles of the store and Fran gets talking to somebody."

She was going to wring Hailey's neck. Slowly. "That was a joke. You know it was a joke, right? I was trying to illustrate how ridiculous the serial-killer thing is by throwing out another equally stupid story."

"I've heard a lot of theories, but porn studio's a new one."

"I know the gossip's probably a pain, but I promise I can keep a secret. I won't tell anybody—even Hailey—what you do."

"Even if it *is* a porn studio?"

The idea of Max Crawford having a sex room in his basement should have made her laugh, but she felt a flush of heat over her neck. He was a good-looking guy, even if he was totally wrong for her, and it wasn't hard to imagine him naked.

"It would kill me," she said, trying not to sound like a woman who was picturing him naked, "but even if you're making porn, I won't tell Hailey."

He flipped a light switch and she followed him down the stairs. When she got to the bottom, she looked around, shaking her head. Trains. The man seriously had a thing for trains.

"I paint model trains, mostly HO scale brass," he said, as if that would mean something to her.

He went to a shelving unit and pulled out a long, thin green box. After pulling off the lid and peeling back the packaging, he showed her an old steam train engine. It was all brass and, as she leaned closer, she could see it was so detailed, it looked real.

"They usually come to me like this," he said. "This is a 2-8-0, which means the wheel configuration is… never mind. Anyway, it's a Consolidation and I'm going to paint it in the B&M livery. In, uh…the colors the Boston and Maine Railroad used. Sorry. That probably makes no sense to you."

"So you paint toy trains?"

He frowned, carefully replacing the packaging and

closing the box. "They're not toys. Model railroading is actually an expensive hobby, especially if you model brass, which most of my clients do. It's my job to take this shiny engine and make it look real, and I'm not cheap, either."

"Do you have one done I can see?"

He looked pleased that she asked and, after replacing the green box, walked over to a corner and turned on a section of overhead lighting. She saw a platform, done up to look like…land. There was a meadow with train tracks running across it, with woods in the background made of tiny trees. The wall was painted to look like a sky and it was all so well done it looked real. On the tracks sat a lone engine and, unlike the shiny brass one, this one was grubby and looked old.

"This is another 2-8-0, but in Union Pacific livery. See how it looks real?" He went to what was obviously his primary workbench and picked up an engine, which he set on the rails behind the Union Pacific train. "Now look at this one."

She didn't have to be an expert to see the difference. The one from his workbench had been painted, but it looked brand-new. Like a Hot Wheels car. "It doesn't look real. It looks like a toy."

"Exactly. See those pictures?" He pointed to a frame hanging on the wall that held side-by-side eight-by-ten photos.

She moved closer and saw that the pictures were almost identical. A steam train pulling cars along the track, through the woods, with steam blowing out of the smokestack.

"One is a photo of a real engine and one is a photo of the brass model that the client sent me after I painted it. I work from historical photographs of the actual engines and rolling stock the clients are modeling whenever possible."

"That's amazing, Max. It really is. So you didn't paint that one, then." She pointed at the new-looking engine he'd set on the tracks.

"No, I didn't. A gentleman sent that little 4-4-2 to a friend of a friend for painting to save money. I'd hoped to be able to weather it for him with minimal work—and cost—but the paint is bad, especially on the detail work. I'm going to have to strip it down and essentially start over."

"You're such a wonderful artist."

"I have a reputation for quality work in the model railroading community."

"That's very modestly put." She wandered to his workbench, looking at the various tools of his trade. "Why do you hide what you do from people?"

"I have the security system because I'll often have thousands of dollars worth of rolling stock in here, and some of them are hard to replace, to say nothing of my equipment. Then the rumors started and I have to confess, I've enjoyed hearing the theories."

She laughed. "You're a little twisted, Max. I like you."

MAX FOLLOWED TORI back upstairs, feeling pretty good about the evening so far. Even though she didn't know anything about trains, she'd recognized the artistry and skill of what he did, and a lot of people hadn't in the past.

Her eyes had never glazed over with boredom and she'd even asked questions about his process and how he'd gotten into it. His dad's brother had done model cars when Max was a kid and had let him help. His love for trains, love of models and natural aptitude for the painting had all come together and that was that. Because of his meticulous attention to detail and willingness to put in hours of research for historical accuracy, it hadn't taken long for his reputation to spread.

Once he'd closed the door and reset the security panel, he led her back to the kitchen, where she took a seat on one of the bar stools at the island. "It should only take about fifteen minutes to make supper."

"What are we having?"

"Marinated steak and mushroom kebobs, with rice pilaf."

"Uh-oh. What if I'm a vegetarian?"

His brain froze for a second and then kicked into overdrive. He should have asked her if she had any dietary likes or dislikes. Or allergies. He hadn't given any thought at all to her tastes and had simply rummaged through the chest freezer until he found something he thought he cooked particularly well.

"Max?"

"You can probably pick out the steak. Or I will, before I put them on the grill. It'll be a mushroom kebob."

She laughed, and he blew out a sigh of relief. At least she wasn't annoyed with him. "I'm not a vegetarian. I just wanted to see how you'd react."

A pop quiz, he thought. And he felt as if he'd failed somehow. "I should have asked you if you have likes or dislikes in advance."

"Relax. Chances are you're going to have at least the first date, if not two, with a woman in a restaurant where you'll be able to see what she orders. If she's a vegetarian or has any allergies, you'll probably find out at that point. Having a friend come to your house is different than taking a woman out to dinner."

That was true. And if, after a couple of dates, he wasn't comfortable enough with a woman to ask her if she had any food allergies or preferences, it wouldn't bode well for their relationship, anyway. He needed to feel as at ease with his date as he did with Tori in order to have a future with her.

Though he'd had a moment of panic over her fake taste in food, he'd been almost totally free of awkwardness this evening. He'd learned at the diner that talking to Tori was easier than talking to other women. It was going to be very hard to replicate how relaxed he was with Tori, no matter where the date took place.

He fired up the indoor grill that was his favorite way to cook and went to the fridge to get the marinated kebobs he'd assembled shortly before she'd been due to arrive.

"Those smell delicious," she said when they'd been sizzling on the grill for a few minutes.

"Thank you. I enjoy cooking, which is why I rarely eat in restaurants."

"But it's nice to get out once in a while. At least twice a month, maybe. Just to see people and socialize."

"I'm discovering that, and I think I'll keep visiting the diner on a regular basis." He turned the kebobs. "I'll go set the dining room table."

"Do you usually eat in the dining room?"

"No. I usually eat here in the kitchen, unless there's something on TV I want to watch. Then I eat in the living room."

"I don't mind eating here. There's no sense dragging everything to the dining room and back."

He put out two place settings on the island and, when the kebobs were done, laid them out on a serving platter. After spooning the rice pilaf from the slow cooker to a serving dish, he set them out and then realized he may have screwed up the place settings.

He'd set the plates and silverware side by side because that's how the bar stools were—all on one side of the island. But it seemed weird to sit next to her. He felt like he should sit across from her so they could make eye contact while talking.

"That food looks too good to let it get cold, so make up your mind," Tori said. "Either move the stool around to the other side, like you want to do, or sit next to me and pretend we're at the counter at the diner."

"Was it that obvious?"

She shrugged. "You pick an object to look at, as if you're pondering something, and I think you do it so you don't make deer-in-the-headlights eye contact when you're anxious about something."

"You're very perceptive." And, because of that, he chose to sit next to her instead of across the island from her. It was weird how she seemed to see him more clearly than other people, who were usually content to see what he showed them.

"I'm an artist. Rendering emotion through body language and facial expressions is kind of what I do, and I've always been a people watcher."

She helped herself to a kebob and some rice pilaf, and then he did the same. The appreciative sound she made after her first bite of the steak and mushrooms made him feel a small glow of pride. The marinade was one of his own making and it was nice to see somebody else appreciate it.

"We're supposed to be chatting so I can get to know you better," she said between bites, "but this is so good, I don't want to stop eating long enough to talk."

"Enjoy your dinner. We can talk after."

They did make small talk while they ate. Mostly about cooking, which wasn't her forte, and their work. It felt nice to have company during a meal and a renewed commitment to finding a wife hit Max while he carried their dishes to the sink. Tori stepped up next to him at the counter with the serving dishes.

"What are the chances of finding a woman in Whitford who's as easy to talk to as you?" he asked without thinking.

"Sorry, Max. I'm one of a kind." She laughed. "But we'll find you somebody awesome, I promise. I think we should go on a mock date so you're not on your home turf. Next weekend, maybe."

"A mock date?"

"Yes. But we'll pretend it's real. You can pick me up and drive me into the city for a nice dinner." She grinned. "I'll even let you pay."

"I'll feel bad if I take up too much of your social time. You probably have better things to do than hold my hand through the dating process, like finding your own dates."

"I'm not interested in dating, by your definition."

He couldn't wrap his head around that. "But you're very pretty and friendly. And you're funny. Any guy would be lucky to have you. And I bet you'd be a wonderful mother, too."

He wasn't the most socially adept knife in the block,

but even Max couldn't miss the way her mouth tightened and the warm humor left her eyes. With his gaze fixed on the faucet, he wondered where he'd gone wrong.

Maybe she'd been in a bad relationship. Or perhaps she couldn't have children, which meant what he'd just said would be highly insensitive. If he'd hurt her feelings, no matter how inadvertently, he would feel horrible.

He wracked his brain, trying to come up with something to say. Should he ask her what was wrong or try to change the subject? Somehow he didn't think *Hey, how 'bout those Red Sox* was the appropriate thing to say at the moment.

"That's not going to happen," she said in a tight voice.

"Oh. I…" He looked at her and then back at the faucet. "I… Hey, how 'bout those Red Sox?"

THE LOOK ON MAX'S FACE made Tori wince and she put her hand on his arm. "You didn't say anything wrong. It's just something I'm oversensitive about."

He was wearing a blue button-down shirt with the cuffs rolled to below his elbows, and his forearm was warm and tense under her hand. "I must have said something wrong. You were happy and now you're not."

"What you said was a perfectly normal, and rather flattering, thing to say to a woman. I just have issues and those are on me, not on you."

He finally stopped staring at the faucet and faced her. When Max made eye contact, it was intense, and Tori thought some lucky woman was going to drown in those green eyes someday.

"If I say something stupid or something that hurts your feelings, I want you to tell me."

She squeezed his arm and the muscles twitched in response. "I will. Especially if it's about something that might come up in conversation during a date."

"Would you like some decaf? We can go sit in the living room and talk."

"Decaf?" Tori didn't even have the stuff in her apartment. What was the point of coffee with no caffeine?

"It's after 5:00 p.m."

Couldn't argue with that. "Sounds great."

He brewed them each a mug of decaf and gestured toward the sugar bowl before going to the fridge for milk. Since she drank hers black, she picked up one of the mugs and took a sip. He didn't cheap out on coffee, which was one more thing to like about him.

She carried her decaf into the living room and shoved the coffee table closer to the sectional so she'd be able to reach it from the corner. When he walked in and saw what she'd done, he smiled.

"I knew you'd be in the corner seat. It's Katie's favorite spot, too." He sat on the far end, slightly sideways so he could see her, while still being able to set his mug on the table.

"So tell me more about your list of desirable qualities in a wife. I need more to go on than intelligent and friendly, since not many people go searching for cranky, dumb people to spend time with."

"I guess at the top would be openness to a relationship with the hope of marriage and children."

It wasn't a dig, but she hoped he hadn't said it because he was still dwelling on what happened in the kitchen. She'd seen how upset he was by the possibility he'd offended her somehow. "I moved here because my parents divorced and there was so much anger and pettiness and, no matter how hard I tried to stay neutral, they kept dragging me into it. I have no interest in that being my future, so I'll live my life the way I am now. Nobody's responsible for my happiness and I'm sure as hell not responsible for anybody else's."

He looked at her as if trying to read her as well as she seemed to be able to read him, and she escaped his scrutiny by leaning forward to take a sip of her coffee. "I've heard the effect divorce has on adult children is often underestimated, but your reaction seems extreme. Swearing off marriage and motherhood entirely?"

She wasn't sure she could find the words to explain how afraid she was that the same thing that had happened to her parents—whatever it was—would happen to her. The stable foundation of her life had been blown apart and she'd become a weapon wielded by and against the two people she loved more than anybody else in the world.

"It wasn't the divorce," she said. "It was the hatred. Watching my mom and dad turn on each other and try to hurt each other after almost twenty-five years of marriage turned my life upside down. If I can't trust my parents not to tear each other—and me—apart, then… Like I said, I have issues."

"With that much hostility, it must have been rough growing up under the same roof as them."

She rubbed the pad of her index finger over a rough edge on her thumbnail, wishing she had an emery board with her. "There wasn't any hostility. Maybe that's why I'm having such a hard time with it. Even though I'm pretty good at reading people, I didn't see it coming."

"They didn't fight?"

"Not really. Sometimes there was tension and I'd notice they weren't really speaking to each other, but they never fought that I can remember."

"Every couple has disagreements. They probably did you a disservice by hiding what is a normal aspect of any long-term relationship from you."

She gave him a wry smile. "Says the foremost relationship expert in the room."

"Admittedly, I've never been married, as you well know. But I've spent a lot of time around married people, including my parents and sister, and I've had several serious relationships myself. Nobody agrees all the time."

"Really?" She propped her chin on her hands. "Several serious relationships?"

"I believe we're talking about your past, not mine."

"But we're not supposed to be," she pointed out. "I'm supposed to be getting to know *you*, not the other way around."

And one burning question she had was why he'd moved to town seven years ago. As far as she could tell, Max didn't do any of the activities that drew people to Whitford who weren't born and raised there. There was no snowmobile, hunting or fishing gear in the garage and nothing about him screamed outdoor activities.

"How did you end up living in Whitford?" she asked, because the only way to find out was to ask and it would, hopefully, change the subject from her parents' divorce. "I mean, you're from Connecticut and you don't seem to have any ties here. Why on earth, of all the places you could live, did you pick Whitford?"

"*You* picked here."

"Because my aunt Jilly lives here, so I have her and Uncle Mike and my cousins. If I didn't have family here, I probably would never even have heard of Whitford, never mind moved here."

"This was my grandmother's house."

She almost dropped her coffee mug. "What? How did I not know you had family here?"

"I'm not in the habit of telling people my life's history."

"Maybe not, but people here had to know your grandmother. I can't believe Fran or Rose or somebody didn't know her well enough to know her grandson bought her house. Or did you buy it? I just assumed…"

"I bought it." He shrugged. "She was aging and, after my grandfather passed away, my mother started worrying about her. It got really bad when they started talking hip replacement but, financially, Grams couldn't move to Connecticut to be near my mom until she sold this house. Unfortunately, the market had tanked and nobody even looked at it."

"So you bought it and moved up here to the middle of nowhere so your mom could take care of her mother." Tori felt an urge to sigh, but she squashed it. That was so sweet.

"Gram couldn't put off her surgery any more. Since I lived alone and already ordered most of my purchases online, there was no reason I couldn't move to Whitford."

He said it in a very matter-of-fact way, but Tori didn't think his decision had been purely rooted in logic. Online shopping was one thing, but moving hours away from your entire family to a place where you had nobody was another, especially for an introvert like Max. Obviously he loved his mother very much.

Then another thought occurred to her. "Did you come visit your grandparents? When you were a kid, I mean."

"A few times, but my dad and Gramps didn't get along very well."

Tori sipped her drink, studying Max over the rim of her glass. He was not only a puzzle, but he was one of those "spilled milk" puzzles where the pieces were all the same color and all a person had to go on were the slight variations in shape. She'd never had any patience for those kinds of puzzles, but she found Max a lot more intriguing than five hundred pieces of spilled milk.

She'd heard a lot of gossip about him, but she'd never heard anything pre-dating seven years ago, when he'd moved into town.

"What's your grandmother's name?"

The corners of his mouth twitched. "Grams."

"Funny."

"Caroline Dobson."

Tori waited for him to elaborate but, of course, he didn't. His tendency to answer questions with only the information requested was probably why she hadn't heard this story. She highly doubted Fran had ever said, "Hey, Max, you wouldn't happen to be related to a woman named Caroline Dobson who used to live in Whitford, would you?"

Before she could ask more questions, he set his empty mug on the table and leaned back against the cushions. "Smart, kind, patient and, of course, wants to be a mother."

"What?" She was lost.

"My list of desirable qualities in a wife. That's what we're supposed to be talking about, right?"

"You said it would be nice if she liked trains, but it's not necessary, and I assume the same goes for sports. And it would be nice if she's attractive, but also not necessary. You are not a picky man."

He shrugged. "We don't have to enjoy the same things. And her looks are secondary to the traits I listed."

Tori sighed and shook her head. "Maybe I'll pick up on some bad habit of yours or something when we go on our mock date but, right now, I can't for the life of me figure out how you're still single, Max."

His smile and the way his eyes crinkled would weaken any woman's knees. "Hopefully not for long."

FIVE

On Wednesday, Max got a call from Josh inviting him to join him and Drew at the diner for lunch.

Josh had told him once they should grab some lunch together away from the televised sports, just to talk, but that had been back while he was trying to win a bet with Katie to see who could discover what went on in the basement first. Since Max wanted Katie to win, he'd taken her downstairs to show her his work space and Josh had run down after them, just in case the serial killer rumor was true. As far as Max knew, they hadn't told anybody else. But before that, when Josh had suggested lunch, Max had told him he wasn't very good at small talk and left it at that.

Since then, he received invitations from his friends on a regular basis, but he almost always begged off, using work as the obvious excuse. He was most comfortable being one of the guys in his own home, with a game on the television to keep everybody entertained.

But this phone call coincided with his plan to get out more, so at one o'clock, he walked into the Trailside Diner for the third time in a week. He looked around, saw Josh and Drew at a booth, but kept on looking.

He didn't see Tori. And when, a moment later, Liz Miller stepped out of the kitchen in a Trailside Diner tee with an apron on, he felt a pang of disappointment. It was probably good that Tori wasn't working, since she probably had jobs backing up on her computer thanks to taking an evening off to spend with him, but he couldn't deny he'd been hoping to see her.

When he walked over to the table, it was Josh who moved over, so Max slid in across the table from Drew. The chief was in his police uniform, so was presumably on a late lunch break.

"Hey, Max," they both said almost at the same time.

"I hope you weren't waiting long." They'd said *about* one o'clock and he wasn't sure if that meant a few minutes before or a few minutes after, so he'd timed his arrival for exactly one.

"Just got here." Josh passed him a menu.

Even though he already knew what he was going to order, Max read through the menu because the others were. And when Liz came through with their drink orders, he asked for coffee like the others. It felt a little strange, since he was used to cracking beers with these guys and yelling at refs on the television. Without the sports, this was weird.

Liz returned with three mugs of coffee and, once she'd set them down, she took out her order pad. "What are you guys having today?"

Max asked for a grilled cheese on wheat with fries, thankful it wasn't a complicated order because Liz seemed more interested in exchanging smitten looks with her husband than what he wanted to eat. Josh went for a burger and Drew ordered a salad with grilled chicken. Obviously with a side of flirtation, Max thought. Drew winked at Liz and she blushed before walking away from the table.

Josh made a sound of disgust in the back of his

throat. "What's with the googly eyes? You've been married awhile now. You should be over that by now."

Drew grinned, shrugging at the same time. "Can't help it. I'm a happy man."

"I'm a happy man, too, but I don't make googly eyes at Katie in public. You should… Oh." Josh looked at his sister, who was refilling coffee mugs at the counter, and then back at her husband. "Is she? Are you?"

Max was lost. He'd assumed Drew was referring to their presumably lively sex life as newlyweds, but Josh's reaction seemed a little out of line for that. Despite Liz being his sister, Josh had to know she and Drew were making each other happy, so to speak.

"We're not supposed to be telling anybody yet."

When Josh leaned across the table, almost knocking over his coffee in the process, to slap Drew on the shoulder, Max got it. Liz was expecting a baby.

"Congratulations," Josh was saying. "I can't believe you're going to be a dad. I can't believe my sister's going to be a *mom*."

"Congratulations," Max said.

"Thanks. We've been trying for a while and…I can hardly believe it."

"Rose knows, right?" Josh held up both hands, as if fending something off. "Please tell me you told Rose first."

Drew laughed. "Rose and my dad know. Other than them, we didn't want to tell anybody yet, but I guess we're not very good at keeping secrets."

"Even I know you can't keep secrets in Whitford," Max said.

Drew snorted. "I don't know. You do a pretty good job."

"True."

Drew knew what Max did because he was the police chief and he'd shown a strong interest in what secretive and lucrative business one of his citizens was running from a basement. That wasn't surprising, so Max had filled him in and headed off any unnecessary suspicion on the part of the Whitford Police Department.

"When's she due?" Josh asked.

"Mid-May. I can't even believe it's finally happening."

Looking at the obvious joy on Drew's face, Max felt a strong twinge of envy. He couldn't wait to have children. Little ones he could share his life and his passions with. Toddlers with little wooden train sets running around the kitchen floor, even though they'd be tripped on, because it was the only room without carpeting. Following real tracks until they found a train coming through. They'd get out of the car and wave to the engineer as the lights flashed and, if his kids were lucky, they'd get to hear the whistle blow.

Then there were sports to watch and books to read and favorite movies to share. He could teach them how to cook and how to organize their schoolwork for maximum efficiency.

He felt like he'd be a great dad.

The other two men talked babies for a few minutes, and Max kept a smile on his face when Josh flagged his sister down to offer hurried congratulations in a low voice. Somehow he'd imagined having lunch with "the guys" would have gone much differently.

Max was glad when their food came because it gave him a reason not to say too much. The discussion moved from Liz's pregnancy to work to the Northern Star ATV

Club, which oversaw the four-wheeler trails that had helped revitalize Whitford's economy.

"We need to revamp the website," Josh was saying. He was the club's president and Drew's dad was the trail administrator. "And get a real logo, not the clip art we've been using."

"That won't be cheap," Drew said.

"I know, but it needs to be done. And once we get the logo, we can sell hats and sweatshirts and stuff. Maybe offset the cost a bit. I hate spending the money, though."

Max set down his coffee mug. "Have you thought about asking Tori for help?"

"Tori?" Josh shook his head. "Can't say that I have."

"She's a graphic designer. Book covers mostly, but this kind of job would probably be easy for her."

"I knew she did something on the computer, but not what. I was hoping you, being an artist, could give us a hand, actually."

"Two different kinds of art, unfortunately. I'd gladly help if I could, but design is beyond me."

Drew shrugged. "It was worth a shot. But you think Tori would do it?"

"I don't know if she *would* do it, but I think she *could* do it."

"Since you know about her work, you and her must be friends, huh?"

Max was pretty sure he could guess where Josh was going with that. "Yes, we're friends."

"Maybe you could run the idea by her? See if she'd be willing to come up with a logo for us. And maybe one of those banner things for our website and Facebook page?"

"I could give her a call."

"Appreciate it," Josh said. "I know you don't ride, but we're glad to get whatever help we can."

"You should come out with us sometime," Drew added.

Max laughed. Meeting them at the diner for lunch was one thing. Riding an ATV through the woods was quite another. He could barely ride a bicycle. "Maybe. Someday."

As the conversation went back to trail conditions and increased ATV traffic with the upcoming Columbus Day weekend, Max thought about his promise to call Tori.

He'd do that later, when he got home, and hopefully not disturb her while she was working. Or maybe he'd text her. He'd have to give some thought to how long the conversation would be before he figured out the best way to contact her.

He'd prefer to call her, though. Texting seemed too impersonal for asking a favor and, besides that, he liked the sound of her voice.

WHEN TORI'S PHONE CHIMED, she gave it a quick sideways glance. Phone calls she let go straight to voice mail, but she didn't have the willpower to not peek at the preview on the lock screen.

It was from Hailey. *Books! Let me in.*

She grabbed her phone and typed in *coming* as she walked across the apartment. Two years ago, when she'd rented the apartment in the old brick building that housed the bank, they'd told her the buzzer system didn't work, but that they'd get around to fixing it.

She was still waiting. But it wasn't that big a deal. Anybody who wanted to visit was somebody who already had her cell number, so whoever it was would simply text. It might have been a problem for deliveries, but nobody delivered in Whitford.

Except for the library, apparently.

After jogging down the stairs, she opened the glass door that was tucked into a recess at the other end of the building from the bank's entrance.

Hailey ducked inside, bringing a gust of autumn air with her. "I can't believe how chilly it is tonight."

"You didn't walk here from the library, did you?"

She held up a tote bag. "With these? My car's two spaces down."

Tori took the bag. "Are you coming up or do you have to get home?"

"I'm coming up, but I'm not staying long. Matt called me a little while ago and he's running late."

Once they were upstairs, Tori emptied the tote onto her kitchen table. Two new romances, a new horror, and an older horror title Hailey had ordered for her through interlibrary loan.

"You have trouble with returning your books on time, so read the ILL book first because the fines are higher."

Tori smiled and put it on top of the stack. "Yes, ma'am. You're so hot when you use that librarian tone. I bet Matt thinks so, too."

"I had my hair up in a bun the other day and shushed him and ended up naked on the living room floor."

Tori wouldn't mind getting naked on the living room floor. Sadly, it had been a while since her last good tussle and, the way things were looking, it would be a while before she had somebody to be naked with.

Hailey sat on the edge of the couch. "So how's *Operation—Makeover Max* going?"

"I had dinner at his house Monday night."

Hailey's eyes narrowed. "Did you go in the basement?"

"We had steak-and-mushroom kebobs that would blow your mind. He's a wicked good cook."

Flopping back against the couch cushion, Hailey sighed. "You went in the basement and you're not going to tell me what's down there."

"I didn't say that."

"You tried to divert me with talk of food. If you hadn't gone down there, you would have just said no."

"Unless I enjoy torturing you."

"Did you learn how to do that in Max's basement?"

Tori laughed. "You're funny. But, seriously, the kebobs were amazing."

"I'm your best friend, remember?"

"I seem to recall that you came in the diner, bummed out that all your friends were in love and, when I said I had no interest in falling in love, you decided we should be friends."

"And now we're besties." Hailey gave her a winning grin.

"But now *you're* in love and you'll be getting married next summer. So by your own reasoning, shouldn't I find a new best friend?"

She frowned. "No. If you find a new best friend, you can't be my maid of honor."

"Matt said your color scheme is camo."

"I'm ninety-five percent sure he wasn't serious about that."

"Regardless, I promised Max I wouldn't tell anybody what's in the basement."

Hailey thought about that for a moment. "But you didn't promise you wouldn't tell anybody what's *not* in the basement?"

"Really? Do you think if he was killing people down there—and he was dumb enough to show me—that I wouldn't have called Drew from my car as I was laying rubber to get the hell out of there?"

"I was thinking more along the lines of porn studio. Because that would pay better. I assume, anyway. When I help the high school kids research career choices and projected incomes online, I've never seen either of those endeavors listed."

"Imagine that."

"Fine. What *can* you tell me about Max Crawford?"

"He's a nice guy. Good cook. Has a comfortable couch."

Hailey's eyebrows shot up. "Really? I'd like to hear more about that."

"About the comfortable couch? It's a sectional. Leather that's just right amount of beat up so it's like butter. The corner is my favorite."

"And what did you do on the couch?"

"I sat on it."

"Come on, Tori. Did you or did you not make out with Max?"

She blew out a breath and shook her head. "I did not. I told you, I'm helping Max find a date. Ultimately, he wants to find a wife."

"You know…if you had a husband, then I wouldn't have to feel guilty about making you be my friend and then falling for Matt."

And here it came. "I don't want a husband. Marriage isn't my thing."

"Because I'm your best friend—at least for now—it's my job to tell you that swearing off marriage forever because your parents divorced is weird."

It went deeper than that. The most solid thing in her life had blown apart and turned her parents into two people who cared more about hurting each other than they did making sure she was okay. It was a betrayal of everything she'd believed about her life and she was *not* okay.

"I don't believe in happily ever after anymore" was all she said. It wasn't the first time they'd had this conversation and Hailey knew how she felt.

"But what about Matt and me? You did a pretty good job of pushing me toward him for somebody who thinks we're going to turn on each other someday."

How she'd gotten herself in this no-win conversation, Tori couldn't remember, but she wanted to kick herself. "It's different for you two. You're perfect for each other, and you're both good people. Even if, God forbid, you did break up, you'd never use your kids as weapons against each other."

"If it can be different for me, it can be different for you."

Obviously there was some logic to Hailey's statement, but Tori shied away from analyzing it too closely. If she thought about committing to a man and allowing him into her life and her heart, she felt almost physically ill. The thing about a couple being together for twenty-five years is that they knew the soft spots—where to hit to inflict the most emotional hurt.

"I'm enjoying my life the way it is" was all she said,

and it was the truth. "And I won't find a new best friend just because you went and fell in love. I draw the line at wearing camo, though."

"Okay. How do you feel about blaze orange?"

AFTER MUCH DELIBERATION, Max decided to contact Tori at six that evening. She was the one who'd suggested that time for their dinner, so he felt he could safely assume that would be the time least disruptive to her work. He was taking a chance on interrupting her dinner, but he'd get right to the point if that was the case. Sitting on the edge of the sofa, he pulled up her number and hit Call.

"Hi, Max."

He liked cell phones. They removed that awkward need to announce one's identity to avoid the embarrassment of being a minute or two into a conversation and hearing *Who is this?* "Hi, Tori. Am I interrupting you?"

"Nope. I just finished eating, so I'm cleaning up before I go back to work for a few hours."

"You said you prefer texting, but phone calls for longer conversation. I don't want to tell you how much time I spent going through how I thought our conversation might go to determine if it would constitute *longer.*"

When she laughed, he leaned back against the sofa and got comfortable. It was something he couldn't quite put his finger on, but when she laughed at him, it's because she thought he was funny. There was nothing mocking or scornful about the sound.

"There's no mathematical formula," she said. "Just don't be offended if you go to voice mail. If I'm at the diner or working at my computer, I don't usually answer phone calls, but I can't seem to resist text messages. So what's up?"

"This is slightly awkward."

"Are you calling to cancel our mock date?"

Even though he heard the amusement in her voice, the need to assure her that wasn't the case was urgent. "No! Not at all. I'm looking forward to it. For the practice, of course. I need the practice."

Her soft chuckle touched him in a way that was almost physical, and he held the phone just a little bit away from his ear. He needed to focus.

"Relax, Max. If you have to try too hard to make a woman like you, then she's not the woman for you. Now, what's awkward?"

"Josh and Drew invited me for lunch at the diner today."

"Really? At this rate you're going to be a regular soon. You might even turn into one of those guys who has a very particular seat at the counter and refuses to sit anywhere else."

"That would be rude," he said. "If somebody was sitting at that spot, would I just turn around and leave?"

"You'd be surprised. Sometimes the regular will ask the person sitting on his stool to move over one. And there's one older gentleman who kind of looms and stares, which is creepy. But he comes in at the same time every morning, so we've started making sure nobody sits in his spot."

"I don't foresee myself becoming that rigid about which seat at the counter I occupy."

"Just one more reason to like you. Let's get to the awkward part."

"During lunch they were talking about the ATV club.

They need a professional logo and a website banner, but I explained to them that's not my kind of art. I suggested they ask you."

There were a few very long seconds of silence. "You volunteered my services?"

"Of course not. I didn't tell them you'd do it. I suggested they ask you if you'd be willing to help." He knew it was an important distinction.

"And they said?"

"They suggested I ask you because you're my friend."

She sighed. "I'll send Josh an email and see what they're looking for. If I can't do it, I can at least connect them with somebody who can."

"Thank you. I hope I didn't impose too much on our friendship."

"You didn't. I do need to get back to work, though. I've worked enough extra hours at the diner, so I need to chain myself to the computer for a few days."

He knew the time she spent with him was also taking away from her working time. "I understand if you want to cancel our date. Mock date. I know you're busy."

"No way. You and I are going to go out and have a good time. It's all part of the plan. So you'll pick me up about four-thirty?"

"At four-thirty, yes." Driving into the city meant starting an evening date a little earlier than was the norm.

"Okay, I'll see you then."

Once they'd hung up, Max pulled her contact info up again and looked at the picture he'd taken at the diner. She was very pretty, even in her work T-shirt and ponytail, so he was going to have to put his best foot forward on Saturday, even if the date was only pretend.

Even he knew a man looking like a schlub didn't take out a woman as beautiful and vivacious as Tori.

SIX

TORI LET LOOSE a string of curses and used a balled-up tissue to scrub the lipstick off of her mouth. Between working at the diner and the time spent at her computer, she hadn't been outside enough and she was too pale for that color. Rummaging through the plastic bin that held her makeup, she dug up a simple lip gloss she liked and called it good.

It wasn't even a real date. She knew that, since she'd reminded herself of it often enough over the course of the day, but she couldn't stem the slight buzz of excitement she'd woken up with. Mock or not, she was going out for a nice dinner with a very handsome man whose company she enjoyed.

That was reason enough to look forward to the evening. She didn't need to read anything else into it, or she'd drive herself crazy.

She stood in front of the full-length mirror that hung on the inside of her closet door. There weren't many opportunities to dress up in Whitford, so she might have gone a little overboard for the occasion. The dress was her favorite, a solid plum that was cut so well it didn't need any further adornment. But in deference to the season, she'd topped it with a black cashmere cardigan and tall black boots that hid her warm tights. With her hair blown out and framing her face, she thought she looked pretty damn good.

A glance at the clock told her she was almost out of time, so she kicked the closet door closed and grabbed the black leather wristlet she'd tossed on the bed earlier. She suspected Max would arrive at exactly four-thirty, which didn't leave her much time to finish getting ready.

At 4:32, she realized she hadn't told Max how to get in.

The buzzer doesn't work, she texted. You have to text me you're here and I'll come down.

I'm here.

Trying not to picture him standing outside her door for two minutes, wondering if he'd been stood up or was doing something wrong, she grabbed her bag and hit the lights on her way out.

When she opened the door at the bottom of the stairs, she almost laughed out loud. He was in a crisp black suit, with a blinding white shirt and black tie. "Did you come straight here from a funeral?"

He looked down at himself. "This suit is a classic. Maybe I should have worn a different tie."

"I'm not sure a different tie would help. It's a nice suit, by the way. Just a little severe. Is this how you always dress for a date?"

He fiddled with the cuff of his coat, lining it up perfectly with the cuff of the white shirt, all the way around his wrist. She recognized that he was feeling off-guard, but she resisted the urge to smooth it over by talking.

"You're wearing a dress," he pointed out a few seconds later.

"Yes, but it's a sundress, not a cocktail dress."

"It seems impossible to dress to complement you

if I don't know what you'll be wearing. And, since I haven't lived under a rock my entire life, I know asking a woman what she'll wear when she agrees to a date isn't the way to go."

"You don't dress for me. You dress for the date. For example, if the restaurant you're going to is nice, but doesn't require reservations, maybe not the full dress suit."

"Should I go home and change?"

She laughed, shaking her head. "Of course not. That suit looks *very* good on you and I won't mind being seen on your arm at all."

When he turned his body and held out his arm, elbow bent, she bit back the urge to point out it was an expression and she hadn't meant it literally. But she looped her arm through his and rested her hand on his forearm. There was something to be said for a guy with nice manners.

When he tucked her arm against his body, pulling her slightly closer as they walked to his car, she tried not to think about how warm and solid his body was. Her arm was pressed just below his ribs and there wasn't a lot of softness around his middle. They didn't have a gym in Whitford and she didn't remember seeing any equipment in his basement, but he obviously found a way to stay fit.

When they reached his car, he freed her arm so he could open his door for her, and then he put his hand on the small of her back to guide her as she stepped off the curb.

The contact, slight as it was, almost made her stumble. Between the affection dream, as she thought of it, and the way his hand on her back sent a warm flood of yearning through her, she must be starving for physical contact more than she thought.

This was Max. Yes, he was incredibly attractive, but he was a sweet, geeky guy she'd felt sympathy for when he bombed trying to talk to Jeanette and she was helping him find a date. No—she was really helping him find a *wife*.

There was no way she was having any sexual feelings toward Max, no matter how good it felt when he touched her.

She sat on the edge of the passenger seat, thankful when his hand fell away, and then turned, pulling her legs in. In the time between him closing her door and sliding into the driver's seat, she took a few deep breaths to steady herself.

Max was not for her. Or, rather, she was not for Max. She would be tempted to invite him upstairs after dinner, but he—or rather *they*—were on a mission that fun, casual sex had no part in.

"It's a power seat," he said as he started the car and put it in gear, "so if you'd like to adjust it, the control panel's on the side."

"It's fine, thank you."

The car was quiet as he navigated through town and hit the main road, and she wondered if he even realized his radio was turned off. A little music turned down low wouldn't be a bad thing.

She let several miles pass, trying not to fidget, but the silence was too much. As tempting as it was to fill it, it was Max who needed to make the effort. "This would be a good time for small talk."

His fingers tightened on the steering wheel. "I'm not very good at small talk."

"I know that, but what we have going on here is called an *awkward silence* for a reason."

He turned the radio on, and it took all of Tori's will-power not to laugh at him. "That's not what I had in mind. Try to come up with something to talk about that's specific to me."

"You're often humming or singing. I've noticed it before at the diner, if you're making coffee or something else that's fairly mindless."

Tori sighed and looked out the window. That wasn't exactly what she'd had in mind, either. "Most of the time I don't even realize I'm doing it. I guess I do it while I'm working."

"You were singing just now."

"Does it bother you?"

"Not really, I guess. But it would probably be less noticeable if you sang the same song the radio's playing."

"I don't know that song."

"What kind of music do you prefer?"

"I'm a country girl."

He cringed. "Yee-haw."

"Wow, what an incredibly original thing to say. Let me guess…you like classical and jazz."

He pointed at the radio. "Does this sound like classical or jazz?"

"I don't know what that is."

"It's The Who. This is… You have horrible taste in music. There. That's something specific to you."

She laughed and, after another shake of his head to show his disbelief she hadn't recognized the song, he joined in. He spent the rest of the drive quizzing her about bands and songs, feigning shock when she recognized one. It probably wasn't great first-date conversation, but they laughed a lot as the miles passed.

Once he found a space in the restaurant's parking lot, Max hurried around to her side of the car and opened her door. She should probably warn him that not everybody was into chivalry and he shouldn't say anything if his date opened her own door before he could get there.

"The space is kind of tight," he said before she had a chance to speak. "I want to make sure you don't ding the other car with my door."

Oh, Max. "You're a true romantic."

He held out his hand to help her out, while keeping a firm grasp on the door so it wouldn't open any further, and she placed her palm against his. Fingers closing around hers, he gave a little tug.

He hadn't been kidding about the parking being tight and with her on her feet and him guarding against door dings, there wasn't a lot of space between her body and his. How she was going to get by him without full body contact was a mystery.

She heard him breathe in deeply. "You smell like fruit."

This time when she laughed he only gave her a puzzled look, which made her laugh harder. He put his hand on her shoulder and pushed her sideways enough so he could close the door, then hit the button on his fob to lock the car.

"That was a compliment specific to you," he said in a confused tone that did nothing to dampen her amusement.

"Was it a compliment? It was hard to tell."

He offered his arm and she took it, trying to compose herself as they walked across the parking lot.

"I was trying to tell you that you smell nice."

She squeezed his forearm. "Then just say that. You didn't need to be so specific."

"So my specific compliments should be vague."

Stopping him before he could open the door to the restaurant, she turned to look up at him. "Just be you, Max. The woman you marry has to love you for who you are, and I shouldn't have laughed. It was just so… adorable."

"Adorable." He growled a little and yanked open the door for her. "Great."

ADORABLE. THAT WASN'T exactly the word a grown man wanted to hear from a beautiful woman wearing sexy black boots. He pulled up the rear, scowling at the back of Tori's head, as the hostess led them to their table.

He might not know how to drive a tractor or wrestle an ATV through the mud or change a woman's oil for her but, by God, he was not *adorable*.

Tori asked for a glass of white wine and Max ordered a glass of water and decaf, since it was after five. Once they had their drinks, Tori ordered baked haddock and he asked for the steak tips. Their server took the menus and went away.

"I'm not adorable," he said as soon as they were alone.

"It wasn't an insult."

"Not if you're a six-year-old or a baby panda bear."

She tilted her head. "How about endearing?"

"How about sexy?"

"You told me I smell like fruit."

"I like fruit."

She took a long drink of her wine. "I should have asked for the whole bottle."

When he smiled, she smiled back at him. "You smell very nice tonight, Tori."

"Thank you." She set her wineglass down. "I've been thinking about who would be a good match for you, and I think you should ask out Nola Kendrick."

He wracked his brain, trying to put a face with the name, but he came up blank. "I don't know who that is."

"She works at the town hall. She's around your age and has blond hair cut at, like, chin level."

"I was at the town hall a couple of months ago."

"Then you probably talked to Nola. She's attractive and very nice. And she's kind of quiet, too, so I think you'd have a very nice time."

He knew should be excited at the idea of having a prospect, but all he had was a vague idea of a nice woman who'd given him a receipt for his tax payment. "So you think I should ask her to have dinner with me?"

"I'd offer to set it up as a blind date, but I don't know her *that* well. And, let's be honest, this whole serial-killer thing might have been amusing to you, but it makes it a little difficult to offer you up for some quality alone time, if you know what I mean."

He leaned across the table so he could lower his voice. "How about a porn studio? Better or worse?"

Tori laughed. "With Nola, I'm honestly not sure. It's the quiet ones you have to watch."

"If I ask her to dinner at the diner, it's not an ideal place for a nice date, but she'll feel more secure than if I ask her to get in my car and head off to the city."

"Absolutely. Unfortunately, that means she has to decide if she's up to the gossip that'll come after or not, but you're a good-looking guy. I think she'll risk it."

He took a sip of his water, watching her over the rim. "You're very good for my ego, you know."

"Just giving you a boost, so you'll be confident when you approach a woman." She paused, taking a quick drink. "I wish there was more to do in Whitford. Something for after dinner, if you both want the date to continue. Like someplace to dance or…something."

"I don't foresee myself going dancing, even if it was an option. I'm more of a dinner-and-a-movie type. Not that Whitford has a movie theater."

"Of course you are. You don't have to talk to a woman when you're watching a movie. And I bet, between chewing and listening to your date, you don't do a lot of talking over dinner, either."

"What's that supposed to mean?"

"Dinner and a movie don't require thought or intimacy. That's all I'm saying."

He wanted to deny he took the easy way out on dates, but she was right. She was also a little annoying, with this ability to see right through all the tricks he used to navigate through life. "I don't have very good rhythm. That's all."

"I've watched you move, Max. I bet you can dance."

He watched the candlelight flicker in her eyes and tried not overthink the words she'd said. She'd told him before she watched people and studied their body language, but that didn't stop the sexual hunger that seemed to be short-circuiting his brain. *Not this woman.*

Tori didn't look away from his gaze and he wondered what she would do if he reached across the table and took her hand. For the first time in his life, Max wanted to dance. He wanted to pull her into his arms and see how she fit against his body.

"Nola," she said quickly, as if it burst out of her mouth, and the name hit him like a bucket of ice water. "We need to figure out what you'll talk about with Nola."

"Okay." He didn't want to talk about Nola Kendrick. He wanted to talk about Tori.

"What do you like to do?" Just as he opened his mouth to respond, she held up her hand. "Nothing to do with model railroading or sports."

He closed his mouth and thought about it. "I like reading."

"Okay. What do you like to read?"

"Everything, I guess. But mostly military thrillers. Historical biographies. Stuff like that."

"Not my kind of stuff, but I like to read, too. Romance. Horror. Almost anything, but those big, epic fantasy series, mostly. Anyway, loving to read is a great quality, but it's not really something you can do as a couple."

"Two people curled up in front of a fireplace on a snowy winter day isn't a bad way to spend an afternoon."

Her expression turned soft and a little dreamy. "You have a point, there. But that's *once* you're a couple. And it's the same as going to a movie, Max. You don't have to make conversation."

"I think all the time we've spent together proves I'm capable of having a conversation."

"Because I'm just me."

He wondered what she meant by that, exactly. Because she was genuinely so easy to talk to or because he wasn't trying to have a real, heading-toward-marriage relationship with her?

Their server brought their dinners and, after delivering their plates, brought them drink refills. There was a lull in the conversation as they went through the process of tasting and seasoning their food, for which he was grateful. Tori challenged him and, while he enjoyed it immensely, he could use the short reprieve.

He had to keep reminding himself this wasn't a real date. It was what he'd like a real date to be—with laughter and banter and that sizzle of attraction—but her purpose in being here was to help him find another woman. It was an odd situation, to say the least.

"This is quite good," he said after a while. "Though I prefer your cousin's cooking, to be honest. Gavin, right?"

Her smile was bright and kick-started an ache that had nothing to do with the meal he was eating. "That's right. And I'm sure he and Paige both would be glad to know you prefer the diner to this place."

The small talk came easy, then. He asked about Gavin and his culinary aspirations. About how Paige had come to buy the closed-down diner and reopen it. Because there were so many people in Whitford they both knew, but she had more stories about, it was easy to not only get through dinner, but the car ride home, as well.

When he pulled up in front of the bank building, he found himself very reluctant to get out of the car. "I enjoyed tonight."

"So did I. I think whoever goes out to dinner with you next will have a wonderful time."

It wouldn't be her, though. "I think being out with

a friend and being out on a first date are two very different things, though."

"Nola's lived in Whitford her entire life, you know. You can ask her about her work and what it was like growing up there as a child. You'll do fine and once the conversation starts rolling, you relax pretty quickly."

Max wasn't sure he felt as optimistic as she did. He got out of the car and walked around to open her door. Once again, he took her hand to help her out. He'd never done it for other women in the past, but he liked the feel of her hand in his and the way her fingers squeezed his slightly as she stood.

"It's good that you have a streetlight here," he said as they walked toward the door.

"Yeah. I feel pretty safe in Whitford. Especially since the bank keeps a couple of administrative offices on the second floor, so I'm the only tenant. They use the top floor for storage."

She pulled her keys out of her small black bag, but stopped walking. This was where she'd thank him for dinner and disappear through the door, but he wasn't ready to leave yet. And if she was going to be his dating coach, they may as well be thorough.

"Is this the part where I'd kiss you good-night?"

Her lips parted and he knew she was probably surprised by the question, but with her face turned up under the streetlight, she looked very much like a woman who should be kissed.

"I...uh, I guess if the date went well and you're getting that vibe then, yes, this is the part where you'd kiss *her* good-night."

"I'm not very good at reading vibes."

"If she puts her key right in the lock or keeps her

hand on the doorknob, so she's kind of facing away, that would be a no."

"What about the way you're standing right now?"

Her keys were still in her hand and she was facing him. She hadn't even moved closer to the door. When her tongue flicked over her lip, as if her mouth had gone dry, he had to stifle a groan. "I guess...yes. If I was your date and I was standing like this, you could move a little closer. If I didn't step back or turn away, you could make your move."

He took a step forward, definitely into her personal space. "Like this much closer?"

She tilted her head back and there was a long moment of eye contact before she ducked her chin and took a step back. The keys in her hand jingled as she grasped the key to the entrance door and shook the others free of it.

"You're better at this dating thing than you think, Max," she said, and even he could tell by the breathless quality of her voice that she'd been affected by the moment as strongly as he had. "Thanks for dinner."

"Thank you for...pretending to be a date." He said it that way deliberately, knowing it would make her smile and pop the tension that seemed to be hovering between them.

And it worked. "It was a very lovely pretend date, but I have plans for another one before you...ask out Nola. Or whoever."

That sounded intriguing. "A second date?"

"A second *pretend* date. Casual this time. With flash cards."

"Flash cards?" That wasn't his idea of a second date. "That sounds...adorable."

"Trust me." She unlocked the door and pulled it open.

"Text me sometime in the next few days and we'll set up a time."

"Will I be graded on this activity?"

"Not a letter grade, but if you ace them and they help you have a great date, you might get lucky."

She was gone before he could respond to that, not that he had any idea what he would have said. But as he walked back to his car, he couldn't help feeling like he'd gotten lucky earlier, when she smiled at him across the table in the soft candlelight.

Now, looking up to see the light flick on in her apartment window before opening his door, he didn't feel lucky at all.

SEVEN

TORI STARED AT her computer monitor, idly wondering how to make the horror author's request for a cover featuring a haunted antebellum home and creepy kudzu on a dark, foggy night look even remotely original.

It was a challenge she was usually particularly good at overcoming, which was why she was in a position to turn away work now. But she was having a little trouble concentrating.

It seemed like every single time she'd closed her eyes last night, she'd seen Max's face as he'd stared down at her, asking about good-night kisses.

She'd wanted one. And so had he.

That was such a bad idea. She couldn't even count the reasons she shouldn't kiss Max.

She had no doubt if she kissed him once, she'd want to kiss him again. Then she'd want to nip at his jawline and unbutton his shirt so she could run her hands over his chest. Then she'd want to get naked.

What she had to remember was that they were wired differently. She could feel a sexual attraction, act on it and then move on with her life when the itch was scratched. Max was on a mission and she suspected he didn't do detours. If she encouraged whatever it was she'd seen in his eyes last night, he might decide he wanted to date *her*—and not just in the casual, having sex way—and that wasn't going to happen.

No more candlelight and wine. No more dresses and makeup. And no more of him walking her to her door.

Her cell phone rang and she picked it up. She'd been waiting all day for Hailey to call, because Tori had no doubt somebody had seen Max pick her up in his car yesterday afternoon, or drop her off, and she would want details. "Hello?"

"So you do know how to answer your phone."

Tori sighed and dropped her forehead to her hand. *Stupid.* She should never answer without checking the Caller ID. "Yes, Mom. I know how to use my phone."

"You never answer when I call."

"I have it automatically send all of my calls straight to voice mail when I'm working," she said. It was a small lie, and one she told often.

"Then you work too much. Anyway, I'm calling about Thanksgiving."

Tori knew where this was headed and wanted no part of it. "It's the middle of October."

"You know I like to plan ahead. Things fall apart when you leave them to the last minute."

No, she was calling over a month in advance in the hope of beating Tori's dad to the punch, which she hadn't. "I'm going to Uncle Mike and Aunt Jilly's."

"Your father said he was going to call you soon to invite you to spend the day with him. Has he called yet?"

One of the many side effects of the divorce was her mother's seeming inability to say *dad* anymore, or use the man's given name. He was always *your father,* said in a tight voice, as if her mom had a mouthful of dirt and wanted desperately to spit.

"He did invite me," she said, "and I told him I'm going to Aunt Jilly's, the same as I'm telling you."

"You haven't been home in months, Victoria. This is getting ridiculous."

"The last time I went home, you complained that I went to Dad's apartment first and Dad complained I was going to have dinner with you, but only lunch with him. *That* was ridiculous."

"I can't believe your father's so hung up on which meal you ate with him."

Almost as hung up as her mother was on who Tori had visited first. "I'm really busy, Mom."

"Busy right now or busy at Thanksgiving?"

"Both." And if she wasn't busy come the end of next month, she'd make something up.

Her mom's sigh was long and loud over the phone. "Maybe I should call Jilly and see if there's room at the table for me."

Tori paused in the act of drumming her fingers on her desk. She hadn't seen that coming. In this post-divorce maneuvering, her mother was attempting to flank her. "Um…"

"I know the divorce surprised you, but you're an adult, Victoria, and you really should be over it by now."

"If age matters, then *you* should be over it, too."

She heard her mother's sharp intake of breath. "Of course I'm over it. Divorcing your father was the best thing I ever did."

They both claimed to be the one who wanted the divorce, of course. As if there was a blue ribbon for being first. "I'll think about Thanksgiving, Mom."

She had no desire to go home, so to speak, for the holiday, but the last thing she wanted to do was bring her mother's horrible attitude into her aunt Jilly's home on a day that celebrated family and being thankful.

n off energy and there was certainly no shortage of
n. He didn't have the patience for bagging or burn-
them, so he usually raked them into the tree line
bordered his lawn. Some drifted back on the breeze,
most didn't. Good enough.

She got out of her car and leaned against the fender,
tching him get rid of the last pile before putting the
e away.

"I guess that's one good thing about not having a
wn," she said when he was done. "No mowing or
king leaves."

"I don't mind mowing. And some years I just ignore
he leaves, but it was too nice to be inside. We won't
ave many of these days left."

"We can sit outside if you want. Enjoy the sun while
t lasts."

It sounded lovely, but he only had two patio chairs
nd he'd already put them in the shed for the winter.
'All I have is the front step or the grass."

"Let's sit on the grass." She walked toward the cen-
er of his lawn, where the sun was bright and not shad-
wed by trees or the house. Before she sat, though, she
ulled a short stack of small index cards out of the back
ocket of her jeans.

She really hadn't been kidding. "Let me just grab a
uple of waters."

Max couldn't remember the last time he'd sat on the
rass—probably when he was a kid—but it wasn't so
d. It probably wouldn't be comfortable for long, but
ing outside was nice.

"You ready for this?" She fanned the index cards,
e same smile she'd given his cell phone camera light-
g up her face.

If Tori could keep her mom from getting herself invited
to her aunt and uncle's house until it was close enough
to the day so it would be rude to invite herself, maybe
Tori could then come down with a mystery illness at
the last minute.

And it was ridiculous, at twenty-seven years old,
to have to fake being sick to play hooky from a family dinner.

"I'll make your favorite foods," her mother said in
a much softer tone. "Since I know how to cook them."

"Mom." Tori sighed and rubbed the bridge of her
nose. "If I go to Portland for Thanksgiving, I'm going
to see both of you. You know that."

"You can have dinner and dessert with me and then
stop by *his* house for coffee on the way out."

"Please stop dragging me into this. You hate each
other. Fine. But you're both still my parents. You're
being really awful."

"Fine. Do what you want. But someday when a man
you thought loved you treats you the way *your* father
has treated me, we'll see how your attitude is."

Not if. When. "I have to go, Mom. I'm filling in at
the diner and I have to leave now."

That was a flat-out lie. She was going to spend the
day catching up on design work. And she'd worked up a
few ideas for the Northern Star ATV Club's new design,
so she'd send those to Josh. If none worked, she'd have
to refer him to somebody else and step out of the project. But what her mother didn't know wouldn't hurt her.

"Let me know about Thanksgiving."

Tori promised she would and hung up the phone.
She not only set it out of easy reach, but she leaned it
up against her printer so she would be able to read the

screen from her chair. Her parents were hard enough to deal with when she braced herself for them. No more ambushes.

With the bitter taste of love gone horribly wrong in her mouth and thoughts of Max and kisses chased away, Tori downed a gulp of cold coffee and went back to work.

BY TUESDAY, MAX was missing Tori. It was probably because he'd spent so much time in her company since the first time he went into the diner, but having no contact with her since dropping her off Saturday night left a void he was antsy to fill.

He'd even caught himself staring off into space, thinking about her, when he was supposed to be researching engine numbers to put on a Santa Fe Railway Prairie class. A little extra time in the shower wasn't enough to cure his restlessness, either.

She'd told him to text her sometime in "the next few days," so it was probably time. Not that he was particularly interested in whatever she meant by flash cards, but he wanted to hear her voice.

Or, more accurately he supposed, see the words she typed into her phone. Texting wasn't the same as a phone call, but he was nothing if not a man who could follow directions.

Because reception could be iffy in the basement, he took the phone upstairs and sat down at the kitchen table.

Hi, Tori. It's Max.

He scowled, then hit the backspace until it was all

erased. It wasn't necessary to tell her w... saved him in her contacts and it would... And if she didn't have unlimited textin... phone plan, it would be a waste of mon...

Are you busy? That was better, so he...

Not too busy. I got the flash cards don... you free?

Anytime, and the sooner the better. T... with going out and being sociable was feelin... you didn't go out and socialize. My schedul...

This afternoon? Or later?

He'd already given up on working anyway. time you show up is good.

Haha. Would drive you crazy not to have a ti... there at one.

You caught me. See you at one.

He had over an hour to kill, so he went to... board to check over his lists. He was on tra... usual. He could even check off *find a date*... probably didn't count.

Not only was it a mock date, but it di... any closer to the goals he may have crosse... wanted to achieve. A girlfriend to eventu... not *too* eventually—become a wife.

By the time Tori arrived, he'd gotten r... to venture outside. Raking leaves was...

"What are we doing?"

"I have here a variety of random interests. You're going to ask me what I like to do in my free time and I'm going to pick one. And you're going to practice being interested in my hobbies until you can converse about them without straightening the silverware or staring off at the wall sconces."

"You're kidding."

"Nope." She leaned forward so she could put her hand on his arm. She did that a lot, he realized. And he liked it. "I know it sounds weird, Max, but I think it'll help. If nothing else, it'll force you to be aware of how you respond in a conversation."

He wasn't sure it would help, but it would keep them outside on the grass in the sunshine for a while longer. "Let's do it."

"I LIKE TO play Bingo."

He didn't even hesitate. "That's wonderful. How many cats do you have?"

"Max!" Tori threw the index card at him, trying not to laugh. "No."

"I was quick, though. No awkward pauses this time. Okay, next."

She pulled a card out of the stack. They'd been at it awhile and the pile was getting thin. "Gardening."

"Flowers or vegetables?"

"That's a good question. Flowers."

He nodded. "Are you more partial to annuals or perennials? Do you grow them from seed or buy them from nurseries? Do you make an effort to attract hummingbirds or butterflies?"

"Perfect." She turned the card over, since there were

multiple words on each. "Though not all the questions at once. Ask one, then let her talk. If necessary, ask another. Knitting."

"My grandmother knits. When I was young she made me hold my arms out so she could wind her yarn around them." When she nodded, he gave her a cocky look. "I'm much better at small talk than I thought I was."

It was time to shake it up a little. She pulled another card, but ignored the benign suggestion written on it. "I like to have sex in public places."

Max opened his mouth. Closed it again. Then he shifted his gaze to something over her shoulder for a few seconds before looking back at her. "Is this public enough or would you like to step out to the sidewalk?"

It was the last thing she'd expected him to say, having anticipated a recap of town ordinances and decency laws, and she almost choked. "You would not say that."

The grin he gave her was pure naughtiness. "You said yourself it's the quiet ones you have to watch."

She laughed and set down the cards to pick up her water bottle. "I guess I did."

Taking a long swig of the water, Tori willed the parts of her body his look had overheated to cool down. She'd gotten so caught up in the game they were playing, she hadn't taken the time to consider how stupid it was to throw the word *sex* into the mix. She'd been thinking about that word entirely too much lately and, no matter how much she tried to imagine any of the sexy models in the stock image sites she browsed, Max's face always ended up in her head.

"You look happier now than when you arrived," Max said. "Not that you looked unhappy, but you looked tired. The sun and fresh air are good for you."

"I definitely need more sun and fresh air." She took a long swig of water and screwed the cap back on. "My dad called just before I left. I told my mom I would consider going back to Portland for Thanksgiving—even though I'll do whatever I can to get out of it—and she told him I was going to her house and I *might* make time to stop in and have a coffee with him. Which is a total lie."

"It's wrong, the way they put you in the middle."

"I kept thinking I'd just get out of the way until they got past it, but two years later, I'm still in Whitford and they're still playing tug-of-war with my emotions."

She watched him pluck at the grass. "If they did get over it and stopped trying to use you to hurt each other, would you go back to Portland?"

Wasn't that the twenty-dollar question? She leaned back, bracing herself on her hands, so she could turn her face up to the sun. It was starting to drop now and it would start getting cold. "I don't know. At first I thought I would. There's so much more to do there. Stores and restaurants and nightclubs and movies."

"But?"

She smiled. "But Whitford's grown on me. And I have good friends here. It's just…"

"It's just what? I consider myself one of those good friends, so talk to me."

"You are." Yes, they were friends. While she may have to keep shoving back that sexual attraction, she and Max had clicked and he was her friend. "I hate what my parents have done. Do you know when I go visit Uncle Mike and Aunt Jilly, I try to look at their marriage and how much they love each other, but all I can do is wonder if or when it's going to blow up. I picture them saying the things my parents have said to each other and it makes my heart hurt."

"Not only does every marriage not blow up, but even the ones that do don't always end up like your parents' has."

"I know that, logically. But…when it ended, my dad said he was taking the newer of the televisions and Mom said he could have it over her dead body. He told her he'd been praying for that moment for years and it hadn't happened yet. She said if that worked, he'd have been dead a long time ago.

"Just a week before, I'd been there for Sunday dinner and everything was fine. They were normal and we were just a normal family eating pot roast. One week, Max. One week later they were screaming about how they'd been wishing each other dead for years. It was… My *family* was a lie."

To her horror, tears spilled over her cheeks and she swiped angrily at them. She rolled to her stomach because playing with the grass gave her something to look at.

She was surprised when Max crawled over and stretched out beside her. "If you'd like to see me at my most awkward and socially inept, crying's a good way to do it. I'm not good at tears and I have no idea what to say except that really sucks and I'm sorry your parents are assholes."

The barking laugh that burst out of her mouth surprised her, though nothing about Max should surprise her. "You're right. I haven't said that because, you know, they're my mom and dad. But my parents are being really selfish assholes."

"Does it feel better to say that out loud?"

"Yes. Though now I feel bad I ruined this fun afternoon we were having."

He leaned close and bumped her shoulder with his. "It's not ruined. Being friends means more than laughing together."

Awareness of how close his body was to hers and how sweet he was and the memory of that smoldering sexy look from early made her melt a little inside and a loud *uh-oh* alarm went off in her brain. She was getting too comfortable with him and was in danger of forgetting why their friendship had started in the first place.

"So," she said, shoulder-bumping him back. "Have you asked out Nola yet?"

For what seemed like forever, he stared at a leaf that had escaped his rake, before shaking his head. "No. I haven't seen her."

"Okay, we need a plan." She gave herself a mental shake and turned her focus to getting them back on track. "Let's start with reasons you need to visit the town hall."

EIGHT

MAX WAS SURPRISED to receive a summons to the Northern Star Lodge from Rose Davis. Everybody knew Rosie, of course, and her baked goods were legendary, but no matter how much he thought about it in the two hours between being invited and arriving, he couldn't make sense of the invitation to lunch.

He walked up onto the big farmer's porch that surrounded the lodge, admiring the big, old house. It had been in the Kowalski family for generations, and he was impressed with the level of care the renovations were given. Obviously they loved their home and had worked hard to bring it back. He knocked on the door and waited until Rose opened it.

She had a baby on her hip and, even if he didn't know Sarah was Mitch and Paige's daughter, the bright blue eyes and the dark hair would have marked her as a Kowalski.

"I'm so glad you could come today," Rose said, leading him in to the kitchen.

"You have a beautiful home," he responded, since he still had no idea what was going on and that's what people always said on television.

He knew Josh and Andy—who was Drew's dad and Rose's boyfriend—worked at the lodge full-time, but he hadn't seen them anywhere. As far as he could tell, it was him and Rose for lunch. And Sarah, who was being strapped into a high chair and didn't seem happy about it.

"Have a seat at the table. Make yourself at home."

He could tell that, as in his parents' home, the kitchen was the heart of this house. It was warm and inviting, and the baby calmed when Rose gave her a toddler cup of juice and a handful of Cheerios.

"I bet you're wondering why I invited you over for lunch," Rose said as she set a bowl of chicken stew in front of him, along with a plate of freshly sliced, home-made bread. The smell alone was enough to make his mouth water.

"I am curious, yes."

She set down a bowl for herself and sat across the table from him. "You've lived here a long time, but no-body really knows a lot about you."

Max dipped his spoon into the bowl, stirring the thick broth. So that was it. She and Fran were good friends and loved to one-up each other with gossip. Rose was obviously going to pull out all the stops to find out what he did in his basement.

"I've been spending a lot of time with Paige lately," she continued. "You know, with Mitch traveling a lot and little Sarah Rose to visit with."

Those two things didn't seem to go together, but Max just waited quietly. Obviously Rose was going to take her time getting to her point and, rather than be thought rude if he interrupted, he'd wait for a question.

"Paige happened to mention you and Tori Burns have been spending time together lately."

When she paused, he realized she was waiting for confirmation from him. "We've become friends, yes."

"Tori can seem like a tough nut at times, but she's

not really. And Paige looks out for her, of course. She's not just her boss. They're friends, too. And she's a little worried, which makes me a little worried."

He paused with his spoon halfway to his mouth and looked her in the eye. "I'm not a serial killer, Ms. Davis."

"Call me Rose or Rosie. And I know you're not a serial killer, though we do have a lot of fun making up stories. I think Josh and Katie know what you do, based on a bet I'm pretty sure Josh lost, and Drew probably knows. If you were up to something criminal, you'd be gone already."

"Then there's no reason to worry," he said after swallowing a mouthful of the best chicken stew he'd ever had.

"You're a puzzle with a lot of pieces missing, Max Crawford. Just because you're not going to hack Tori into pieces and shove her in a freezer doesn't mean we don't have to worry."

Sarah threw a Cheerio at Max, as if to show her agreement with Rose. It landed near his bowl and he looked at it for a moment, wondering if or how he should react. Then he picked it up and reached over to set it back on her tray. She threw it at him again. Since his first reaction hadn't seemed to satisfy her, he ate it.

And she cried. Or screamed, actually.

"I'm sorry," he said as Rose got up. "I assumed she wanted me to have it."

"No, she wanted you to throw it back at her like her uncle Josh does when he thinks I'm not looking."

Rose cut a banana into chunks and added those to the pile of Cheerios on the tray. Sarah stopped screaming and mashed a piece into her mouth. And her nose.

Max turned his attention back to his stew, wanting to eat as much as he could while Rose was fussing with the baby. All too soon, she was back in her chair and ready to resume the conversation.

"I know you like to have your secrets and, believe it or not, I keep the ones that need keeping, but I'm asking you straight out what you do for a living."

He set down his spoon. "I custom-paint brass engines and rolling stock for model railroaders. My work space is in my basement because it offers space and was the easiest way to manage climate control and ventilation. It has its own security system due to the value of the models and my equipment and maybe a slight degree of paranoia on my part. Drew, Josh, Katie *and* Tori all have been in my basement and can confirm that."

"Really? Now isn't that interesting." She leaned back in her chair. "My uncle had some model trains. What were they called…garden scale?"

"Yes, ma'am. G scale is significantly larger than what I usually work with, but I've done a couple of engines and a boxcar in the past."

"Thank you, Max. I feel better now. We all care about Tori, and this friendship seemed to come up rather suddenly…"

While she might have been direct in asking about his business, the way she trailed off now let him know she wanted him to fill in some details about their friendship. "I'm not sure *sudden* is the right word. I simply hadn't crossed paths with her before. We met at the diner and we enjoy each other's company."

"That's good." She ate a few bites of stew, giving him a brief reprieve.

It was tempting to tell her that Tori was helping him

in his quest to go on a date. She would be reassured that he had no nefarious intentions toward Tori and it would explain why she'd been spending time with him all of a sudden.

But he'd heard about Rose Davis and he was definitely familiar with Fran Benoit. He suspected if he said he was wife-hunting and those two women put their heads together, he'd be subjected to a matchmaking campaign that would steamroll over him and he'd end up married to somebody's cousin's daughter's best friend before he knew what hit him.

He figured this was best treated like a police interrogation. Answer only the questions asked of him and, if it looked like it was going south, run like hell.

The door opened and Josh walked in. He'd taken off the thick sweatshirt he was wearing and his boots before he saw Max. When he frowned, Max just waved and went back to eating his stew. It was almost gone, so he picked up the bread and starting sopping up the broth.

"Rosie," Josh said, "I told you to mind your own business."

"And I told you to not to have food fights with Sarah. I guess neither of us listens worth a damn."

Josh looked at the baby as if she'd ratted him out and Max chuckled. "She threw a Cheerio at me and I ate it."

"That pisses her off."

"I know that now."

"Paige is the sweetest woman I've ever met, but that child right there is a mini-Liz. We're all going to lose sleep during her teenage years."

"You all turned out fine," Rose said. "And she will, too. Won't you, pumpkin?"

Sarah squealed and threw a Cheerio at Josh.

"What she needs," Rose said, "is a pack of cousins to help her run off the excess energy. Liz is doing her part, but she can't have a whole pack."

Josh shook his head and picked up the Cheerio which, under Rose's watchful eye, he threw in the garbage can. "Your daughter's not having a whole pack, either. Not with me, anyway. Unless one or two is a pack."

Max licked the last of the bread crumbs from his fingers and knew he'd made the right decision not to tell Rose he wanted a wife. This was not a woman who knew how to watch from the sidelines.

"Thank you for lunch, Rose," he said. "It was delicious, but I really should get back to work."

"Of course you should. Those bodies won't bury themselves." He was surprised when she kissed him on the cheek. "You're welcome to stop by anytime, you know. There's always something in the goody jar."

He said goodbye to Josh and Sarah, then escaped to his car. Once he was on the road home, he laughed. Rose was quite a woman. It would be easy to be offended by her, except he suspected, since he was a member of the community and a friend of Josh and Katie, that she'd be just as quick to rush to Max's defense if she thought he needed her.

It wasn't a bad feeling.

TORI HAD ALWAYS liked her aunt and uncle's home. It was nothing special—a small ranch on the outskirts of town—but it was a house full of love and laughter. Or so it had always seemed during childhood visits.

She stopped by early Wednesday afternoon when she knew Uncle Mike and Gavin would both be working. Todd would be getting out of school soon, but he had a part-time job helping out at the hardware store and wouldn't be home until later in the evening.

"This is a nice surprise," Jilly said when she answered the door. "I was just going to brew a cup of tea. Do you want one?"

It wasn't her favorite drink, but it was Aunt Jilly's thing, so she nodded. "That would be great."

Tori sat at the kitchen table while Jilly put more water in the kettle and prepared another cup.

"There's been some talk about you around town lately," her aunt said.

"If it's scandalous, it's not true. I've done nothing scandal-worthy. Not in public, anyway."

Her aunt laughed. "No, nothing scandalous. But interesting, I guess."

"About Max Crawford and me?"

"That would be the talk."

"I'll tell you why, but you have to keep it to yourself. I don't want Max to be embarrassed."

"And it gets more interesting by the second. I'll keep your secret."

Tori told her aunt how Max had come into the diner and about his botched attempt to talk to Jeanette. She chose not to mention her growing attraction to the man, focusing instead on their mission to find a lovely woman for him to marry.

"I think it's wonderful," Jilly said, setting a mug of tea in front of her before taking a seat. "I was starting to worry about you, so I'm relieved you still believe in love and marriage."

Tori shook her head. "How *I* feel about it hasn't changed. But if that's what Max thinks he wants, I'm going to help him get it. He's a sweet guy and the least

I can do is help him find a woman who's the least likely to turn into a shrieking harpy."

Her aunt winced. "I'm sorry that's become such an accurate description of your mother since they split up. I try to be supportive because she is my sister, after all, but sometimes I don't pick up when she calls."

"That's actually why I stopped by."

"Tell me she didn't call you to complain that I didn't answer my phone."

"No, it's worse."

Jilly held up a finger, motioning for her to hold on, and went to rummage in the cabinet under the sink. From behind packages of napkins and paper towels, she took a plastic container, which she set in the middle of the table. When she took the lid off, Tori smiled at the sight of chocolate chip cookies.

Jilly took a bite, then motioned for her to continue. "Okay, hit me."

"She called about Thanksgiving. You know, the same drama we've gone through every year. And I told her I was coming here." Tori reached into the bucket for a couple of cookies. "She got pissy about it and said she might call you and see if there was room at your table."

"Oh." Jilly started shaking her head, slowly at first, and then with vigor. "There isn't."

Since they were sitting at a butcher-block table surrounded by six chairs, Tori laughed.

"I need to go buy a smaller table," her aunt said. "How the hell am I supposed to tell her no?"

"Without setting her off? I don't know. That's why I wanted to give you the heads-up."

"I can't do it, Tori." The amusement faded, and Jilly looked tired all of a sudden. She looked a lot like Tori felt whenever her mother called or came up in conversation, she thought. "She's my sister. She's your mother. She should be welcome in my home, but she's so…"

"Miserable," Tori said. "And she wants everybody to be miserable with her."

"If I tell her we're going out of town for Thanksgiving, she'll expect you to go home."

"Don't worry about me, Auntie. Save yourself."

Jilly snorted. "I appreciate your noble sacrifice, but no. We're entitled to have a relaxed, happy Thanksgiving dinner as a family."

"I'm thinking a last-minute flu."

"That has possibilities."

"It's risky, but I don't see Mom driving three hours to help nurse us back to health."

"At least she can't blindside me now and surprise me into inviting her. But enough about your mom. I want to hear more about Max."

Speaking of blindsides, an image of Max lying in the grass next to her and laughing popped into her head. Even with her little breakdown over her parents, it had been a fun afternoon.

"Does he have a date in mind already?" Jilly continued.

"He's going to ask Nola Kendrick to dinner."

"Hmm. She's a nice woman. Kind of quiet. They're probably a good match."

"I think she'll enjoy his company and, from what little interaction I've had with her, she doesn't seem prone to sarcasm or anything like that. Max has a good sense of humor, but he's still a pretty literal person, so somebody who's snarky could hurt his feelings without meaning to."

Jilly took another cookie out of the basket. "You sound very protective of him."

She shrugged. "Remember back in high school, how you felt watching a guy ask a girl out and get shot down? It was kind of like that. She wasn't mean or anything, but I still felt bad. And then, when I was talking to him, he's...sweet and funny. I want to help him find a date who'll appreciate that."

"Okay." Jilly took a bite of the cookie.

"Stop it. Don't do that."

"Don't do what?"

"You're planning my wedding to Max Crawford in your head right now."

Her aunt sipped her tea, the picture of innocence. "I'm just eating my cookie. I have no idea what you're talking about."

Tori rolled her eyes and took the whole cookie bucket. She was surrounded by hopeless romantics.

NINE

MAX SMILED AT Fran Benoit as he closed the door to the Whitford General Store behind him. She was in her usual spot behind the counter, knitting what looked like a sock. Or maybe a mitten. She had on a checked flannel shirt and her long gray hair was in a braid, as usual.

"Good afternoon, Max."

"Hello."

That was usually the only conversation they had, until it was time for her to add up his purchases and give him his total. Despite her penchant for gossip, especially where he and his basement were concerned, he liked Fran. He often heard her conversing with others and she seemed warm and friendly, and she genuinely cared about the people in town.

He wandered the aisles with a handheld basket, grabbing a few perishable items. Like most people in Whitford, he drove into the city once or twice a month to stock up at the big grocery stores, but there were always things like milk and ice cream that didn't keep well, long-term.

Skipping the ice cream, because eating at the diner had the numbers on his bathroom scale creeping upward, he grabbed two half-gallons of milk and a package of American cheese. He also picked up a loaf of regular white bread, as well as a loaf of the raisin bread somebody in town had been baking for the store to sell.

It made thick, delicious toast in the mornings. After a moment's consideration, he grabbed a second loaf.

As he unloaded the items onto the counter, he realized that, after seven years in Whitford, being something of an outsider was starting to bother him, and that was his own fault. It was time to stop talking *at* people and start forming relationships. Plus, he was trying to put off going to the town hall, even though it had been two days since he and Tori had come up with a reason to drop in.

"Did you know Caroline Dobson?" he asked.

Fran looked startled for a second, almost dropping his cheese. "Sure. She and Pete lived out… Well, in the house you live in now, actually. He passed away some time ago and she moved south to live with her daughter. What was her name…Brenda! That was it. She went off to college and met a boy. Never moved back. Nice enough people, though I didn't know them well. Caroline would come in, of course, but she was a bit of an… she was a quiet one. Kept to herself, mostly."

She was a bit of an odd duck. The fact she hadn't said the words meant she'd used them about him—not that he blamed her—and she felt bad about it. It wasn't the first time he'd been compared to his grandmother, though. The apple didn't fall far from the tree, even if it came from a higher generational branch. "I'm Pete and Caroline's grandson. Brenda is my mother."

She narrowed her eyes, planting her hands on her hips. "All this time you've been here and you didn't tell anybody?"

"Nobody asked."

"You're a quiet one, too, aren't you?" she said, and he laughed, not missing what she was saying. "I know she sold the house and moved down with Brenda because her health was suffering, but nobody ever mentioned it was her grandson who bought it."

"Nobody else would buy it and she was trying to hold off on the surgery, so I bought it. My parents moved into my old room and Grams moved into their first-floor master bedroom."

Fran's eyes softened and she covered his hand with hers in a surprising gesture. "You make it sound so practical, but you're a good boy, Max Crawford."

He made it sound practical because it *was* practical, but he wasn't going to argue with her. "Anything for Grams."

"So you came to Whitford as a boy, then?"

"Not very often and, as you said, we kept to ourselves mostly. But I remember going to the diner for ice cream once. That was a long time ago, and it wasn't as nice as it is now."

She shook her head. "All this time, I had no idea you were one of us."

He opened his mouth to point out he was not only born in Connecticut, but had spent the majority of his life there, but he thought better of it. This was obviously the beginning of a new relationship with the General Store's owner, and he wasn't going to ruin it. Being *one of them* didn't sound so bad.

The bell over the door rang and he was surprised to see Tori walk in. She was wearing a Trailside Diner T-shirt, but she'd pulled the ponytail holder out of her hair. He could still see a slight ridge across her hair where it had been cinched.

"Max!"

She sounded happy to see him, which thrilled him

in a way he couldn't really define. Maybe it was simply nice to have friends who were glad to see him. "Hi, Tori."

"Hi, Fran. Do you have any cream of chicken soup?"

"There should be a couple of cans on the shelf. The mushroom's gone, but I had ordered extra of the chicken."

Max turned to watch Tori walk down the aisle, his gaze drifting slowly south. She kept herself in shape, that was for sure. It was probably a side effect, in addition to socializing, to working at the diner.

Fran cleared her throat and he whipped around to face her. She had an eyebrow raised and the speculation was clear as day as she looked from him to Tori and back. Busted.

Thankfully, she didn't say anything, but went back to ringing up and bagging the last few items he'd bought. He pulled out his wallet and waited for the total.

Tori came back, setting two cans of cream of chicken soup on the end of the counter. "I'm taking both so, with the cream of mushroom gone, there's a big gap on the shelf now, Fran."

The other woman shook her head. "I hate that. My order best come in soon. And now whoever keeps messing up my canned goods might be tempted to screw around again."

"Somebody's messing with your canned goods?" Max asked. What could one do to canned goods?

"I like the cans in alphabetical order. *Somebody* in this town likes them shelved by color. *Color!* Does that sound normal to you, Max?"

He couldn't say he'd ever been asked to define normal before, but he had to agree with Fran to a point.

His canned goods were shelved by type and then alphabetically from there. "I think you should shelve them however you like, since you own the store."

"Damn straight." She pointed a finger at Max, but turned her gaze to Tori. "Max here's a good boy."

While Fran made his change, Tori poked him in the side with her elbow. He looked down at her—realizing for the first time he was quite a bit taller than she was—and she gave him a questioning look. He just gave her a small smile, reverting to his man-of-mystery shtick.

"Here you go." Fran counted back his change, giving his hand a little squeeze after that crumpled the paper bills. "You know, if there's something you'd like to have that I don't stock, you just let me know. I can probably order it. And you give your grandmother my best."

"Thank you, Fran. I will."

He stepped out into afternoon air that was quickly cooling and sat on the old wooden bench to wait for Tori.

"You should snap that man up."

Tori looked toward the door, thankful it had already fully closed behind Max. "I'm not looking for a man right now."

"A young, pretty girl like you?" Fran shook her head, taking the money Tori held out to her for the soup. "You could have any man you wanted."

"If I wanted one."

"I know you went out with that young man who tried to open the tanning salon down the road—as if anybody around here's going to pay money for fake sun—so I know it's not a matter of you liking men or not."

"I'm just taking some time to work on me, Fran."

The older woman frowned and handed Tori her change. "Did you read that in one of those shiny magazines with the supermodels on the cover?"

Tori just laughed and shrugged. "Maybe. I have to run, but I'll see you later."

Max was sitting on the bench outside the store, with his bags at his feet. She sat next to him, cans of soup on her lap, and leaned back. "Aren't you the golden boy all of a sudden?"

"I asked her if she knew Gram. The more I come into town, the more I like it. I guess I should start being part of the community."

"Have you gone to town hall yet?"

"No."

"I practically wrote you a script, Max. You're considering building a garage, though you haven't decided yet, and you'd like to know what the fees are for a building permit so you can add those to the projected costs."

"Why can't I just ask if I can…get a fishing license or something? That's simple."

"Because everybody gets their fishing licenses at the General Store. And because you don't fish. If she does, you're screwed. It's easy enough to think about building a garage, but then change your mind. And not many women want to talk about construction over dinner."

"I need to put my groceries in the cooler."

"You have a cooler?"

He looked at her as if she'd lost her mind. "Of course I have a cooler. It's in the trunk. How else do you keep your perishables cold until you can put them in the fridge?"

"I leave that errand for last, but I'm not usually procrastinating about asking somebody out to dinner."

She got up and followed him to his car. He popped the trunk, then carefully packed his milk and cheese in the cooler with multiple ice packs. Then she laughed at the look he gave her when she tossed her cans of soup in next to the cooler.

"I'm going to walk with you. I'm not going into town hall, but I'll hold your hand to the front door." When he arched his eyebrow at her, she rolled her eyes. "Not literally."

He slammed the trunk lid. "I feel ridiculous."

"It's nerve-racking, asking somebody out on a date. But I feel like if I don't push you, you're going to chicken out and then you're going to give up and go hide in your basement some more."

They followed the sidewalk around the town square, moving at about half of Tori's regular pace, and it was hard not to hold his hand in the literal sense. The poor guy was so nervous.

"It's childish to make up a story to talk to a woman."

"Trust me, Max. It's perfectly normal. Have you ever been to a bar? At least you're just telling a little fib about a garage and not lying about who or what you are."

"It would be nice to have a garage. The shed's small and I have to half-empty it just to get the lawn mower out. Then I have to drag everything out and repack it with the snowblower in front when winter comes."

"Well, there you go. Now it's not even a little fib. Though I think actually building a garage so your excuse to talk to Nola is legit is a bit extreme."

He stopped walking suddenly and shoved his hands in his pockets. She followed his gaze and didn't see anything but the barbershop's pole. He'd seen it before, since he got his hair cut there, but he was staring at it as if it was the most interesting thing on the planet.

"What's the matter, Max? What are you trying to figure out?"

"We've gone all through how to ask her out and how to talk to her and we even covered knowing if I should try to kiss her good-night or not. But what do I do if she says no?"

"Hey. Look at me." She put her hand on his elbow and forced herself to be silent until he gave up on the barber pole and looked at her. "If Nola isn't interested, we'll find somebody else who is."

"No, I mean, what do I actually say if she says no."

"Have you *ever* asked out a woman? You said you've had previous relationships."

"They asked me out."

"Okay." No pressure, there. No wonder he was treating the walk to the town hall like he was on his way to the gallows. "Let's go sit in the park for a few minutes."

There was a bench in the middle of the town square, which was thankfully empty at that time of day, and they sat down. Because they were literally in the middle of Whitford, she sat at the opposite end of the bench instead of closer to him. The gossip squad thinking they were a couple wasn't going to help Max's dating prospects any.

"Nola is a wicked sweetheart," she said. "So if I had to bet money, I'd say if she's not interested, she's going to say she's really busy. Or that she's seeing somebody, which she's not, but you wouldn't really know that. So smile and say maybe another time."

"Maybe another time."

"Or just smile and thank her for the information

about the building permit. Just smile. You have a great smile."

He flashed it for her and she was relieved to see him relax a little. Though she understood he was feeling out of his element, she also thought he was putting way too much pressure on himself.

"Okay," she said after a few minutes. "Are you ready?"

When they got close to the town hall, she wished him luck and kept on walking. But she didn't get very far before she looked back to make sure he actually went inside. She turned in time to see the antique wooden-and-glass door close behind him.

Part of her was tempted to keep on walking, right to the bank building and her apartment. But she knew he'd want to talk to her about how it went when he came out. Plus her soup was in his trunk.

So she found a good vantage spot to wait, which allowed her to see through the big glass windows along the front of the town hall. They were talking, no doubt about the hypothetical garage, but she could tell by his body language that Max was slowly relaxing.

Then Nola handed him a slip of paper, on which Tori assumed she'd written the information he'd requested, and she watched his shoulders stiffen a little. It was go time.

Through the window, Tori saw Nola smile and nod. They talked for a few more minutes, and then she watched Max take out his phone. Nola smiled as he took her picture and Tori's stomach tightened up.

They were exchanging contact information, which meant Nola had agreed to go on a date. *Operation— Makeover Max* was on its way to being a success.

But as she watched Max smile at Nola, Tori couldn't shake the feeling she was on the losing end of this proposition.

MAX PEERED THROUGH the magnifying glass suspended on a telescopic arm to paint the tiny trim of a headlight mounted on the smoke box of an N scale 2-6-6-2. Though he usually preferred to work in HO scale, he occasionally painted N scale engines—which were so small they fit in the palm of his hand—as a special favor or for more money.

Using a single bristle snipped from a regular house-painting brush, he focused on the meticulous detail, trying to keep his shoulders and back relaxed. If he tensed up too much, which was easy to do, his hand would shake and there was no room for error with such a small scale.

Normally, he found his work soothing. He had since his uncle had discovered Max's painting skills and brought him model cars and airplanes to paint. His quiet focus, need for accuracy and attention to detail had all been funneled into the childhood hobby that became his career.

His mind wasn't in it today, though. He wasn't able to lose himself in the details so completely that he lost track of time.

Tomorrow afternoon, he was going on a date with Nola Kendrick. She was attractive, as Tori had said, and she dressed nicely. She seemed kind. And, even though he'd felt awkward asking her if she'd like to have dinner at the diner on Saturday evening, she'd seemed flattered and hadn't hesitated before accepting his invitation.

That was a good thing. And Tori had certainly been happy for him. When he'd left the town hall and told her how it had gone on the way back to his car, she'd whooped and high-fived him like a buddy would.

Then she'd retrieved her soup from his trunk, wished him luck and walked away.

With a sigh, Max put away the engine and cleaned up. Then he covered his work space with a drop cloth and took Josh's tractor off a shelf. Years of grime were built up on the toy, so he took a wire brush and started gently sloughing it off. It required a light touch, but not much in the way of concentration, and at least he could still feel as if he was being productive.

About twenty minutes later, his phone—which was sitting on the top step where it could both get a signal and be heard—chimed. After dropping the brush and wiping his hands on a rag, he picked it up and locked the basement behind him. The text was from Tori.

Don't wear the funeral suit tomorrow.

He smiled, having gotten that point when she laughed at him the night of their mock date. I have a casual suit coat my grandfather gave me. It would look nice with khakis.

I'm coming over tomorrow. Don't get dressed until I get there. Before he could respond another text came through. I mean get dressed. Don't be naked. But don't dress for your date.

It's a nice coat. I think you'll approve.

Fair warning, I'll be going through your closet. If

there's anything in there you don't want me to see, move it now.

He laughed, wondering what a guy would keep in his closet besides clothes, belts and shoes. Considering myself warned. We're meeting at five. Nola likes to eat early.

Six o'clock was his preferred time, but he knew flexibility was the way to go. Perhaps she had shows she liked to watch in the evening or pets to feed.

I'll be there at three-thirty.

Max smiled and grabbed an apple to snack on before he went back to work. He already knew what he'd be wearing on his date and he was fairly certain Tori would approve of his choice, but he liked pushing her buttons.

And, to be honest with himself, he just wanted to see her. Poking through his closet was as good a reason for her to come over as any.

TEN

"YOU OWN AN overabundance of long-sleeve button shirts." Tori stared into Max's closet with her hands on her hips.

"I like long-sleeve button shirts."

She didn't turn around to talk to Max because he was sitting on the edge of his bed. His very large bed, which was covered by a soft comforter in a dark sage green. The bed skirt, and therefore presumably the sheets, were a light taupe, as were the tiebacks on the sage drapes. Both colors were in the braided rug, along with some shades of blue, covering the hardwood floor.

It was all very attractive and neutral, except for the distraction of Max. As he'd very matter-of-factly led her to his closet, it had belatedly occurred to Tori that going through his closet would require being in his bedroom. With him.

Not the best planning on her part.

Now she was staring at his impressive collection of dress shirts while trying not to imagine him naked. It wasn't the first time she'd had to resist, but from now on she was going to be able to imagine him naked *in his bed*.

"What about a sweater?" she asked, desperate to get her mind back on clothing. Clothing was good and the more layers, the better.

"Third drawer down."

"You don't need to be. Let me know how it goes, okay?"

She left then because there didn't seem to be anything else to say and there was no sense in lingering. It was almost time for him to leave, since he planned to arrive slightly early and pick a nice table. He had the insane idea he might find a place for them to sit that would offer some privacy and shield Nola from the gossip.

Tori knew better. She'd probably be hearing about his date before he was even home, and she'd no doubt hear the details repeatedly during her shifts at the diner in the coming days.

And she'd smile and look happy for him.

MAX WOULD BE the first to admit he wasn't an expert on social niceties, but even he knew it would be rude to call another woman while sitting across the table from his date.

It was too bad he didn't have spy gear that would enable him to communicate secretly with Tori, like a 21st century Cyrano de Bergerac, so she could feed him witty and charming lines to woo Nola with. He wasn't doing a very good job on his own.

His life would probably be a lot easier if he just dated Tori. Unfortunately, she didn't have the most important quality in a future wife, which was a desire to actually *be* a wife.

Nola was very nice. Pleasant, even. And she'd arrived only a few minutes after their arranged meeting time.

"What do you like to do in your spare time, Max?"

He moved some of Gavin's lasagna around on his plate with the fork before forcing himself to set it down. "I like to watch sports, I guess."

She laughed, putting up her hands. "I'm not rummaging through your dresser drawers."

"Not all of them. But the third one down only has sweaters in it."

Since it didn't sound like he had moved, she sighed and moved to his dresser. There were a few ceramic steins on top that looked like some kind of railroad collectibles. Other than that, just the normal debris. Some change. A comb. A few buttons that probably came as extras with his fancy shirts. It was pretty boring as far as dresser tops went.

She pulled open the third drawer down and removed a heather blue-colored Irish knit sweater. It was incredibly soft and, with this coloring, it would look amazing on him. "This one."

"There are quite a few sweaters to choose from in there."

"Nope. This one." She turned to face him, sweater in hand, and then froze.

He'd started out sitting on the edge of the bed, but at some point he'd leaned back onto his elbows. Stretched out like that on the comforter, he looked so very tempting. Max, in his element and totally at ease, was a delicious sight to behold.

And she was helping him dress for a date. With Nola.

"With jeans," she said, not wanting to dwell too much on why she wasn't happier about their plan being a success so far.

He wrinkled his nose. "Jeans? Doesn't that seem rather casual?"

"You're going to the Trailside Diner."

"It's still a first date. Our lack of dining options shouldn't impact the thought I put into it."

He was probably right. "You're wearing this sweater, though. Let's look at the pants."

"There's a reason that sweater was on top. And the shirt I usually wear under it is the freshly ironed one hanging offset from the others. You'll find the pants with it."

When she realized what he was saying, she threw the sweater at him. He caught it easily, but without his hands to prop him up, he fell back on the bed, laughing.

Tori's breath caught in her throat and she turned back to the closet, hoping like hell the thoughts in her head didn't show on her face. Her cheeks felt hot, though, so she took her time picking through to grab the shirt and pants he'd ironed.

"Why did you tell me you were wearing your grandfather's hand-me-down suit coat?"

"Because I thought it was funny."

"You already knew what you were going to wear."

"It never hurts to have a second opinion," he said, and his voice was closer.

She didn't turn. He'd be too close to her and she was too unsettled to trust herself not to touch him. If she touched him, she wasn't going to stop touching him until he told her no or she'd had her fill. Either way, it would mess up his date.

"So I came all the way over here for nothing?"

"No, you didn't." His voice was definitely close enough so she shouldn't turn around. "Instead of sitting at my table being anxious and watching the minutes tick by, you're making me laugh."

There was something about the way he said it that made her shiver. Holding out the hangers for the shirt and pants in the direction of his voice, she stepped away

from it so she could get the hell out of his l[...]

"Here. I'll wait in the kitchen while you get d[...]

She was gone before he could say anythi[...] practically fleeing to his kitchen. She poured h[...] glass of water and drank the entire thing, and th[...] poured some more.

Sitting at the table, she closed her eyes and st[...] listing off the single men of Whitford in her hea[...] wasn't a super-appealing list, but she needed someb[...] to take her mind off Max. Some sweaty sex, a few [...] gasms and she'd be right as rain again.

"What do you think?"

She opened her eyes as Max stepped into the kitchen. He looked as hot in that sweater as she'd imagined he would, and it was just the right blend of casual and made-an-effort. "Perfect."

He looked at the clock. "I wish you were working tonight."

"I think me being at the diner would make it worse, not better."

"If you were there, you could send me signals or something."

"No." She had no intention of spying on his evening out with another woman, whether it was at his request or not. "You're going to have a good time eating a good meal with a very lovely woman."

"I hope you're right."

She dumped the rest of her water down the dra[...] and set the empty glass beside the sink and not i[...] because that's how Max liked it. "I'm going to ge[...] of your hair. Just relax and be yourself."

"I'm not very good at being anybody else."

"I like watching tennis."

Of course. One of the few sports he didn't care for, along with golf and bowling. He picked his fork back up. "I don't follow tennis, but I've seen a few matches. They're amazing athletes."

She smiled and some of the tension in his gut uncoiled. So far, so good. "I've heard all about your television, of course. And how you're the haven for all the guys whose wives don't care for the yelling at the TV."

"I guess I'm the closest thing Whitford has to a sports bar. Maybe I should institute a cover charge." He took a bite of lasagna, giving himself a few seconds to think. "What do you do when you're not at the town hall?"

She talked for quite some time, requiring only slight encouragement from him. He liked her voice. It was quiet and she was well-spoken, and he found her to be very intelligent. And she had good table manners.

Frowning, Max looked at his plate. Those were all nice qualities in a woman—or in anybody, for that matter—but he thought he'd feel more...excitement. Anticipation. Something.

"Are you okay?"

He looked up and noted the worried expression on her face. With a sinking feeling in his gut, he realized he'd zoned out on her. "I'm fine. I apologize. This lasagna is so good, but it's filling and I'm trying to decide if I should keep eating or surrender."

She had a soft laugh, more polite than happy. "It *is* delicious. I'm going to take the rest of mine home and have it for lunch tomorrow."

"Are you thinking about dessert?" he asked, since she seemed to have signaled she was finished eating.

"No, but I wouldn't mind having more decaf. Unless you're ready to go."

"I'd like more decaf." He didn't want her to think he was eager to end their evening.

And he honestly wasn't. Nola was nice company and, when he wasn't overthinking things, he enjoyed talking to her. Lingering over another cup of decaf sounded like a good idea.

When Ava, the waitress who usually handled dinner, stopped by, he asked for two boxes and a refill. He wasn't a big fan of leftovers, but she was taking hers home and he didn't want her to think he was wasteful. Besides, he was confident that Gavin's lasagna would taste just as good after a trip through the microwave.

"I'm glad you came into the town hall," she said, once their cups were refilled. "It's nice to get out once in a while."

"I probably could have found the fees on the website, but then I wouldn't have been able to talk to you."

The blush of pink across her cheeks felt like a win to Max. He'd said the right thing. "You can come in and talk to me anytime."

"I was afraid you'd say no because…well, I have a reputation, from what I hear."

That made her laugh again. "Yes, you certainly do. But you know if anybody in town actually thought you were up to no good, somebody would have put a stop to it a long time ago."

"This isn't exactly the kind of place where everybody turns a blind eye."

"No, it isn't. I might have to take my phone off the hook tomorrow because everybody's going to want to hear about my dinner with the mysterious Max Crawford."

"I would have taken you somewhere else, where we wouldn't be the center of attention, but I wasn't sure you'd want to spend two hours in the car with a rumored serial killer."

"That's very considerate of you." She was really pretty when she smiled. Not as sparkly as Tori, but... well, she wasn't Tori. But she was still pretty when she smiled.

There was more small talk and then Max paid the bill. Once outside, he saw that they'd managed to park at opposite ends of the parking lot, which meant parting ways immediately.

He couldn't kiss her good-night right in full view of everybody in the diner. And he wasn't sure that, although they'd had a nice dinner, they were in a kissing-good-night stage yet.

Nola pulled her keys out of her jacket pocket, and he noticed her body was half-turned in the direction of her car already. She must not think they were in a kissing-good-night stage yet, either. "Thank you for supper, Max. It was fun."

"Thank you for sharing your evening with me. I hope we can do it again."

She nodded slightly. "That would be nice. You know where to find me."

He waited in his car until she pulled out of the parking lot, since it was the gentlemanly thing to do, and then he headed toward home.

Nice. It was the first word that came to mind and it seemed to fit. The evening had been *nice*.

Once he got home, he changed into sweatpants and

brewed another mug of decaf for himself. Flipping through the television channels, he looked for something good—but not too exciting—to watch. It was time to start winding down or he'd never fall asleep.

Finally settling on a show about a pawn shop in Las Vegas, he settled back to drink his decaf. And thought about Tori.

TORI STARED AT her television, wishing one of her favorite comfort movies—*Armageddon*—was enough to distract her from wondering how Max's date was going.

She was nervous for him and now she wished she'd urged him to make a reservation in the city. Even though it meant quite a drive for Nola to meet him, it would have been better than eating in a fishbowl. If he made a wrong move, all of Whitford would know by lunch tomorrow.

When her cell phone rang, she snatched it off the table and smiled when she saw his face and number on the screen. "Hello."

"You said to let you know how it went. It didn't occur to me until after I hit the call button that you might have meant tomorrow. Or some other day."

She paused the movie. "Now is good. I've been thinking about you tonight, wondering how it went."

"It was nice."

Nice? "Is that a good nice or a bad nice?"

"There's good nice and bad nice?"

She laughed and stretched out on her couch. "It's a very blah word that needs voice inflection to really have meaning."

"It was a pleasant nice."

Ouch. That translated to boring in Tori's mind, but

she didn't say so. "So what kind of things did you talk about?"

"She likes tennis."

The way he said it, even filtered through the phone as it was, made it clear he didn't share that interest. "And you said something nice about tennis, right?"

"I did. We talked about a lot of things and I complimented her and she blushed. It was very nice."

Tori grimaced. Maybe she'd been wrong about Nola. The date sounded so bland, he might have been describing a business meeting. Of course, some of that might just be Max, but it definitely wasn't *her* kind of date.

"Do you think you'll go out again?"

"Possibly. I said I'd like to and she said that would be nice and that I know where to find her."

"Everybody needs to stop using the word *nice*. It's not a very exciting word."

"But it's the good nice."

At this point, Tori was leaning toward the bad nice but, again, she kept that opinion to herself. She didn't want to discourage him when he was feeling good about how his date went.

But she was going to get together with Hailey and try to come up with some more possible dates for Max. The idea of him and Nola being nice for the rest of their lives depressed her.

"I'm glad you had a good time."

"Me, too. I'm going to watch TV for a while and then head to bed."

The bed with the soft green comforter and the light taupe sheets. She squeezed her eyes shut, trying to shake the image, but it didn't help. "Do you have big plans for tomorrow?"

"Tomorrow's Sunday."

He said that as if it explained everything. "Oh! Sunday. Right. Big game?"

"Not big. Just a game. But that's what we do on Sundays."

"Enjoy the game, and I'll talk to you soon."

Once they'd hung up, she resumed *Armageddon* and sighed. It had gone well. Maybe it wasn't her idea of a great date, but Max and Nola had enjoyed themselves and that's what mattered.

She should probably leave Hailey out of it. Between the diner and the library, she and Hailey knew pretty much everybody in town by varying degrees and she was sure they could come up with more single women. But if Max was content with Nola, she should leave it alone.

Her phone rang again and she looked at the screen. Her dad. With a heavy sigh, she paused the movie again and answered it. "Hi, Dad."

"Hi, doll." He'd always called her doll. Her mother had always hated it, but it had made Tori feel special and treasured. Now she wondered if that was a lie, too, and he called her that just to annoy her mother. "I know you're probably working, but I haven't talked to you in a while. What have you been up to?"

She smiled. "Work. Between the diner and the computer, I haven't had much time to do anything else."

Except hang out with Max, but there was a zero percent chance she was going to tell either of her parents about him.

"You can't work all the time. You need to relax, too, or you'll end up old and gray, like your old man."

"Rumor has it I'll eventually end up old and gray

no matter what I do, so I'll work hard now and play hard later."

"That's my girl. I have a small favor to ask you."

Here it came. Even though she'd expected it from the second she saw his number on the screen, the disappointment hit her hard. Every single time, she let herself hope this time would be different. That the worst was over.

"I can't find my collapsible fishing rod, and I think it's in the garage. Your mother won't let me in and refuses to look for it. I was hoping that, the next time you visit her, you could poke around for me?"

"Sure, Dad," she said, because it was the easiest thing to say.

"You're the best, doll. I'll let you get back to work, but I'll talk to you soon. Love you."

After severing the connection, Tori pulled up the to-do app she used on her phone and made a note to find the fishing pole. She tried not to wonder if he hadn't needed her to intercede with her mother, how long would have passed before he called her, but she couldn't help it.

She'd thought moving three hours away would remove her from the middle of their battles. And, while it was definitely better than when she'd lived in the same city as the two of them, all it meant was more time on the phone and less time in person. They were just as draining long-distance.

Once she'd made the note to do her daughterly duty, she hit Play on the remote. One of the benefits of not having neighbors was the ability to crank the television as loud as she wanted, and she cranked it loud. Then she stretched out on her couch and watched Bruce Willis save the world.

ELEVEN

BUTCH BENOIT WAS always the first to arrive to watch football and this Sunday was no different. Max wasn't sure if he wanted first choice of parking spaces or to get away from Fran, but he was never late.

Butch handed over the pepperoni-and-cheese plate Fran had sent him with, then grabbed a beer from the fridge. "Heard you were out with Nola Kendrick last night."

"We had supper at the diner. Which you already know, of course."

Butch snorted. "How was the lasagna?"

Heaven forbid the gossips not get the details right. "It was good."

"Fran told me more, of course, but the only thing I really paid any attention to was lasagna. Then I realized she didn't mean she was making it for me and I stopped paying attention again."

Josh and Katie arrived together, with Gavin on their heels. Max took the basket Katie was carrying so he could lift the corner of the towel and inhale the delicious scent of Rose's baking.

"I think Rose should be the one who gets to watch the game," he said.

"Trust me, you do not want to watch sports with my mom," Katie said. "She's not a fan, but she'll try to enjoy it, which means she asks a thousand questions."

He laughed, then turned to Tori's cousin. "I'm glad you could make it today."

"Me, too." Gavin held up the glass baking dish covered with foil. "Where should I put this?"

"Is that buffalo chicken dip?"

"Of course. I swear, I can't go anywhere in this town without it."

Max put a trivet on the island and gestured for him to set the dish down. "I think I have some tortilla chips for that."

"Tori said she'd bring them."

For a few seconds, Max wasn't sure he'd heard Gavin correctly. Tori didn't follow sports. Why would she want to watch a game with them? His gaze fell on Katie, who was checking out the food, and he realized she and Tori would both be watching the game, but only one of them could sit in the corner of the sectional.

Game day was supposed to be easy. He wasn't supposed to wonder about social niceties because guys didn't really care. As long as Butch got the recliner, the men were always happy.

Matt showed up with his slow cooker of Swedish meatballs. He and those meatballs had become a regular addition to the crowd when he moved to town in the spring. And he was engaged to Hailey, who usually made plans with Tori on Sundays, according to Matt.

By the time Tori arrived, the game had started. With everybody in the living room and already yelling, thanks to a crazy opening drive, he was able to meet her in the kitchen.

"Sorry I'm late," she said, holding up a bag of chips. "I hope people aren't in there eating the buffalo chicken dip with spoons."

"I had a half a bag, but we'll need those, too." He set the bag on the counter and faced her. "Katie's sitting in the corner."

"Um…is she being punished?"

He sighed and tried again. "I mean she's sitting in the corner of the sectional. Where you like to sit."

"I'll sit somewhere else." She snatched a brownie out of the basket from Rose. "Have you been worrying about that?"

"Not worrying, exactly." Not much, anyway. "I guess I tend to overthink things when there are a lot of new things in my life."

"You can cross Katie and I coming to blows over your couch off the list of things to worry about today."

She filled a plate and followed him into the living room, where everybody gave her some variation of a hello. Max had left his plate on the coffee table, and he watched Tori place hers between his and Gavin's. Once she sat next to her cousin, Max was free to take his spot again.

It was a cozy fit, with his thigh pressing the entire length of hers. He tried to ignore it, but the warmth slowly became heat and he was so aware of the contact, he could barely concentrate on the game.

This was even worse than having her in his bedroom and that had almost killed him. He'd spent the entire time she was going through his clothes reminding himself that the only reason she cared what he wore was that she'd made getting him a date a challenge and she wanted to win. And winning meant him dating Nola.

He wolfed down the last snacks on his plate just to have an excuse to get up and throw his plate away. When that was done, he became a roaming host, refilling plates and grabbing drinks. He'd perch on the arm of a couch or lean against the doorjamb to watch the game, but mostly he mingled.

During halftime, Josh pulled him aside. "Hey, we're going to have a Halloween party at the lodge on Saturday the first, since the town trick-or-treating is Friday night. It's a fundraiser for the ATV club. You in?"

"A Halloween party? You mean with costumes?"

"Well, yeah. If you don't have costumes, it's just a party. It loses that whole Halloween thing."

Max had never been invited to a party by somebody he wasn't related to, if he didn't count elementary school, when parents forced their children to invite their entire class. Even the kids who didn't fit in.

"I know you don't have an ATV to decorate," Josh continued, "but you can still come and have a good time. Hey, maybe you could be a judge."

"No." When Josh's eyes widened, Max realized he'd been rather blunt. "I'm sorry. I would like to come to the party, but I'd rather not be a judge. I'm not very good at telling people their work is better or not as good as somebody else's."

"I get that. So just come and have a beer and a good time. I know two weeks isn't a lot of notice, but the idea just came up at the last club meeting. And it's Whitford. It's not like everybody has big plans."

"That would be movie night, wouldn't it?" From what he'd heard, movie night was taken very seriously.

Josh laughed. "So I was told. But the women agreed to skip a month for the cause. Katie said they're thinking about revamping it anyway, and voting on a movie schedule. I guess Hailey made them watch some old musical last time."

My Fair Lady. Max didn't bother telling Josh that one was his fault. That would lead to an explanation he didn't care to give. "I'll be there."

"Excellent." Josh slapped his shoulder. "I'm going to take a leak before the second half starts."

And Max was going to try to find a seat that didn't involve his body being in contact with Tori's.

THE BUZZ ABOUT Max so often fell into two camps—the people who didn't know him and thought he was weird, and the folks who watched sports at his house and said he was a good guy.

Now that she'd gotten to know Max, the game day stories had seemed at odds with everything she knew about him, and she didn't think he was that good an actor, so when Gavin had mentioned he was coming, she'd thought she'd come see for herself.

At least it was a football game today. She'd dated a football player in high school, which had meant sitting in the stands watching high school games and sitting on his couch watching professional games. She really didn't care about the game, but she had a basic idea of what was going on.

And the buzz was accurate. Sports-watching Max was quite different from everyday Max. But she was sure neither was an act, which just confused her. He was so at ease with the guys and with Katie, and she didn't see any of his little quirks on display.

Tori had been at ease, too, until he sat down and everything except the fact that his leg was pressing against hers became background noise. When he got up to throw away his plate, she'd almost sighed in relief. Then he'd been too busy being a good host to sit back down.

Somehow during the halftime seating shuffle, she'd ended up next to Katie. "Is it always like this?"

"It has been lately. At the rate he's going, Max is going to have to build an addition soon and buy more couches. So are you coming to the Halloween party at the lodge?"

"I saw the flier taped to the door at the diner, and then Hailey texted me and told me I have to go."

"You may as well. Everybody else will be there. Paige even said she's going to close the diner early, even though it's a Saturday night."

Everybody else would be there. She wondered if Nola would be going. If Tori was a good friend, she'd probably tell Max he should call her and ask her if she was going and, if she was, if she'd like to go with him.

Maybe they could even get cutesy matching his-and-hers costumes.

"What's the matter?" Katie asked.

"What?"

"You just made a horrible face."

"Oh." She was going to have to watch that. "Nothing. I remembered something I forgot to do today. Work."

The game started up again and Katie lost interest in Tori's facial expressions. Even though Katie's daily attire usually advertised one of Boston's sports teams in some way or another, Tori had no idea she was as rabid a fan as she was.

Her phone vibrated in her pocket and she pulled it out to see a text from Max.

Are you okay? You keep making faces.

She looked up and found him off to her right, leaning against the wall. *The text is coming from inside the house.*

She watched his brow furrow and had to stifle a laugh. Obviously he needed to watch more horror movies.

How many beers have you had?

This time the laugh escaped and everybody in the room turned to glare at her. Apparently the Patriots had just done something on the television that wasn't very funny.

"Sorry. Funny text," she muttered, holding up the phone to prove she wasn't amused by their football misfortunes.

Zero beers, she texted back. It was a joke. And I'm fine. I was thinking about work and made a face.

When she looked over, he smiled at her and then tucked his phone back in his pocket. It was sweet that he was worried about her. It was also interesting that he'd been watching her enough to notice she was making faces.

"I'm going to see if there are any of Matt's Swedish meatballs left," she told Katie. "You want anything?"

"I'm good. And good luck on the meatballs. They go fast."

After getting to her feet and making her way through the room, trying not to block anybody's view for more than a few seconds, she hit the bathroom. Then she took the last two meatballs. She stood at the island and ate them so nobody would ask her for some and force her to admit she'd eaten the last ones.

She wasn't surprised when Max stepped into the kitchen. He peered into the empty slow cooker, then raised a questioning eyebrow.

"Yes, I ate the last one," she said. "But don't tell them. It's bad enough I had to ask what an ineligible receiver is. They might throw me out."

"It's my house."

She put the lid back on the slow cooker, as if she could hide the evidence. "Good point."

He dug through Rose's basket until he found a couple of peanut butter cookies and winked at her on his way back to the living room.

Tori was glad his back was to her because she was pretty sure the smile on her face defined goofy.

As MUCH AS he enjoyed the company, it was always a bit of a relief when the game was over and his house emptied out. Everybody was good about picking up after themselves, but it still took him a while to put things back to rights.

He didn't mind. It was part of the routine and it calmed him down after several hours of excitement. He especially didn't mind today, because Tori stayed to help. She made herself busy, puttering around and picking up, so nobody seemed to think much of her not leaving. Before long, she was the only one left.

"What made you decide to come today?" he asked once they were alone, since he'd been wondering all afternoon.

"Gavin said he was coming and that it was kind of an open-door thing, so I decided to come."

"You don't even like sports."

She walked to the garbage to throw away a couple of paper plates. "Is it okay that I came?"

"Of course." It was not only okay that she'd come, but he was *glad* she had. "I just notice when people change their habits, that's all."

"Speaking of people and habits, you're why I came, actually." For a few seconds her words made his heart beat faster, but she wasn't done. "I've heard about Max the possible serial killer and Max the sports guy and they sounded like two different people. I wanted to see Max the sports guy."

"I'm just Max. All the time."

She shook her head, taking a seat at the island. "No, you were different when the guys—and Katie—were here to watch the game."

"I doubt that."

"You were comfortable with them, laughing and cheering and trash-talking."

"It's notable that I behaved the same way as all the other men in the room?"

She propped her chin on her hand, tilting her head a little sideways as though she was studying him. "Yes, it is. But when Josh and Matt were in the kitchen, talking about trucks, you were more like yourself. You looked like you were paying attention, but you weren't really part of the conversation."

He shrugged. "I don't have a truck."

"How are you such a guy's guy when it comes to sports, but so awkward when it comes to everything else? No offense."

"None taken. My dad and my two brothers are big into sports."

"That doesn't really answer the question."

"It was pretty obvious from the time I started talking that I was different from my brothers. At first they thought it was a 'being the baby and mama's boy' kind of thing, but I'm just…different. Then I started school and I was a little different from most of those boys, too. Then I was a nerd." He stopped when he looked up from the leftover baked goods he was wrapping in plastic wrap and saw her face. "Should I stop telling this story? You look like you want to punch somebody in the face."

"I do… But, no, you shouldn't stop."

"Okay. I realized that whether a guy was six or sixteen or sixty, he could always talk to other guys about sports. No matter where I went, I saw men—some of whom were strangers to each other—talking about sports."

"So you started following sports."

"I know what you're thinking," he said, because he could see it on her face, "but I honestly love the games. The strategies and statistics combined with luck and athletic performance is fascinating to me."

"But it also made you feel more like your father and your brothers?"

He shrugged. "I'll never be like them, but I was able to be part of their conversations. I could sit at the supper table and argue about who had the best chance to win the Series just like they did."

"Well, today was definitely a side of you I hadn't seen before."

"I'm with people who share a love for sports and are watching a game. If they also shared a love for model railroading, you'd see that side of me then, too."

The way she was looking at him gave him an urge

to squirm, just as his elementary school teachers' looks had. Maybe Tori had missed her true calling. "That's why, when you talked to Jeanette at the diner, you opened with sports. Because it's instant camaraderie."

"You say that like it's a bad thing."

"Of course it's not, since you really love sports. But it's a rather different side of you, so make sure she likes *both* sides."

"Let's watch a movie."

She must have recognized his signal that he didn't want to talk about it anymore, because she shrugged. "What did you have in mind?"

"We could see if *My Fair Lady* is on streaming."

"Ha, ha. Action or horror."

"Drama?"

She made a face. "Depends on the drama."

"Let me finish this up and we'll see what's on."

She helped him finish the kitchen and he said nothing when she loaded the dishwasher differently than he usually did. It was nice to have somebody to talk to, which was what he'd been hoping to achieve when he went to the diner the first time.

Meeting a friend like Tori was the unexpected bonus. He stopped wiping the counter and frowned. That was something to take into consideration. If he was going to have a serious relationship with a woman, she'd not only have to not mind having her living room occasionally overrun by sports fan, but she'd have to like Tori.

"Are you trying to set the toaster on fire with your eyes?" Tori nudged him in the side. "That only works in the movies, you know."

"I was thinking about something."

"I could tell. Something serious?"

Guessing she might think it was ridiculous for him to factor how a woman felt about Tori into the equation, he shook his head. "Nothing serious."

She looked skeptical, but didn't push. "If you're trying to find a way to twist my arm into watching an old musical, don't even try."

In the end, he let her have her choice because he was a gentleman and she was company, so they watched *The Avengers*. He didn't bother to tell her he'd seen it many times already, and he laughed when she quoted some of the dialogue just ahead of the actors. She'd seen it a few times herself.

He didn't mind. There were definitely worse ways to spend an evening than watching a favorite movie with Tori.

TWELVE

Late Tuesday morning, Tori punched her time card at the diner, then went back out front to grab a soda in a to-go cup. She'd stayed up very late working, so the early morning phone call from Drew had been unwelcome. The explanation of morning sickness, complete with background noises, had been worse. She'd jumped at the chance to work Liz's shift just to get off the phone.

She was seriously dragging now, though, and she knew no matter how much soda she drank, there was a nap in her near future.

"Thanks again for coming in," Paige said. With her dark hair in a ponytail and the same Trailside Diner T-shirt they all wore, nobody would guess Paige was married to a guy with a bunch of money.

Mitch Kowalski owned a controlled demolition company that imploded big buildings all over the world, which apparently paid well. But the diner was Paige's pride and joy and, even after they married and had Sarah, Paige had no interest in walking away from it.

Which was especially good right now, because Tori really wanted to sit down. And sleep.

"I told you I don't mind filling in beyond my regular hours if you need it. I was at my computer until two, though, so I'm glad you're doing lunch." Paige would fill the gap between Tori and Ava. When Tori got called in without warning, she usually tried to keep the hours to a minimum.

"I'm going to talk to Rose later, and call Mitch. I'm thinking if I bring a playpen in, I can bring Sarah in with me to open and then Rose can pick her up here once it's a decent hour."

"If we change up the schedule, I can cover for Liz. If it's planned in advance, I can change my schedule accordingly."

Paige smiled and shook her head. "I appreciate you and I'm so glad you're here, but a person who works until two in the morning doesn't become somebody who gets up to work at four-thirty in the morning just like that. You're a night owl. I'm a morning person."

There was no denying that. "Schedule me however you think it'll work best for everybody and I'll work around it. But, yeah, I'm not sure the customers would like the version of me that gets up at four-thirty every day."

Taking her soda, Tori went out through the kitchen door into the parking lot. She'd gotten a text from Gavin earlier, asking her to stop by his place on her way home. Since his place was a very small mobile home at the back of the diner's parking lot, it wasn't much of a detour.

She knocked on the door and wasn't surprised to find him dressed and ready for his shift at the diner. He always went in early because he truly loved his job and nothing excited him more than cooking whatever he had planned for the day. There was a good chance he'd already been over there, tucked away in the prep area while she was out front.

She sat on his couch and looked around. "Have I

ever told you this is the tiniest trailer I've ever seen that wasn't hooked to the back of a pickup truck?"

"Every time you come in. And I'll say what I always say. It takes like five minutes to clean the entire thing."

Paige had lived here until she moved in with Mitch, from what Tori had heard. The trailer had come with the diner and Paige hadn't cared that it was small and not…recently renovated. It was all hers and it was home.

"So what's up?" she asked, because it was obvious he was looking for somebody to talk to.

He leaned against the fridge. Thanks to the floor plan, he was still only a few feet away. "I have an opportunity to cook for a restaurant in Kennebunkport."

Tori's eyebrows arched. "Holy crap, that's amazing, Gav! Maybe you'll get to cook for former President Bush."

"I have to prove myself. It's like a tryout, I guess. But it's a fancy place, Tori. For a lot more money. And he also owns two restaurants in Boston."

"When do you go? Do you need my car?"

He laughed, holding up his hands. "I have my truck."

"The exhaust is held up with a wire coat hanger and you get about six miles to the gallon. You can't show up in Kennebunkport in that. Take my car to save on gas, if nothing else."

"I'm not sure if I'm going to go."

"Whoa." She sat forward on the couch, seeing the conflict in his expression. "This is a great opportunity for you. It's a step toward living your dreams. What do you mean you're not sure if you're going to go?"

"What if I get the job? If I leave, who's going to cook at the diner? Carl only does breakfast but, even if he did dinners, he can't work that many hours every day. His wife would kill him."

"Paige can hire a new cook."

"Who? Where is she going to find somebody? After all she's done to support me, I can't just leave her like that."

Tori grabbed his hand, squeezing it and pulling him down on the couch next to her. "It's *because* of all she's done to support you that you have to go. She's so proud of you and she wants you to follow your dreams. Why do you think she's bought all those weird ingredients and let you test recipes on her customers?"

"I talked to Carl this morning. I know you had to come in and cover for Liz. She could have morning sickness for months, right? I can't tell Paige that, on top of that, she's going to lose her dinner cook."

"We'll make it work. I can cook. Paige can cook. Hell, I bet Rose would help out."

"Rose has enough on her plate. And she doesn't need to be on her feet that long."

"She believes in you. We *all* believe in you—the whole freaking town, Gavin—and we'll figure it out."

"You can't run a kitchen with rotating, untrained staff. There's quality and consistency and—"

"Gavin." She sighed and leaned back. "I love the diner and I know you do, too, but you have to take this shot."

"The chef came here. You see these guys ride into town on their ATVs in muddy jeans and you don't give them much thought. I guess one of them is some super-rich banker guy who knows the chef and he kept talking up my food. The chef stayed at the lodge and came in three times and nobody knew. He came to Whitford to taste my cooking, Tori. Can you believe that?"

"That just proves my point."

"I guess this chef isn't hung up on formal training because anybody can be taught to cook. He's big on instincts and passion and the ability to take whatever you have on hand and make it a meal a customer won't forget."

She shook his arm, unable to contain her excitement. "That's what you *do,* Gavin. When are you supposed to go?"

"A week from Thursday. They'll put me up in a bed and breakfast and I'll have the weekend to show them what I can do. That way, if they offer me the job, I can acclimate during the off-season and be at full strength for next tourist season."

"That's great timing for us, too. The ATV season's about over, but the sledders won't start coming in until mid-to-late December, so we can look for a cook during the slow time. Gavin, tell me you're going to do this."

He took a deep breath and, when he exhaled, she could hear the tremor. "I'm going to do this."

She wrapped her arms around him and squeezed. "I think you'll have to make this town at least a year's worth of buffalo chicken dip to freeze before anybody will let you go."

"I'll leave you the recipe. Or you can find it on the internet. It's not exactly a secret gourmet dish."

She waved her hand dismissively. "It won't be the same. It's never the same if you have to make it yourself. And I confess I tried to make it and screwed it up."

"Says the woman who offered to cook in my place."

She grinned. "Hey, we'll make the Trailside Diner

the first potluck restaurant in Maine if that's what it takes."

The nap was put on hold while she helped him plan what he'd take and what he'd wear. She also taped a note on his fridge reminding him to go see Katie for a haircut. The closer it came to next Thursday, the more nervous he was going to get.

She was getting pretty good at taking care of other people, she thought. *Tori Burns, helping men get their shit together.* Too bad she was barely keeping up with the two jobs she already had. And Max.

MAX FINISHED HIS LUNCH and pushed his empty plate back toward the edge of the counter. Paige snagged it as she walked by with a coffeepot and dropped it into a bus pan under the counter without even slowing down.

He'd hoped Tori would be working, but Paige had told him she'd already left. It was disappointing and he'd thought about texting her, but during a lull, Paige had told him how their morning had gone. Tori had enough going on without dealing with him.

Nola was a conundrum. He wasn't sure how to handle the follow-up to their first date. Should he call her? It seemed like if he called to thank her for a lovely evening, there would be an expectation of asking her for a second date. If he wasn't the best at taking social cues in person, he was even worse over the telephone.

He paid the bill and then walked outside, debating on his next course of action. He'd parked in the municipal lot, which meant walking by the town hall to get back to his car.

He could go in, thank her for the information and inquire as to the next step. While it may have begun as a way to talk to Nola, actually building a garage made sense. He wouldn't have to arrange things like a jigsaw puzzle in the shed, his property value would go up, and there would be less lawn to mow.

As he went by the town hall, he turned sharply and went through the door before he could change his mind. It wasn't fair to ask Tori to keep holding his hand—figuratively, of course—and he needed to stand on his own two feet.

Nola's smile was warm and genuine when she saw him step up to the counter. "Hi, Max."

"Hi. I was walking by and I thought I'd come in and thank you for the information you gave me. I think I'm going to go ahead with the project, so I need to research the next step."

She held up a finger, then rummaged through a file drawer behind her. Then she handed him a form across the counter. "Fill out this building permit and the building inspector will look it over and then you'll talk. You need to know your property lines and the setback and such."

"Okay." His grandmother had given him a fat folder of house papers, so he made a mental note to go through it again. He thought that information was in there.

"I should warn you, he's only here every other Wednesday because it's part-time so it could be a slow process."

"That's fine. It wouldn't make sense to start the construction until spring, anyway."

"Okay, then."

There was an old-fashioned industrial clock hanging on the wall and Max could literally hear the seconds tick by. "I also want to thank you for having dinner with me. It was very nice. The good kind of nice."

She looked confused. "Is there a bad kind of nice?"

"So I'm told." Now what? "I'd like to do it again, if you're so inclined."

"That would be lovely. I have plans Saturday, but I like the fish fry at the diner on Friday nights. If that's not too soon."

"No." He frowned at the pen chained to the counter, wondering if people actually tried to steal them. "I mean, no, that's not too soon. I haven't had their fish fry yet."

"So five o'clock Friday?"

He was aware of somebody coming through the door and was grateful for the interruption, which effectively ended the conversation. "I'll be there. And thank you for the form."

Once he was outside, he took a deep breath and started the walk back to his car. There. He'd done it. He had a second date with Nola Kendrick, who was a very nice woman. The good kind of nice.

It was unfortunate the diner was their only option, no matter how much he liked the place or how good their fish fry was. It wasn't very romantic, like the place he'd taken Tori to on their mock date. There had even been candlelight, which had seemed very romantic when reflected in Tori's brown eyes.

He paused in the process of unlocking his car. It seemed odd that, despite several conversations and a dinner date, he had no idea what color Nola's eyes were.

He'd have to remedy that lack of knowledge on Friday.

THE NEXT MORNING, Tori was once again filling in for Liz at an obscene hour of the morning. But she'd been ready this time. After leaving Gavin's yesterday, she'd gone home and made a list of everything she had going on, professionally.

The first thing she'd done was put a notice on her website that she wasn't accepting new clients for the remainder of the year. Then she prioritized the jobs she had in the queue and sorted them into tasks that required a lot of time and concentration, and smaller jobs that could be done in short bursts between everything else.

She was going to get everything done, but it would be a delicate dance. Then she'd foregone the nap and gone to bed earlier than she had in years, anticipating that early morning phone call.

What she hadn't anticipated was Max walking through the door at eight o'clock. As far as she could tell, breakfast at the diner was yet another break in his routine. The guy was living on the wild side now.

She poured him a coffee and snagged a wrapped silverware bundle. "What brings you into town so early?"

"I've asked Nola for another date."

She set the cup down, then cursed under her breath when the hot liquid sloshed over the rim onto her hand. "At eight in the morning?"

"No. A breakfast date would be weird, wouldn't it?"

She shrugged. "I guess it depends on why you're together for breakfast. But I meant, did you ask her at eight in the morning?"

"Oh. No, I asked her yesterday. I'm going to build a garage, so I went to see what the next step was and she gave me a building permit form. And I asked her if she'd like to go out again."

"And? What did she say?"

"We're going to have dinner again. The fish fry here on Friday. I haven't had it, but she says it's very good."

"I'm happy for you. A second date is kind of a big deal."

"By a third date, we should be comfortable enough to make the drive to the city and back together."

The smile on her face felt incredibly fake, but he didn't seem to notice. "You'll be dancing with her before you know it."

"And I owe it all to you."

"No, you don't. I might have boosted your confidence a little and we had some fun with it—helped you relax—but you're the same Max now that you were before you met me."

The way his green eyes captured and held hers made her stomach do a flip. "No, I don't think I am."

She wasn't the same, either, but the coffee counter at the Trailside Diner was not the place to have deep personal revelations. Especially unwelcome ones. With a glib laugh, she reached under the counter and grabbed some sugar packets even though his didn't really need refilling, just to break the eye contact.

"Hey, if you want to give me the credit, I'll take it. You can name your first kid after me."

"Then let's hope it's a girl."

She could tell by the slight curve of his mouth that he was teasing. He wasn't really mentally naming the children he might have with Nola, which was a good thing. Max could be intense and, if he moved too fast, he'd scare off any woman.

"Do you know what you want for breakfast?"

He looked at the menu, but didn't pick it up. "What's good?"

"Everything's good. Carl isn't a fancy cook, but his breakfasts are amazing."

"Paige lucked out with Carl and Gavin from the sound of it."

It was on the tip of her tongue to tell Max about Gavin's opportunity in Kennebunkport, but she kept her mouth shut. She wanted to talk to him about it, especially the chaos it would bring into her own life, because he was so logical and calm when it came to facing a problem, but it wasn't time yet. As far as she knew, Gavin hadn't had an opportunity to talk to Paige yet and she didn't want their boss and friend to find out through the grapevine.

"Just write something down for me."

She arched an eyebrow, considering him. "It's not like you to just roll with things."

"I'm broadening my horizons."

"Anything you don't like?"

"No seafood and no beans."

She wrote out an order for a veggie omelet, home fries and raisin toast, which she handed over to Carl. Then she did a circuit of her tables, refilling coffees and checking up on everybody. Three parties came in and two tables had food go out before Max's appeared in the window.

When she set it down in front of him, his eyes got big. "Carl doesn't skimp on portions."

"It's the best breakfast in the state of Maine. Trust me, you'll eat it all."

"Raisin toast is an interesting choice."

She topped off his coffee. "You bought two loaves of this raisin bread the day I ran into you at the market."

"This is the same bread?"

"Yup. Carl's wife bakes it at home and sells it to Paige and Fran. The cinnamon buns, too."

He slid his knife through the omelet and a bounty of cheese and vegetables oozed out. "I really like this town."

THIRTEEN

On Friday, Max worked until he would have just enough time to shower and dress for his second date with Nola. Hanging around watching the clock wouldn't help him relax any.

He should be more excited about the coming evening. It was a second date, with the awkwardness and formalities of the first one out of the way. They would both be more at ease and, hopefully, they'd both want to keep going toward an exclusive relationship.

He really wished Whitford had a movie theater, though. Or a bowling alley or even a mini-golf course. Sitting across from a woman with nothing to do but hold a conversation was a lot of pressure.

He arrived at the diner ten minutes before five and found the table they'd sat at the first time was open. He took it, wondering if it would become "their" table. Women seemed to like things like that.

"Just you tonight, Max?"

He smiled at Ava and shook his head. "Nola's joining me."

"That's twice," she said, giving him a sassy, raised eyebrow. "Might be getting serious."

He liked Ava. She was older and always worked the evening shift. He'd heard, maybe at the General Store, that she'd taken the job at the diner after her husband passed and requested the evening hours because that's when she missed him the most. She was funny and bold and he could imagine Tori being like her some day.

"She said the fish fry was good and I haven't tried it yet, so here we are" was all he said. Besides being funny and bold, Ava was also one of the pivotal links in Whitford's gossip chain.

He stood when Nola arrived, and she looked pleased by the gesture as she slid into her side of the booth. "I'm running a few minutes behind. Sorry about that."

They both ordered decaf and the fish fry, and then they talked about her day while waiting for Gavin to work his magic. She told him a few funny stories—without names, of course—from her years of working with Whitford's public.

"What about your work? You haven't told me what you do yet."

It was tempting to make a joke, but this was their second date. "I paint models. Trains, to be exact. For people who do model railroading."

"Really?" She made a *huh* face, which didn't give him a lot to go on. "And that's your job? Like your regular job?"

"Yes. It has been for about ten years. I did it part-time while working for a tax firm, but I made the jump to full-time several years before I moved here."

"That's interesting."

He should offer to show her his workshop, but he didn't. While she'd said the right words, there hadn't been a lot of enthusiasm behind them. He knew from experience she would be one of those whose eyes glazed over with boredom mere minutes into a tour of his basement.

Luckily, fish fry was a fast dish and Ava appeared

with baskets of fish and fries, and dishes of coleslaw. "Max, if you haven't had Gavin's slaw yet, hold on to your socks. And don't forget, fish fry is all you can eat."

"I'm pretty sure this *is* all I can eat," he said, staring at the food in front of him.

"If you change your mind, just holler. I'll be right back with more decaf."

The coleslaw was as good as promised, the fries were freshly cut, and he could tell Gavin had breaded fresh fish himself rather than relying on frozen. As much as he'd regret not having feasts like this at the diner, he really hoped the kid made good on his culinary dreams.

Neither of them had seconds, but he asked Nola if she'd like dessert or more decaf.

"I don't think so. Not tonight."

She sounded a little odd, and he had a feeling he wasn't going to have to worry about her good-night kiss body language. "Okay."

"I...I like you, Max. You're funny and sweet and I like spending time with you. But..."

But. Max knew what that meant. He waited for some sign of distress or disappointment or something in himself, but all he felt was relief. He liked Nola, but he didn't want to spend the rest of his life with her. It was all too...polite. He'd finally figured out Tori's reaction to the word *nice.*

"I don't think there's any spark between us," she continued. "Not a romantic spark. I genuinely would like us to be friends, though."

"I'd like that, too." When she started to pull her wallet out of her purse, he waved it away. "I'm still paying."

She kissed his cheek on her way out, and Max sighed. She really was a nice person.

He still had half a cup of decaf, so he decided to stay and finish it. Ava had already cleared the other dishes, so he was surprised when she slid into the booth across from him.

"That was painful to watch," she said.

"It was mutual. More or less."

"I don't mean the leaving. I mean the date. You two have less chemistry than two two-by-fours."

He laughed. "I should probably be insulted by that."

"Not talking about your personalities. There's no chemistry between the two of you. Don't even try to pretend you spent the entire dinner trying to figure out how to get her naked."

His fingers tightened around his coffee cup and he stared at the liquid lazily swirling inside. There was no possible way for him to respond to that statement.

"I've known Nola her entire life and she is the sweetest thing. Love her to death. But she needs a rowdy, loud man to shake her up and turn her neat, orderly life upside down. And you need the same in a woman."

"Does the advice come with the fish fry, or do you charge extra for that?"

"Oh, you do have teeth, Max Crawford. I was beginning to wonder." She leaned forward and grinned. "You can show your appreciation in your tip. And speaking of tips, here's one for you—stop pussyfooting around and smash your way through that wall Tori built up around herself."

"I…" If he squeezed the coffee cup any tighter, it was going to shatter in his hands. "I…don't know what to say to that."

"I know she's younger than you and probably the last

woman on earth you'd think is your type, but trust me. That girl is exactly your type."

"I think I'll have a slice of Boston cream pie."

She laughed, the kind of big and booming laugh that made everybody in the diner look. "Don't want to talk about her, huh? That says a lot."

He took his time eating the pie and had two more cups of decaf. He shouldn't, but he wasn't in any particular rush to get home. Now that he was back to square one, he wasn't in the mood for the quiet. Sometimes silence was comforting, but sometimes it was isolating.

After all the food and coffee he'd consumed, he decided he'd take a walk around the square before heading home. He could work off some calories and soothe his soul at the same time.

When Ava brought him his change, she couldn't resist one last shot. "You need shaking up, kiddo. And so does Tori. If you're a smart man, you'll be the one doing the shaking."

He only gave her a polite smile, because he had no intentions of discussing how he felt about Tori with a woman who had a voice like a megaphone and no tact, but he tipped her thirty percent.

TORI IGNORED THE kitchen timer telling her it was time to get up and move around until she couldn't take the sound anymore. Then she twisted it to the off position and tossed it back on the desk.

Then she went back to the sci-fi cover she was working on. Screw a break. She needed to work. It was the only thing that could distract her from the fact Max was out on a second date with Nola Kendrick.

Even without looking at the clock, she knew it was

getting late. They'd be done with dinner by now and maybe they'd gone for a romantic walk around the square. Maybe the date had gone so well she had invited him back to her house for a drink, or vice versa.

Maybe, right that minute, Max was making love to Nola.

Swearing viciously, Tori hit the undo button to fix what she'd just screwed up and tried to shove Max out of her mind.

She zoomed in on the nose, working with the pixels until she achieved the shape and shading she was looking for. Then she worked on the eyes for a while. It was painstaking work, and she could already feel the pull in her shoulders that would become a painful reminder of ergonomics.

Once she was satisfied with the eyes, she zoomed back out to the full cover view.

And swore again.

She'd made the guy Max Crawford. The hair wasn't quite right, but there was no mistaking the features. Since this was the fifth book in the author's series and the leading man had previously *not* looked like Max, that was a problem.

She deleted her work back to her evening starting point and closed up shop. It was time to acknowledge to herself how much she hated Max going out with Nola. She was jealous and she didn't like sharing him, even if her own relationship was supposed to be strictly friendship.

She wanted Max. There was no denying that at this point. But she wanted him temporarily and it wouldn't be fair to pull him away from a woman who might want to keep him forever.

The worst part was knowing—or at least strongly believing—that she could have him. She could get Max into her bed, or his, and satisfy the hunger for him that had been building inside her.

But Max wasn't a fling kind of guy and, when she'd had her fill and it was time to cut him loose, he'd be hurt. She could imagine all too well how he'd look while trying to figure out what he'd done wrong and how he could fix it.

She couldn't do that to him. All she could do was be his friend and help him go after what he *really* wanted, which was a wife.

And what she could do right now was get out of this apartment before she lost her freaking mind. She pulled on a hoodie, shoved her keys in one pocket and her phone in the other, then went downstairs.

Unfortunately, once she was on the sidewalk, she realized she had no place to go. She walked aimlessly in the dark for a while, before ending up on the bench in the town square, where she'd sat with Max before he asked Nola to have dinner with him.

Taking out her phone, she scrolled through her contacts, looking for somebody to text. But they were probably all snuggled up with their guys and, though Hailey or Liz or even Paige would be willing to be a shoulder for her, she wasn't going to bother them.

So she sat, trying to get her head on straight so the next time she saw Max, he'd never guess she considered—however briefly—torpedoing the serious relationship he was trying to build.

Maybe she needed some flash cards like the ones she'd made for Max so she could practice reacting to his dating successes. Going on a third date. *That's great,*

Max! She's finally invited me to her place. *Go, Max!* We made love for the first time.

Okay, no. Hopefully he'd realize some things were for discussion and some things weren't.

The next step. A ring. The proposal. *That's great, Max. I'm so thrilled for you. I hope you're both very happy and that you never yell at her that you wish she was dead.*

She couldn't picture Max ever doing that, but if you'd asked her several years ago, she wouldn't have been able to picture her father doing it, either.

Movement in the corner of her eye caught her attention and she looked over to see Max walking across the grass toward her. Considering where her thoughts had been for the last few hours, she wasn't sure she could manage it, but she gave herself the world's fastest pep talk.

Max was her friend. He was a great guy and he wanted to find that special someone to spend the rest of his life with. She *would* be happy for him, dammit.

"Were you waiting for me?" he asked as he sat on the bench next to her.

"No. I went for a walk and ended up sitting here. I thought you'd be home already, actually. Or…with Nola."

"After she left, I stayed for dessert."

"You didn't leave with her?"

He gave a little shrug. "We've decided to be friends."

Disappointment for him pushed back anything else she might have felt. "I'm sorry, Max. I thought she was such a good match for you."

"Perhaps too good a match. We'd make very good companions and we could probably have years of polite conversations but, as she said, there was no romantic spark."

"I really wanted it to work out." It wasn't a lie. While she might be conflicted about her feelings, she'd wanted it to work out for *him*.

"It was good practice, and now I have another friend. Besides, it helped me refine my list. I'd underestimated the need for chemistry, I suppose."

Tori turned sideways on the bench so she could see him, pulling her knees up. The temperature had bypassed chilly and gone straight to cold. "Maybe if you were eighty-five, companionship and polite conversation would be enough, but you definitely need spark. Sparks are good."

"I also need somebody who challenges me. Somebody who gets my sense of humor and pushes me out of my comfort zone."

Somebody like her. As soon as the thought entered her mind, Tori tried to crush it. The last thing Max needed was somebody like her, with her issues and her determination not to tie her future happiness to the fleeting concept of love.

"She's out there, Max."

For once, she had a hard time deciphering the look he gave her. "I know she is."

MAX HAD A SMALL CROWD for the game on Sunday. There were usually a couple of weekends each time a new season was almost upon them that the men had to stay home and do chores. And this wouldn't be the most exciting game on the schedule, with the Patriots so heavily favored to win nobody was even talking about it ahead of time.

Butch was there, of course. Being semi-retired, since Fran handled the money for the gas station and there wasn't a huge call for tow trucks in Whitford, he got his honey-do list done during the week so it wouldn't interfere with his weekends. Josh and Katie showed up, and it looked like that would be it.

Max was sorry there wouldn't be any Swedish meatballs. Or buffalo chicken dip. He sure hoped, if Gavin did go off to pursue his culinary aspirations, he'd give somebody the recipe first.

In an unheard-of turn of events, Butch's cell phone rang during the second quarter. He listened for a few minutes, scowling, and then shoved it back in his pocket.

"I've told Margie Walsh five times she needs to change the alternator in that junk she drives. I shouldn't have to miss the game because it finally shit the bed."

Katie gave him a stern look. "You're not leaving Mrs. Walsh stranded until the game is over."

With a groan, Butch shoved himself out of the recliner. "No, I'm not. But if she doesn't let me change the alternator this time, I'm washing my hands of her."

"It doesn't sound like she has much choice this time," Max pointed out.

"You'd be surprised. She's a very stubborn woman. Even worse than Fran. You watch. Now that I'm leaving, the Pats'll start blowing it and I'll miss a nail-biter."

Once he was gone, Max turned the TV down. Since Butch was losing his hearing and refused to admit it, for the first few minutes of every game, all they heard was *Hey, turn that up a bit, would ya?*

"So, Max," Josh said, once it was halftime. "Nola told somebody who told somebody else who told Fran who told Rosie who told Katie who told me you went on a second date with her."

"We did. The fish fry at the diner is really good."

"This is probably a dumb question, but why are you dating her instead of Tori?"

Max pretended he didn't see Katie kick Josh's leg. "Why would I date Tori?"

"According to, well, *everybody,* you guys spend a lot of time together and you seem to enjoy being around each other. And maybe the fact you barely took your eyes off of her when she came over to watch the game last Sunday."

Max stared at the remote in his hand, wondering what he was supposed to say to that. Apparently everybody in Whitford thought Tori was the right woman for him. "I'm not dating her because she doesn't want to date *me.*"

"Are you sure about that?" Josh asked. "Let's just say she wasn't exactly ignoring you, either."

"I know she doesn't want to *marry* me."

"Not yet, but you haven't known each other *that* long."

"No, she doesn't want to marry anybody. Ever."

"I've heard that," Katie said in a soft voice. "She's had some family issues, so she's a little cynical right now. She'll come around."

"Maybe she will." Max shrugged. "But Tori and I are just friends. And, actually, Nola and I will be just friends, as well."

He supposed that was the silver lining. He had more friends now. Actually, he had enough so it was hardly remarkable anymore. He was just part of the community now, he guessed.

"Do you have a costume for the party yet?" Katie asked, probably to change the subject.

"Yes, I do." After much anxiety, the answer to the costume problem had recently come to him at two o'clock in the morning and struck him as so amusing, he'd gotten out of bed to order it online.

"Are you going to tell us?"

He shook his head. "No, I'm not. What are you going as?"

"We're still hashing it out," Josh said, and he didn't sound happy about it. "I want to go as a football player and get Katie in a cheerleader outfit, but she won't."

Max tried not to imagine that, since Katie's fiancé was a good friend. And he was sitting right there. "How about Captain America and the Black Widow?"

Katie gave him a look that should have torched his eyebrows off. "Black leather bodysuit, Max? Really?"

"I'm not wearing tights, dude," Josh added.

"I'm sure you'll come up with something great."

Katie gave them each a stern look. "And child appropriate. Family party."

Max wondered what costume Tori would choose for the party. She didn't strike him as the cheerleader type, but she could pull off a black leather bodysuit. With high-heeled black boots, like the pair she'd worn on their mock date.

She could definitely pull that off. Shifting on the couch, he tried to focus on the halftime report and hoped the second half was about to start. He needed the distraction.

FOURTEEN

On Wednesday, Tori talked Hailey into putting a sign on the library door announcing she was taking a lunch break and joining her at Jeanette's consignment store. It was the closest they had to shopping in Whitford and she didn't have time to drive into the city.

"I am going to find a costume here," she announced as they walked through the door.

Hailey snorted. "Unless you want to go as a crocheted toilet paper cover doll or an eighties bedspread, I think you're out of luck."

"There's all kinds of things here. We'll find something."

"You spend most of your life on the computer. Why didn't you order something online?"

"I meant to, but I kept putting it off and now the party's in three days." Tori pulled an honest-to-goodness suede jacket with fringe off a rack. "Huh."

"It's Village People, not Village Person, and your friends already have costumes. Put it back."

She didn't need to be told twice. They wandered through the aisles, pulling out random items of clothing and putting them back. Worst-case scenario, she could go as a fortune-teller. The last resort of procrastinators roaming consignment shops, looking for a costume.

Hailey pulled out a long black gown with a plunging neckline. "Elvira?"

"Or Maleficent." It had possibilities.

"Both bad-ass sexy women." Holding it up so they could see it better, Hailey frowned. "This dress is three feet taller than you are."

"I'm not *that* short. And the hem can be cut off. It's the neckline that's a problem. I don't think my belly button's supposed to show."

"If you wore this, Whitford would totally have something more exciting to talk about than Max Crawford and Nola Kendrick."

Tori sighed. "I hope nobody's saying anything mean. Having to date in this town sucks."

"Nobody's being mean. Everybody likes Max and Nola, so we're being discreet…ish."

"Great."

"We're missing an important question here." Hailey looked at the gown again. "Who do you think wore this? And how do you think it ended up in a thrift store in Whitford?"

"I don't know anybody who could pull that off. And I don't want to imagine anybody I know wearing it and *not* pulling it off, if you know what I mean."

With a sigh of regret, Hailey hung the gown back on the rack. "Hey, I have an idea. You could go as a cheerleader."

"Really? I'm not the pom-pom shaking type."

"Guys who like sports like cheerleaders. And Max likes sports."

"Leave it alone." When Hailey's eyebrows shot up at her tone, Tori rolled her eyes. "I'm not hooking up with Max. I like him too much for that."

"That makes no sense to me."

"When it comes to fairy-tale romances, he's Disney and I'm Grimm."

"Hey, funny timing."

Tori glanced over and saw Hailey holding up a Snow White costume. "That's for a kid."

"Yeah, but you're short."

"Again, I'm not *that* short. Also, I have boobs."

Hailey put the costume back and pulled out another hanger. "Here we go. A housecoat that looks like it was made from olive green drapes."

Tori was about to call it quits, but something about the cut of the coat or robe or whatever it was supposed to be flipped the light switch in her head and she snatched it out of her friend's hands. "I need this. Where are the hats? Does she have a hat section?"

"You can't be serious, Tori. That is *not* sexy."

That all depended on whose buttons you were trying to push. "Trust me."

"Based on that robe, I'm thinking no. You can't be trusted anymore."

"Says the woman who asked how I'd feel about a safety-orange bridesmaid gown to match her camo wedding."

"That was a joke. You know that was a joke, right?"

Tori just laughed and walked around the end of the aisle, almost running smack into Nola Kendrick. "Oh. Hi."

"Hi, Tori." She looked like she was going to keep walking, but then she hesitated. "How's Max?"

It made Tori uncomfortable that Nola would think Max came to her after their second and final date at the diner. He had, of course, but she hadn't realized their friendship was that well-known around town. Which was stupid. She should have known better.

"He's fine. He had a nice time with you and he's glad you'll be friends." There. That was bland enough.

"Me, too. I'll be honest. I think one of the reasons I'm not the one for him is that he's really into you."

"Told you," Hailey muttered.

"We're friends," Tori said.

"That's what I've heard." Nora's smile was slightly on the tight side. "I have to run, so I'll see you later. Nice robe, by the way."

When she was gone, Hailey nudged her in the ribs. "That was a dig."

"And so subtle, too." Tori took a deep breath and shoved Nola out of her mind. "Hats. Where are the freaking hats?"

MAX WAITED PATIENTLY for Miranda to line the shipping box up on the postal scale *just so,* careful to keep his expression neutral.

Rumor had it not a single living soul in Whitford could remember a time when Miranda hadn't run the post office, and he could believe it. She had to be looking down the barrel at three digits if she was a day.

She asked him the required questions as to whether there was anything in the package there shouldn't be, glared to let him know she didn't believe him and then squinted at the insurance form. One of the biggest adjustments, business-wise, when he'd moved to Whitford had been the lack of shipping options. When he had to ship to Canada, he'd drive to the city because he was a patient man, but not that patient. For everyday shipping, though, the easiest and quickest method for returning models to their owners was Miranda.

It had been clear since day one she thought he was up to no good. He'd tried everything. Pleasant manners. Cool business professional. He'd even tried charming once, but she'd called him a *cheeky monkey* and that had scared him even more than her cantankerousness.

He was a creature of habit, so he'd been shipping boxes the way he always had. But today he made a mental note to research doing the postage online so all he'd have to do in the future was drop the packages and run. For now, he simply waited patiently while she very slowly went through the steps necessary to ship his box, just as he did every single time. While he'd never seen any signs she'd opened a package meant for him, he'd taken extra care in packing them since his first trip to the Whitford post office because he was sure she'd at least shake them.

Once that errand—admittedly his least favorite— was done, he walked back to his car and used his phone to photograph the receipts she'd given him before tucking them into an envelope in his glove box.

Lunch, he decided. He was getting spoiled by the food at the diner and would probably put on a few pounds if he wasn't careful, but since he was already in town, lunch couldn't hurt.

Because it was a little past lunch rush time, the diner was almost empty when he went in. He sat at the counter, on his usual stool, and plucked the menu out of the holder.

"Hey, you."

He looked up, his pulse jumping at the sound of Tori's voice. "Hi. You again, huh?"

"Disappointed?"

"Pleasantly surprised."

She smiled and held up the coffeepot. When he nodded, she poured him a cup. "I work all kinds of weird hours, filling in where needed. You never know when I'll be here."

"I'm looking for something light. Between Carl and Gavin, I'm going to need new pants if I don't watch it."

"We always have the half-a-sandwich and a cup of soup special. How about turkey on wheat and some chicken noodle?"

"Sounds perfect." He put the menu back and fixed his coffee while she handed in his order.

A few minutes later, he heard a female voice yelling for Tori. He watched her lean into the pass-through window. "What's the matter?"

"Where are the damn crackers?"

"We have the crackers out front. You just give me the soup and I'll put the crackers on the plate."

"That makes no sense."

"We give out crackers for more than soup. Toddlers love them and sometimes people ask for them to hold them over if we're busy. We can't be asking the cook for crackers all the time."

He saw the dishes appear in the window and Tori brought them over to him, then grabbed several packages of crackers from under the counter.

"That was fast," he said.

"The soup's in a steam table so it's just a matter of making half a sandwich."

"Dare I ask what's going on?"

"What's going on is Rose." She smiled a fake smile. "She's helping out for a few days."

"Is your cousin okay?"

"I guess it's not a secret now since he's not here."

While he ate, she filled him in on Gavin's trip to Kennebunkport. It sounded like a great opportunity. "I hope he gets the job but, selfishly, I'll really miss him being here."

"You and everybody else."

"You said Rose is helping out for a few days. What if he gets the job?"

"Paige will advertise for a cook and we'll keep our fingers crossed. Until she finds one, it'll be a little crazy, but at least it's the slow time of year. Everybody will chip in and, even if all we can do is burgers and fries for a while, we'll make sure Paige has what she needs. But what about you? Isn't all this time you're spending in town cutting into your work time?"

He shrugged. "Like the diner, I have a slow time. I'll get a few jobs intended for Christmas presents, but mostly I fall into that category of unnecessary money to spend so close to Christmas and winter heating bills. It's built into my budget, so it's not a big deal."

She sighed and stretched, hands to her back. "Ava should be here soon. I can't wait to get out of here."

Max did *not* want to still be there, talking to Tori, when Ava arrived. She was almost as scary as Miranda. "You want to go for a walk after work?"

That was a dumb question. It was obvious she was feeling some fatigue from being on her feet, and he'd invited her to go for a walk.

"That sounds good," she said. "I could use the fresh air."

"Tori!"

"Coming, Rose!" She rolled her eyes and took the money Max handed her so she could make change.

"I'll wait for you on the bench," he said when she brought it back.

"I'll be there."

He took his time walking to the bench, since even once Ava arrived, it would take Tori some time to get out of there. It was a sunny day, but there was a nip in the air, and he was glad he'd put on a sweater before leaving the house.

He realized it was the sweater he'd worn on his first date with Nola and frowned, fingering the cuff. But it was also the one Tori had chosen. She'd obviously liked it.

Sighing, he turned his face up to the sun. How he, a man who'd botched trying to talk to a woman so badly he'd ended up with a dating coach, was going to convince a woman who hated the idea of love and marriage to give him a chance was beyond him, but he was going to try.

He hadn't needed Ava's advice to know he was pursuing the wrong woman by taking Nola out. He'd known it. But maybe the woman's thoughts on the matter had been the push he needed. And Josh and Katie had said essentially the same thing.

He wasn't crazy in thinking Tori might be the woman for him. Other people thought so, too.

Now he just needed Tori to believe it.

TORI KNEW IT WAS WEIRD, standing at the edge of the town square, watching Max, but she couldn't help it. With his arms stretched out along the back of the bench and his face turned up to the warmth of the sun, he was a sight to behold. And she did love the look of that sweater on him.

Eventually she realized she might be spotted staring at Max and started across the grass. Whether he sensed her coming or got bored, she didn't know, but he picked his head up and looked at her when she was two-thirds of the way to him. His face lit up.

"You survived."

"It doesn't take but five minutes with Rose to figure out how she survived raising five Kowalskis plus Katie."

He stood up and starting walking as she fell in beside him. "I've pieced together a little of that story, but not the whole of it."

"I don't know the specific details. Rose went to work doing housekeeping for the Kowalskis when Katie was a baby because Mrs. Kowalski let Rose bring Katie with her. Then Mrs. Kowalski died when the kids were young and Rose stayed. She helped their dad and raised Katie along with those five. If you ask her, she'll tell you she's the housekeeper, but she's way more than that."

"Doesn't that make Josh and Katie's relationship a little weird for them?"

She shrugged. "Hailey said Katie always loved Josh and everybody knew they'd end up together. It just took Josh a long time to figure it out."

"Love works in mysterious ways." When she snorted and looked sideways up at him, he smiled. "I read that somewhere."

"You're going to the party tomorrow, right?"

"Yes, I am. It sounds like it's going to be the social event of the year."

It was nice, walking around the town with Max, and she wondered how many laps they could do before they got conspicuous. "I don't think it'll beat Old Home Day, but it'll definitely be the social event of the fall."

"Do you have a costume yet?"

"Maybe." She had no intention of telling him what she'd come up with at the consignment store. It was going to be a surprise.

"Katie rejected my suggestion of the Black Widow. You should feel free to borrow that."

She laughed and shoved him away. "Got a thing for black leather, Crawford?"

"Have you ever met a man who doesn't?"

"I'm not sure it's come up in conversation. Do *you* have a costume?"

"Yes, I do."

She waited, but he didn't say more. "Are you going to tell me what it is?"

"Nope."

"Such a mystery man."

"I like to keep people guessing." He stopped walking and she realized they were in front of the bank. "You probably want to get off your feet, and I should probably get home. Slow season doesn't mean off season."

"Yeah, I'm pretty beat. And this *isn't* my slow season, so I need to make up some hours on the computer. But I'll see you tomorrow."

"If you can guess who's behind the mask."

She smiled and slid her key into the lock. "I bet I'll find you."

"Tomorrow, then."

Because he was a gentleman, he waited until she'd secured the door behind her before continuing his walk. That gave her time to run up the stairs and unlock the interior door. Tossing her keys on the counter, she went to her window that looked out over the town square. It only took her a second to find him. Not only because he was tall and blond, but because there weren't many people walking.

Tori watched him until he got to his car, which was parked a few spaces down from the post office. He unlocked it and got in, taking the time to put on his seatbelt before he turned the key in the ignition. Then, after he'd eased onto the street, he looked up at her window.

She knew he couldn't see her—or didn't think he could—but she waved anyway.

FIFTEEN

THE PARKING AT the Northern Star Lodge wasn't as bad as Max had anticipated and he was able to stick his car at the end of a row of trucks. He backed it in, hoping to be able to get it back out without having to ask people to rearrange their vehicles.

Once he was out of the car and could see beyond the wall of pickups on the other side of the drive, he realized that not only was much of the town there, but many of them owned—and had arrived on—four-wheelers.

It only took a second to put his costume on, and then he walked toward the table set up in front of the lodge. The flier had said the festivities were free, but it was a five-dollar donation to eat, with a twenty-dollar max per family.

A pirate, played by Josh Kowalski, manned the table. He did a double take when he saw Max, and then grinned. "Well played, Crawford."

Max smiled, even though Josh probably wouldn't be able to see it through the Hannibal Lecter mask he was wearing. He'd paired it with a long-sleeved shirt that was probably called melon, but passed for orange in poor lighting. "It seemed apropos."

Josh looked down at his own costume. "Katie wouldn't bend on the cheerleading thing, so I agreed to be a pirate just to get her into that pirate's wench costume she's wearing."

Following Josh's look, Max saw Katie out in the yard in a very sexy—though not inappropriate—wench's getup, complete with scarves, jewelry and a hint of cleavage. "I think I speak for all the men present when I say it's unfortunate you didn't dress up as Jabba the Hut."

It took Josh a few seconds, but then he laughed. "Wish I'd thought of that. Little chilly for gold bikinis and chains, though."

Max handed over a twenty. "Put the change in the donation bucket."

"Appreciate it." He flipped open an ink pad and stamped a fluorescent orange pumpkin on the back of Max's hand. "Tori's around here somewhere. She's… I don't know. I think she's some kind of bag lady or something, but I'm not sure."

"I'm sure I'll run into her," he said, not wanting to sound too eager to see her.

There was a good chance he'd run into everybody, since it looked like everybody was there. There were kids everywhere, princesses and superheroes with costumes bought or made too big so they fit over warm clothes. He saw Josh's brother Mitch dressed in a farmer's outfit and he didn't have to look far to find Paige in a matching farmer's dress. It looked like Sarah was bundled up under a fat strawberry costume with a green knit hat, complete with stem and leaves. With them was Liz, dressed in a police uniform, but he didn't see Drew.

The first person he ran into that he knew well was Matt, who was dressed as a game warden. Hailey was next to him in a disturbingly good zombie getup. He hadn't thought she could be unattractive, but he'd been wrong.

"Warden Barnett, that's a remarkably authentic costume you have."

Matt laughed. "Yeah, I know. I'm here in a somewhat official capacity. There are ATVs and kids and a party, so I'm just serving as a visual reminder not to get stupid. If somebody does, my capacity will become very official very quickly."

"And Hailey, how many kids have you made cry tonight?"

The bloody zombie mouth, complete with flaps of... something, grinned. "Most of them. Have you seen Tori yet?"

"No, I—"

Then he spotted her across the yard and it was like everybody around him disappeared. She was wearing a white dress—or maybe it was a nightgown—that went almost to her shoes, with a long green coat over it. Only the top few buttons were done, letting the dress show. She had on a black, flat-topped hat and was carrying a basket of flowers. Her face was smudged with black. Eliza Doolittle from *My Fair Lady*.

It wasn't the sexiest costume he'd ever seen, but it still took his breath away. She'd chosen her costume for him.

"Excuse me," he said to Matt and Hailey as he walked away from them.

It seemed to take forever to get to her, and the look in her eyes when she saw him coming could have set him on fire. She didn't move, but just waited for him to get through the crowd.

"Do you have slippers for me in that basket?"

"Ha." She lifted her chin defiantly, which made him

want to kiss her and he didn't care who was watching. "This is my horror movie costume."

He laughed. "The ending's not that bad."

"Mmm-hmm."

"You look gorgeous."

"It's the soot, isn't it? Really does wonders for my complexion."

"Everybody seems to have coordinated their costumes. I should have come as the professor."

"I think the world's most famous serial killer mask suits you." She wrinkled her nose. "It's pretty creepy, actually."

"Have you eaten yet? I wonder if there are any fava beans."

She punched his arm. "Don't do that. And no, I haven't eaten yet."

He offered the arm she'd just walloped and she shifted her basket to the other hand so she could take it. They took the scenic route to the back side of the lodge so they could admire the "costumes" on the four-wheelers. One of the first in line looked somewhat like a pirate ship, so he guessed that was Josh's. There was also a space ship and what looked kind of like a banana.

"The parade will be fun to watch," Tori said. "They're going to ride around the property, I guess, and some of the businesses donated prizes."

"Josh asked me to judge, but I passed. I'm not good at picking and choosing."

She bumped against him, chuckling. "It's because you're such a softie."

"That's a funny thing to say to a guy in a Hannibal Lecter mask."

Behind the house, Andy and Drew were manning the

big kettle grills, handing out burgers and dogs. There were three tables laden with chips and salads of every variety and several coolers at the end.

Tori and Max ate and mingled, chatting with everybody, and Max realized it didn't seem to occur to either of them to separate. When the parade went by, they applauded and cheered along with the spectators, especially when one family went by on one ATV doing an impressive, if precarious, reenactment of the hillbilly Clampett family's arrival in Beverly Hills.

"I hope they have that rocking chair strapped down tight," he yelled to Tori over the roar of the crowd.

Nobody was surprised when *The Beverly Hillbillies* family won the grand prize, which was a generous gift certificate to the Trailside Diner. As the families with children started heading home, the party took a turn and it wasn't long before the sound of beer can tabs being popped punctuated the chilly night.

"Are you warm enough?" he asked Tori, worried about her being in a dress.

She lifted the hem enough so he could see the tops of her ankle boots, and the wool covering her legs. "I'm wearing long wool underwear under this getup. It's not my first outdoor Halloween party. What about you?"

"This *is* my first outdoor Halloween party, but not the first time I've been outside in November. I'm wearing thermals, too."

"Good. We can both stay longer, then."

He nodded and put his hand on her back to guide her as they moved through a crowd of people. Usually he couldn't wait to make his excuses and leave any kind of function, but tonight he wasn't going anywhere.

TORI HAD KNOWN the party would be enjoyable. Whitford knew how to have a good time, whether it was Old Home Day or the Fourth of July, and coming together for a fund-raiser at the Northern Star Lodge was no different.

She hadn't anticipated enjoying it quite so much, though. Good food, good fun, good friends and Max. He was having a good time, too, and it showed in how relaxed he was. Everybody thought his Hannibal Lecter mask was hilarious, and he'd probably spoken to more people in the last few hours than he had in all the years since he'd moved there.

Now, as the adults mingled and did their best to ignore the fact they could see their breath when they talked, they made their way toward the fire Andy had started in a metal ring. It wasn't a big bonfire, but everybody could warm their hands for a few minutes before giving somebody else a chance.

Tori hardly felt the cold. With Max's hand on her back and desire pumping through her veins, it would take more than the chill of an autumn night to cool her off.

They squeezed in next to Liz and Drew, who didn't seem to mind getting closer to each other to make room. She looked exhausted, which didn't surprise Tori. She'd been the star of the night, since word had spread fairly quickly about her pregnancy. Drew had wanted kids for a long time and baby-watch fever in Whitford had rivaled that of the royal family for a while.

"How come you're not in costume?" Max asked Drew.

"Dad and I cooked, so we were exempt. As the chief of police, I felt it was my civic duty to point out manning the grills in any kind of costume could be dangerous."

Liz snorted. "Please. You guys whined and Rose and I gave in. There was no civic duty about it. I'd found the best prison jumpsuit online, too. We would have matched."

"Speaking of that, don't let me forget those handcuffs Monday morning."

"Maybe I should put them on you so you can't miss them."

"I'm ready to go home. You?"

Tori laughed and then hugged Liz when she announced she was done for the night. "Congratulations."

"Thanks. Paige is covering the early morning, just in case, but I'll be working tomorrow morning. You should come and..." Her gaze flickered to Max and back. "Visit."

Once they were gone, Tori set her basket next to her and held her hands over the fire.

"Are you cold? I have a coat in my car. I can run and get it."

"No, I'm fine. My hands are getting a little chilly, but the fire's nice."

Butch and Fran wandered over and chatted for a while. Butch was wearing his work uniform, which wasn't very original, but at least he'd tried for the spirit of the occasion. Fran was wearing a fancy cocktail dress, with her hair up and jewelry glittering in the moonlight, though at some point she'd conceded to the cold and had a flannel shirt over the dress.

"I'm a Real Housewife of Whitford," she explained, and Tori laughed. Max just looked confused, which didn't surprise her.

"Oh, like those women on that show," he said about two minutes later, and they all laughed. "I was flipping through the channels one day and there was a show called the Real Housewives of...somewhere. I dropped the remote over the end of the couch and watched fifteen minutes of it before I got the ambition to get up and fish it out."

While Fran, who was obviously not on her first beer, recapped a television franchise none of them watched, Max looped his arms around Tori's shoulder and pulled her close. He was warm and she pressed against him.

"I feel bad for everybody who has to ride home on four-wheelers," she said when Fran paused to take a breath.

"Most of them already left," Butch said. "But there will be a few who'll need cocoa and a hot shower when they get home."

Tori noticed a couple of women edging toward the fire and she and Max had been there awhile. "We should move on and give somebody else a turn."

When they were out of earshot, Max dipped his head close to hers. "Now we know what Fran does all day at the store."

"I knew she'd taken to having a TV on under the counter, where she can see it from her knitting chair, but I've never paid any attention to what she was watching."

"Now you know."

"In detail."

They wandered for a few minutes, before Max pointed toward a group clustered near the edge of the house. "It looks like Matt and Hailey are getting ready to leave, if you want to say goodbye to them."

"Matt and Hailey brought me, actually. Gavin took

my car to Kennebunkport and, when he stopped by to switch vehicles, he put his truck keys in his pocket out of habit and because he was so nerved up, he forgot about them. And Uncle Mike can't find the spare set."

"You have no vehicle?"

She shrugged. "It's only for the weekend and I can walk almost everywhere. He felt bad and was going to drive all the way back, but that would have been stupid."

"So you have to leave with them?"

Tori knew she should say good-night to Max and leave with Matt and Hailey. They'd drop her off at home and she'd go to bed and tomorrow, when she woke up, everything would be the same. That was what she *should* do.

"Unless you want to drive me home."

He locked gazes with her and she wondered what he was thinking. With Max, she couldn't be sure. He could be contemplating the fact she'd spent the entire night at his side and was inviting him to drive her home. Or he could be calculating time and gas mileage to determine who would be the more logical driver for her.

"Of course I'll drive you home."

"I should tell them."

"I'm going to find out where people are getting those cups of hot chocolate. I'll meet you back here."

Hailey saw her coming and met her halfway. "I was just coming to find you. Matt had a long day and I hate to drag you away from the party, but he's ready to go home."

"You can go. Max is going to drive me home." She said it casually, like it was no big deal, but that didn't stop Hailey's eyes from widening.

"Seriously? Like…he's driving you home or he's taking you home? Or going home with you?"

"He's driving me home. That's what I said." She blew out a breath, which hovered in a white cloud for a second in front of her mouth. "It's not a big deal. Instead of you and Matt driving me home, Max is driving me home."

"Hailey, you coming?" they heard Matt call.

"You'd better call me tomorrow," Hailey said. "And tell me everything."

"I'll be able to do that by text. *Max drove me home.*"

Hailey gave her a look over her shoulder, then hurried to join Matt. Tori laughed and went in search of Max. She found him deep in conversation with Mitch, a foam cup of hot cocoa in each hand. When she stepped up beside him, he handed her one of them. After cradling it in her hands for a moment to warm them up, she took a sip. It was delicious.

"We were discussing trestles," Max said. "Um, train bridges and such."

"I've seen some done in HO scale, at expos and such, and they're pretty remarkable," Mitch said. "And since you're here, Tori, I want to thank you for being there for Liz. And for Paige, of course."

She was going to brush it off as nothing, but they were his wife and his sister, so it wouldn't be nothing to him. "I'm glad my other job is flexible, so I can help as much as possible."

"Where is Paige? I haven't seen her for a while."

"She went in to put Sarah to bed and I haven't seen her since, so I'm guessing she went to bed, too. She's working in the morning, but she's not taking the baby since I managed to free up a couple of weeks at home.

That means I'll be getting up at the ass-crack of dawn, too."

"I offered to do it, but Paige doesn't think I'm a four-thirty in the morning kind of girl."

He laughed and shook his head. "Paige has opened at the diner since she bought the place and we were all raised here at the lodge, so we're a whole family of early risers. Though Sarah's taking it to a whole new level."

Tori laughed, but a chill hit her and she shivered. Instantly, Max's arm was around her shoulders, offering her warmth.

"We should get going," Max said, and he let go of her just long enough to shake Mitch's hand.

Her teeth were starting to chatter by the time they'd said all their goodbyes and reached his car. Max opened her door for her, then hurried around to get in. It seemed like forever before the engine started generating heat and he would hold his hand in front of the vent every few seconds. Once he deemed it warm enough, he cranked the fan up. She didn't miss the way he pointed the vents in her direction and she put her hand over his where it rested on the gear shifter.

"Thanks," she said when he looked over at her.

He just smiled and rubbed the side of her hand with his thumb. Tori breathed in the warming, Max-scented air of the car and felt her good intentions crumbling around her.

SIXTEEN

MAX PULLED HIS CAR into the bank lot, which was considered overnight tenant parking after the businesses were closed, and parked next to an old beat-up truck he assumed was her cousin's. He killed the ignition and put the keys in his pocket as he walked around the car. He grabbed her flower basket from the backseat, where he'd tossed it along with his serial killer mask, then opened her door.

She laughed when he offered his hand. "I just got warm and now it's back into the cold."

"Only for a minute."

Once she was on her feet, he tightened his fingers slightly, not letting her hand drop away as they walked around the corner of the bank to her door. She had her keys in her other hand, though she made no move toward the lock. But Max was hoping for more than a quick good-night kiss on the sidewalk.

"I should walk you up," he said.

"You didn't last time."

"But it's Halloween. People get up to no good on Halloween."

She smiled and shook her head. "Last night was Halloween night. Tonight was just the party."

"Call it curiosity, then. It doesn't seem fair that you've rummaged in my closet and dresser drawers, but I've never seen where you live."

She didn't totally buy the excuse that rolled so easily off of his tongue. He could see that in her eyes. "That's true."

"Plus I'm carrying your basket." Which weighed less than a hardcover book, but it was the chivalrous thought that counted.

He had to let go of her hand so she could unlock the door and let them in. After following her up the stairs, he had to wait while she unlocked the interior door, too.

"It's a little messy." She flipped on the light switch as they entered. "Actually, compared to your house, it's probably a lot messy."

It was essentially a wide-open space, like a loft, which meant he could not only see the living, kitchen and her work areas, but—*bam*—there was her bed. And unlike him, making it wasn't the first thing she did in the morning.

She had one of those old-fashioned quilts made of bright-colored blocks stitched together, but it was shoved back so he could see the tangle of white sheets. She was a restless sleeper who liked a lot of pillows, and knowing that sent heat rushing below the belt.

"See?" She waved a hand. "You can see the whole thing from right here. Except the bathroom, of course, but it's pretty standard. Sink. Shower. Toothbrush. All that bathroom-type stuff."

She was nervous. It wasn't really a nervous babble that gave her away, because she was a talker all the time, but he could sense it in her. It surprised him because she was always so confident and he hadn't guessed having a man in her apartment would throw her off.

"It's warm in here," he said, setting the basket of fake flowers on the floor next to the door.

"I have one of those programmable thermostats and I'm usually working this time of night. I sit still most of the time, so I have it set a little warmer. I'm going to go wash this crap off my face. I don't have any decaf, but I have hot cocoa cups for the brewer, if you want one."

He wandered a little while she was in the bathroom, not being too nosy, but wanting a feel for her home. Despite what she'd said when they entered, it wasn't messy. It suffered from a lack of closets and storage spaces, so more of her belongings were out than his, but she was tidy and he'd guess there was a method to her organization.

Especially at her desk. While the blue couch and the battered wooden coffee table, and maybe even the bed, were hand-me-downs or thrift store finds, she'd spared no expense on the massive L-shaped desk. Nor the computer equipment that covered half of it. He had no idea what it all did, since his technical ability was limited to making his laptop do invoicing, email, research and being Facebook friends with his family so he could see photos of his nephews. He noticed the only photograph on display in her apartment was a picture of her and Hailey stuck on the fridge with a magnet.

He brewed them each a mug of hot cocoa. He wouldn't drink very much of his because of the caffeine content, but she'd given him an opening to stay longer and he was taking it.

When she came out of the bathroom, he didn't choke off his laughter in time. She'd scrubbed her face clean of the soot, and her hair was brushed out. She'd lost the hat, robe and—judging by the bare feet and ankles—the wool underwear. That left her in the billowing white dress. Or nightgown. He wasn't sure how that garment had started its life.

"Ha, ha." She rolled her eyes.

"You're like the heroine of an old gothic novel."

"If you go get your Hannibal Lecter mask, we could film an indie horror movie." When he shifted, intending only to show her the mugs of hot cocoa, she held up her hand. "I was kidding."

"I made cocoa."

The mug lured her back into arm's reach, but he didn't touch her. He could smell the soap she'd used to wash her face, combined with a faint smoky smell that probably lingered in the dress from the fire.

Tori picked up the mug and took several sips, but she didn't carry it to the couch or step away with it. She put it back on the counter, though her hands remained curled around the warm ceramic.

"Did you have fun tonight?" she asked, tilting her face up to look at him.

"It was one of the most fun nights of my life."

"You need to get out more if hanging out in the cold, watching dressed-up ATVs is a highlight."

"I think it was the company."

The blush across her freshly scrubbed cheeks made his pulse quicken and he turned so he could put his hand on her waist. The blush darkened and he moved closer, so their bodies were almost touching.

Bending his head, he brushed his cheek over hers, feeling her breath in hot bursts near his ear. "I want to kiss you."

"That's such a bad idea."

She hadn't pulled away, though. "Why?"

"None of this—especially tonight—is part of the plan."

"There's a plan?"

"We're supposed to be finding you a wife."

"Oh, that plan. I've lived this long without one. I can wait a little while longer."

She put her hand against his chest. "Define a little while."

"However long this takes."

"This?"

"Every time I look at a woman's mouth, I wonder what it would be like to kiss you. Every time I think about having a woman in my life, I wonder what it would be like to spend a night with you. I'm not going to make any forward progress until I stop looking at women and thinking about you."

She relaxed her arm a little, but the hand against his chest was still resistance and not a caress.

"I'm tired of fighting this, Max. I want you and I've tried not to because it's not fair to you, but I'm not going to say no tonight. But you need to know that I might let you sweep me off my feet tonight, but they'll be firmly planted on the ground again tomorrow."

"I know where I stand." He thought he actually knew better than she did, but if he pushed, she was going to push back. As in pushing him right out the door.

Patience was something he was good at, and if she wasn't ready to admit she had feelings for him, he'd wait. And he'd worry about tomorrow when tomorrow came.

She relaxed her arm, her palm sliding over his chest, and he turned his head to capture her mouth. Her kiss tasted like hot chocolate, with a hint of minty tooth-paste, and he ran his tongue over her bottom lip.

Her fingers curled in his shirt and her other hand slid into his hair, holding him to her. He ran his hands up her back, hating the bulky dress that had amused him earlier.

He savored the kiss, wanting more, as she unbuttoned his shirt. Her hand slid under the fabric, only to encounter the thermals.

"You have too many layers on," she muttered against his mouth.

He'd been thinking the same thing. Unbuttoning the outer shirt and peeling it off didn't take long, and then he yanked the thermal shirt free of his jeans and pulled it over his head.

The feel of her palms gliding over his bare chest practically seared his skin.

"That's better," she whispered, and then she took his hand and led him toward the bed.

TORI PUSHED THOUGHTS of tomorrow out of her head as she crossed to her bed, Max's hand in hers.

The turning point had come hours before, when he'd touched her and she'd let him. When he'd put his arm around her and she hadn't laughed and found a reason to step away and shrug him off. Definitely when he'd offered to drive her home and she'd accepted.

She threw back the sheets, wishing she'd made her bed for once, and then turned to face him. "Still too many layers."

He put his hands on her waist, drawing her close. "Are you in a hurry?"

She laughed. "A little bit, yeah. It's been a while."

"I'm not a man who likes to rush things." He hooked his finger in the neck of the dress. "This thing has a lot of tiny buttons."

"I'm lazy, so when I put it on, I only undid enough so I could pull it over my head."

He popped the top button open and then another. It was enough so he could dip his finger into the hollow of her throat. A third button and he could part the fabric enough to kiss the same spot.

She threw her head back and he sucked gently, undoing two more buttons. Then he lifted her and set her on the bed, where he gently pushed her back onto the mattress.

"I'm starting to really like this dress," he murmured.

"More than black leather?"

She could tell by his sharp intake of breath it only took one more button for him to realize she wasn't wearing anything under the dress anymore. "I don't think black leather would be nearly as fun to take off."

Tori wasn't going to argue with that sentiment. As he undid enough buttons to push back the fabric and bare her breasts, she raked her nails over his back.

Then his mouth closed over her nipple and she arched her back off the bed. Burying her hands in his hair, she moaned as he sucked gently at first, and then harder. When he gave the same attention to the other breast, and he flicked his tongue over each nipple in turn, she squirmed.

As each button revealed more skin, he stroked her and kissed her. Never hurried, he took his time exploring her body until she wanted to scream.

Then he got to the buttons below her naval and she

sucked in a breath as his mouth followed his trailing fingers from her stomach to...

"Undo that button," she pleaded.

"You're rushing me."

"You're *killing* me."

His chuckle vibrated against her skin. "I thought my attention to detail was one of the things you liked about me."

"Bigger picture, Max. Let's think big picture. Like the fact you still have your pants on."

He sighed and moved back up her body. Looking down at her, he smiled a wicked smile. "You made me lose my place. Now I have to start over."

She groaned, whacking his shoulder. "I know where you left off. I'll show you."

Resisting easily when she tried to guide his hand to that button at the junction of her thighs, Max bent his head and kissed her throat. Then he ran his tongue over her collarbone before blowing lightly across the moistened flesh.

By the time he reached her naval again, Tori was almost burning with a hunger she thought would consume her. She was used to sex that was fast and hard and sweaty. This slow, excruciating exploration of her body was new and she reveled in it.

The sweet ache was almost too much, though, and she whimpered when his fingers freed that pivotal button. Then another.

"You're like my favorite book. I linger turning the pages because I don't want to reach the end, and I want to read passages over and over, savoring the words."

"Turn the damn page," she said, her voice pleading.

He made quick work of the rest of the buttons and

the dress fell away. She pulled her arms free, and then fisted her hands in the sheets as his mouth closed over her mound. His tongue flicked over her clit and she groaned, opening her legs to him.

The man wasn't kidding about attention to detail. He teased and licked until she lifted her hips off the bed, needing more. "Please, Max."

He kissed his way down her thigh, almost to her knee, before he stood. "I have to get these off."

Tori sat up, intending to hasten the process of removing his pants, but he shook his head. "If you touch me right now, it's over."

As tempting as it was to make Max lose control, she had bigger plans for him. She watched as he removed his jeans and the thermal bottoms, then his socks. The boxer briefs went next and Tori was happy to see Max was as eager as she was to move on to the next chapter of this book.

He leaned over her, probably to push her backward onto the bed, but she put a hand on his chest. She didn't want any more interruptions.

"Do you have a condom?" She could tell by the way he tensed, he didn't have one right at hand.

"I left it in the glove box."

"Frozen condoms. Just what every girl wants." She laughed and pushed at his shoulder. "I have one in my nightstand."

He sat up, but when he reached for the drawer, she slapped his hand. "I'll get it, Max."

"Is that where you keep your secrets?"

She pulled open the drawer enough to slip a condom packet out. "Never ask questions about a lady's nightstand drawer."

Because she was stretched across his lap, her back was to him and he pressed a kiss to the base of her spine. Heat flooded through her and she slammed the drawer closed.

"Here." She handed the condom off to him and moved back into the middle of the bed.

When he joined her there, she wrapped her arms around his neck and pulled him down to kiss him. Biting at his bottom lip, she wrapped her legs around his hips and urged him forward.

He filled her as slowly and deliberately as he'd unbuttoned her dress and she dug her fingernails into his back.

"You're not a very patient woman," he said, his voice husky as he moved his hips slowly. Very slowly, giving her just a little bit more each time.

She tried lifting her hips, but he only chuckled and pulled back. "Please. *Please,* Max."

He thrust forward, filling her, and they moaned in unison. She ran her hands down his back to his hips, urging him to move faster. This time he listened. Her breath quickened and she met each thrust with one of her own as he drove deeper and harder.

He groaned what sounded like her name and hooked his hands under her knees. Yanking her body upwards and toward him, he drove into her and she closed her hands over his forearms.

"Yes," she said, over and over, as the orgasm wracked her body.

His body shook as he pumped into her, until all that was left were the aftershocks. He collapsed on top of her and she wrapped her arms around him, panting in quick breaths that made the hair over his ear twitch.

After a moment, he reached between them to hold the condom as he slid free of her body, and she ran her hands over his back. She was perfectly content to lie under the weight of him.

Several minutes later, she realized that while she was slowly melting into a puddle of sated, boneless exhaustion, Max's body was tensing a little.

She chuckled against his shoulder. The man overthought everything. "There's a box of tissues on the nightstand and a wastebasket under it."

The bed creaked as he disposed of the condom, and then his warm body pressed against hers again. It took some effort, but he untwisted the sheets until he'd freed enough to cover them and pulled the quilt up to their shoulders.

She snuggled against him, loving the feel of his tall body cradling hers and the weight of his arm over her. When he kissed her hair, she smiled and closed her eyes.

SEVENTEEN

MAX WOKE BEFORE TORI, the sun peeking through her curtains hitting his side of the bed first. He breathed in deeply, contentment coursing through his body, and then rolled onto his side. Very gently, hoping not to wake her, he shifted closer and put his arm over her.

She stirred slightly, but then nestled against him and quieted again. Max smiled and closed his eyes. He wouldn't fall asleep again, but he wanted to savor this moment for as long as it lasted.

Which he already knew would be until she woke up. She'd made that pretty clear last night. And he'd made the decision to accept what she was willing to give him...for now.

He gently untangled himself from the sheets and slid out of bed. If she needed space to come to terms with what was happening between them, waking up in his arms might freak her out. This way, she could set the tone of the morning and he would follow suit. It was a plan that usually worked for him out in the world.

After using her bathroom and pulling on his clothes from the night before—minus the thermals, which he dropped on the floor by her front door—he hit the power button on her brewer. The smell of coffee would probably wake her up, plus he really needed the caffeine boost.

He was putting milk and sugar in his coffee when

he heard the bathroom door close. While stirring it, he wondered what he should do with it. He could put both mugs on the coffee table, implying they'd sit together on the couch. If he had to guess, he'd say her habit was to sit at her desk and fire up her computer while drinking her morning coffee, but he wasn't sure. Finally, he left hers on the counter and took his to the window, where he looked out over Whitford.

When the door opened, he turned. She'd put on a pair of sweatpants and a long sweatshirt, and brushed her hair into a ponytail. It definitely wasn't a *hey, let's have morning sex* look.

"I made you a coffee," he said.

"Thanks."

He waited to see if she'd detour to the window and give him a good-morning kiss. Maybe he should have stayed near the counter, where he'd be right there in reach. It might have been his imagination, but he thought she hesitated for a second before heading straight to the mug.

"I wonder how many people ended up crashing at the lodge last night," she said after she'd had a few sips of her coffee. She didn't move to the couch or her desk. Instead she leaned against the counter, cradling her cup in her hands.

"More than a few, I'd say. Between beer and staying too late, there were probably some who opted to stay."

"It was fun. Everybody had a good time and I'm sure they raised a lot of money for the ATV club."

He nodded, dread forming a hard, heavy lump in his stomach. Tori didn't sound like herself. She sounded... polite. Not that she was ever rude, but she sounded like she was talking to a stranger.

Sipping his coffee, he tried desperately to think of a way to make things better—to make her look at him the way she had last night—but she seemed so far away. Not just physically, but emotionally.

"Is there a football game on today?" she asked after a few minutes of heavy silence.

"Yeah. Big game. It's the four o'clock game, too, which is good. Leaves more time open during the day." He wondered if she had plans for today, but couldn't bring himself to ask without it sounding as if he was presuming they'd spend the day together.

"I have so much work to catch up on it's not even funny," she said, which answered the question he hadn't had the nerve to ask. "Nobody ever brings me Swedish meatballs, though."

He laughed, then drank the remainder of the coffee in his cup. "I don't have Swedish meatballs, but I'd be happy to buy you breakfast. Unless you'd rather get right to work."

Her gaze fixed on his face for the first time, as if she was trying to figure him out. "I guess I should get right to work."

It was a mistake, he realized too late, to give her the easy out. He should have stopped talking after offering to buy her breakfast. "I'll get out of your way, then."

He had to go by her to set his mug in the sink, then he paused. "So how does this work? Do I get to kiss you goodbye or not?"

Her smile didn't have its usual brilliance, and she didn't set her coffee down. She stood on her tiptoes and pressed a quick kiss to his mouth. It wasn't enough and it left him even more unsettled than before.

"Enjoy the game," she said.

"Thanks. I'll…see you soon."

He picked up his thermals on his way out the door, wishing he knew what he could have done differently. Or maybe this *was* how it was done. He'd never been in a situation like this before.

Once he was on the sidewalk, he realized he should have told her how much he'd enjoyed spending the night with her. Or something. Anything more personal than "I made you a coffee." But it was too late now. The door had closed behind him and he wasn't going to text her and ask her to let him back in.

Turning the corner toward where his car was parked, he cursed himself for a fool. He should have stayed in her bed and held on to her until she made him let her go.

Four scoops of ice cream—two chocolate, one coffee, one French vanilla—three pumps of chocolate syrup, a mountain of whipped cream, a ridiculous amount of jimmies, six cherries and one spoon.

Tori picked up the spoon and prepared to do battle with her emotions. They may have snuck up on her—all strong and messy and inevitably painful—but she was going to vanquish them or make herself sick as a dog trying.

"My cousins' kids would call that an ice cream sundae of doom."

She looked up at Liz, who'd said nothing while Tori had gone around the counter and made her own dessert. One of the perks of being an employee, even when it wasn't her shift. "I have feelings. I intend to kill them with ice cream."

"Would these feelings have anything to do with the tall, blond guy with the impressive…television?"

"Nobody in this town can keep a secret."

"Oh, were you and Max supposed to be a secret? I might not be the best person to offer this advice, since my attempt to keep my relationship with Drew a secret from my family lasted like a hot minute and ended up with my brother punching him in the face, but the next time you're at a party with most of the population of Whitford, you guys might want to chill on the smoldering looks, the touching and the leaving together."

"There was no smoldering." Tori shoved a huge spoonful of ice cream, chocolate and whipped cream into her mouth, glaring at her coworker over the spoon.

"You looked like a frumpy bag lady with coal smudged on your face and still, when Max looked at you, I wanted to cover Sarah's eyes."

"I wasn't a bag lady. I was Eliza Doolittle. You people have no culture."

"Every time I looked, he had his arm around you."

"I was cold. Some idiots decided to have an outdoor party the first night in November and he was trying to keep me alive. As friends do."

Liz laughed at her and reached under the counter for a stack of napkins, which she set next to Tori. "It's too bad we don't have any of those disposable bibs the rib places give out. And zip that hoodie up the rest of the way or you're going to have jimmies between your boobs."

Scowling, Tori yanked the zipper up enough to protect her cleavage from falling chocolate sprinkles and shoveled another bite into her mouth. So maybe she should have kept Max at arm's reach. There *was* a lot of touching at the party. They'd probably looked like a couple, just without the matching costumes. If she was honest with herself, they'd *felt* like a couple, and she'd liked it.

And that was the four-scoop problem. It was one thing to like sex. It was another to like couple-type touches—walking around with his hand at the small of her back or his arm around her. That was *affection* and affection grew into other things. Things that would eventually hurt both of them.

She was halfway through the so-called sundae of doom when Gavin walked out of the kitchen, drying his hands on the full apron he wore.

He looked at her and winced. "This isn't a good look for you."

Tori pointed the business end of the spoon at him. "Do I look like a woman who wants to discuss looks right now?"

"You have whipped cream on your nose. And your chin." He paused. "And your sweatshirt."

She grabbed a couple of the napkins and swiped at her face. The hoodie she didn't bother with. The deeper she got into the dish, the more melted the ice cream was and the messier she got.

"You want to talk about it?"

Tori shook her head. What, exactly, would she say? *Well, there's this awesome guy I'm into and I guess he's into me and we had sex and it was incredible and now I'm drowning myself in ice cream because…*

Just because. The disappointment she'd felt when she didn't wake up cuddled against Max was a problem, as was her annoyance that he'd played the morning-after game so cool. He'd been dressed and ready to walk out the door by the time she woke. Stabbing at a cherry, she swore under her breath. She'd made the rules and now she was moping because he'd played by them.

"I don't want to talk about it. But I want you to sit down and tell me how the tryout went," she told him. "You didn't even text me to tell me you were back."

"I was going to call you on my break, but Liz said you were out here demolishing our ice cream stock." He paused, and then a slow grin lit up his face. "They offered me the job."

Her happiness for him chased away her bad mood. "Gav! That's wonderful! Congratulations!"

"It's a huge step. A new job. A new town. It's three and a half hours away, Tori."

She reached across the counter and grabbed his hand. "You're ready for this, Gav. I know you are. This is the opportunity you've been waiting for."

"Your hand is really sticky." He pulled his free and wiped it on his apron. "I already told Mom and Dad. And Paige. I have two weeks to help her figure something out."

They talked for a few more minutes, mostly about how they'd have to get together and plan his big move. Once he'd succumbed to the ice-cream-coated hug she insisted on giving him and he'd gone back to work, she walked around the counter to get rid of her half-empty dish before the melting caused a dairy tidal wave down the counter.

After washing the counter and her hands, she waved goodbye to Liz and Gavin and walked outside. Whitford was a quiet place on Sundays and she had no idea what she was going to do with the rest of her day.

The library was closed and Matt rarely worked on Sundays, so she didn't want to bother Hailey. Max, even if she was ready to face him again, would have a house-ful of people. She ran through a mental list of her other friends, but Sundays were for couples.

With a sigh, she walked back to her apartment, slowly, since her stomach wasn't sure about ice cream sundaes of doom for brunch. As soon as she closed her door, her gaze fell on the bed and her mind filled with memories of last night.

She needed to work. But first she yanked the quilt off the bed and tossed it onto the couch. Then she stripped the sheets and pillowcases, shoving them into the laundry hamper in the bathroom. Taking another set off the shelf, she remade her bed with crisp white sheets that wouldn't smell like Max. She smoothed the quilt over the top, then brewed a cup of coffee and prepared to get her head screwed on straight.

MAX SPENT THE MORNING worrying and overthinking, until he finally caved and hit the button to call his oldest brother, Colin. He and Ben were both married, but Colin had had more experience with women before settling down. And, when push came to shove, he was the oldest.

"Hey, Max! How the hell are ya?"

Colin's voice was deep and booming in his ear, and Max smiled. His brothers were definitely loud. "I'm good. Do you have a few minutes?"

"Sure. Let me head out to the man cave." Which was a garden shed the size of a half-bath, but it worked for Colin. "What's up?"

"I need some advice. About a girl."

"I had this talk with you when you were like twelve years old."

"I remember. I also remember Chelsea something-

or-other punching me in the face because girls do *not*, in fact, like when a boy pinches her ass to get her attention."

"Ben must have told you that one. I'd never steer my little brother wrong."

Max laughed and refrained from reciting the many entertaining moments Colin had engineered for his own amusement thanks to having a gullible and very literal younger brother. "In all seriousness, there's a woman I want to spend the rest of my life with."

"Damn, Max. It's about time. Does she know about this?"

"She knows I'm attracted to her."

There was a long silence. "Because it's you, Max, I have to ask. Are you sure? How have you expressed your attraction?"

"We had sex last night."

"Oh. Well, that's a good indicator. So what's the problem?"

That was a complicated question. "She was helping me find a wife, but now I don't want to find somebody else. I want her, but her parents are assholes and she doesn't believe in love anymore."

"Whoa." Through the phone, Max heard the pop and hiss of a can being opened. "Slow down and start from the beginning."

He talked for twenty minutes, starting with his growing awareness of being lonely and wanting somebody to share his life with and meeting Tori and his dates with Nola and, finally, the Halloween party and taking her home.

"She was very firm about it being a casual thing, because that's all she wants. So this morning I behaved very casually, and she was disappointed. I should have stayed in bed. I should have pushed."

"Are you *sure* she was disappointed? You know sometimes you're not good at reading people."

"I know her and I can tell. That's the thing, Colin. She knows me, too. She *likes* me. She doesn't think I'm boring and weird. She recognizes when I need a minute to process what's going on and she doesn't push me. She drags me out of my comfort zone, but it's okay because she's with me and she makes me laugh."

"Wow." His brother was quiet for a long moment. "She sounds like she might be the one for you."

"She is. Should I send her flowers? I don't think Whitford has a florist. I could order them online, but… Should I send her flowers?"

"No. That's too generic. It's easy. I think you need to spend time with her and put the friendship back on solid ground. That's the foundation of your relationship."

Max sighed. "What about the fact she doesn't want to get married ever?"

"That sounds like something only time and trust between you can make happen. But the opportunity for that to happen will only come if you keep the friendship solid."

"I don't know how to do that."

"What have you been doing together for the last month?"

"Practicing me going on a date with another woman."

"Oh. You should probably stop doing that."

Max laughed. "It's something of a unique situation."

"You've always been unique, little brother. Can't expect anything less when it comes to problems with women. So we need a reason for you two to get together, but not something that puts too much pressure on you."

Max felt some of the tension ease out of his shoulders. Colin would help him. Sure, his brothers had had a lot of fun at his expense growing up, but there was never a minute they didn't have his back when it came to the rest of the world.

"Maybe you should just stop in the diner for a meal when you think she's going to be there," Colin said. "Not today, but don't wait too long. Tomorrow if you can. It's a normal interaction for you guys, it allows her to set the tone and you can see how she's acting. And you'll have coffee and food and stuff to focus on, rather than just being in an awkward situation you can't manage. Bring a book or a paper to read if it seems like she's avoiding you, so you don't feel too self-conscious."

"I can do that." He exhaled slowly. "I have a plan."

"Don't be too rigid about the plan, though," Colin cautioned. "You have to be flexible, Max. I know it's hard, but you have to try. She sounds really special."

"She is. Thanks for the talk. I have to get ready for the game, but I feel better now."

"Anytime. Love you, Maxi Pad."

He rolled his eyes at the old childhood nickname. "Love you, too, Colon."

Colin barked out a laugh. "Mine's still funnier."

"Remind me to thank Mom and Dad for that."

Feeling better than he had since walking out of Tori's apartment that morning, Max started preparations for company coming. He wasn't sure how many people would come, due to the party last night, but he'd be ready, just in case. It was a big game against a conference rival and nobody would want to miss it if they could help it. With it being the four o'clock game, there was time to get stuff done before start time, too.

He caught himself whistling while he moved around the kitchen, and the song from *My Fair Lady* made him smile. Tori had made for an exceptionally charming Eliza Doolittle and Max knew he'd never see the movie or even a photo of Audrey Hepburn again without thinking of last night.

The first car pulled in well before game time, and it didn't sound like Butch's truck. He popped the tray of pizza rolls into the oven and set the timer before turning to see who it was.

When the door opened and Tori walked in, his carefully orchestrated plan fell apart and he froze.

EIGHTEEN

IT WASN'T THE first time Tori had run into a man with whom she'd spent a night, but it was the first time that man's reaction could only be described as horror.

The look on Max's face when he saw her walk in the door would have been comical if it hadn't taken all of her nerve to get in the car and make the drive over. "I guess I shouldn't have come."

He recovered quickly and reached for her arm, maybe to stop her if she tried to leave. "Why wouldn't you come? You enjoyed yourself last time."

"I saw your face, Max. Let's not pretend you were happy to see me."

"I had a plan."

She waited, but he stopped talking. He clasped his hands together near his waist, his right thumb pressed hard against his left palm, and she recognized his method for not fidgeting under extreme pressure. "What was your plan?"

"I wasn't sure where our friendship stood now and I didn't know what to do, so I called my brother. And he said I should go to the diner when you were working because I'm comfortable there. And I'd be able to tell if you wanted to talk to me or not and I would bring a book to read if you didn't, so I wouldn't feel awkward. So I had a plan. And then you walked in and...I don't have a plan anymore."

It hurt her heart to watch him stare at the cupboard door over her shoulder. "Max, look at me, not at the cabinet. We're friends. I know you're not very experienced with the whole friends-with-benefits thing, but that's where we went last night. It happened. It was amazing and, no, we're not letting it change our friendship."

"You seemed different this morning."

Because she *was* different this morning. No matter what she might say, what she felt for Max wasn't casual anymore. But seeing him so wound up now just reinforced that she was doing the right thing in keeping him at arm's length emotionally. The potential for hurting him was too great.

"I was fine, Max. You know, I was a little worried about our friendship, too, so I was also feeling it out. And I think we were both so careful, we made it weird."

His hands relaxed. "So we're okay."

"Of course we are."

"Amazing, huh?"

She rolled her eyes. "Give me a knife and I'll help you chop those vegetables for the platter."

They started working, standing on opposite sides of the island, but he paused to look at her. "I'm glad you came today."

"I am, too." She chopped the ends off of a carrot and then sliced it lengthwise. "I was trying to work, but I knew the guys would be coming over for the game. I wasn't sure if you'd be prepared for how much ribbing you'd get about last night and if you get overwhelmed, you get tense. I didn't want you to say the wrong thing and damage a friendship because they don't know when to quit. I figure if I'm here, it'll be kept to a minimum."

"Will you stay after and watch a movie again?"

She looked up from the carrots and grinned. "I had Hailey grab me *Thor: The Dark World* from the library last week. It's in my car."

"Excellent. Thor or Loki?"

She snorted. "Loki, of course."

"You can have the sectional corner today."

Laughing, she went back to the carrots, hoping he wouldn't notice the slight tremble in her hands as she sliced. She hadn't wanted to come today. After her failed attempt to kill her feelings with ice cream, she'd tried to work. She'd actually managed to finish off a job before Max invaded her head again.

It was Sunday and all she could think about was how much teasing he was going to have to suffer through. And they were all his friends and it would all be in good fun, but if it went too far, she knew Max might not be able to cope. Best-case scenario, he went to his room or the basement and collected himself. Worst case, he'd say something wrong and put a strain on friendships that were important to him.

The one thing that would keep them from acting like gossiping frat boys about last night was her being in the room. So she'd sucked it up, put on a happy face and driven to his house.

Back when they were little kids, her parents had brought her for a visit to Whitford. Even though she was a bit older, Tori and Gavin had run wild outside for the entire day, his younger brother, Todd, still being too young, until they'd been called in for dinner. Gavin had then discovered a tick on his testicles and the face he'd made was almost identical to the face Max had made when he saw her. Like he'd found a tick on his balls.

Not one of her finer moments.

But the important thing was that they were back on an even keel, more or less. She just needed to keep it that way.

Butch showed up while she was combining dip mix and sour cream in a bowl. He looked a little rough today, and she wondered how many beers he'd had, trying to keep the cold at bay. For that matter, she wondered how Fran looked today.

"Some party last night," he said, snagging a pizza roll from the plate Max had just set out. But other than a quick glance at Tori, he said nothing else about it.

Mission accomplished, Tori thought.

Everybody showed up for the game, which kind of surprised her since they'd all had a late night at the lodge. The game was a close one and there was a lot of yelling at the television, but other than a few speculative glances, nothing was said about Max bringing Tori home last night.

Of course, the flip side of the coin was that everybody would consider them a couple now. They'd looked like a couple at the party and then left together. And today she'd been at his house, in his kitchen, like she belonged there.

But being a real couple wouldn't be as interesting to the gossips, so things would quiet down eventually. As long as she and Max knew what was going on, nobody else mattered.

She breathed a sigh of relief when everybody left. Since she didn't follow football, she wasn't sure what was so intense about the game—other than a close score—but they'd been like a pack of feral wolves today. It was so bad she hadn't even been able to grab a minute with Josh to talk about the ATV club's logo. They'd chosen one of her designs and he'd wanted to talk to her about the next step in the process, but it was obvious today wasn't a good time. She was pretty sure she saw Butch actually foam at the mouth at one point.

Paying attention to the movie proved to be a challenge, though. She was in the corner of the sectional and, although he'd chosen the same sofa, he was on the far end. It was like being a million miles away from him and she didn't like it.

About a half hour in, he hit the pause button. "You seem agitated."

"The polite thing to do would be pretend you didn't notice."

"It would be hard not to. And I thought it would be polite to pause it in case you need to use the bathroom."

"I don't have to pee, Max. It's mental agitation, not physical."

"Oh." He started the movie again, then almost immediately hit Pause again. "Do you want to talk about it?"

Not really, but she had to do something. "I'm sorry I was distant this morning."

"You made it clear it was…a friends-with-benefits thing."

"To be honest, I was a little thrown off. I guess I have more experience with acquaintances with benefits than good friends, because I felt awkward, too. And when I came out of the bathroom, you seemed so closed off. And I know—I *know*—you do that when you're not sure how to act, but I wasn't thinking about you. I guess I'm not so good at friends with benefits."

"We could make flashcards."

She laughed, relief coursing through her. His sense of humor was definitely intact. He set the remote on the table and moved down the couch so he was sitting next to her.

"After I woke up, I held you for a few minutes, but then I got up because I didn't know if that would bother you. If it was too…intimate. I wish I'd stayed in bed."

"I wish you had, too," she said before common sense could stop the words from coming out of her mouth.

"We could try again. Practice this whole friends-with-benefits thing until we get it right. It might be a handy life skill to have."

"Max, I—" She made the mistake of looking into his eyes, and she knew she was lost. "Just practicing friends with benefits."

"Just practice."

She might have given more thought to his verbal loophole of not specifying *what* he was practicing, but he leaned over her and pulled her face to his for a kiss. When she put her arms around his neck, he gripped her waist and pulled her over and onto his lap without taking his mouth from hers.

His hand fisted in her hair and she moaned against his lips. His tongue flicked over her bottom lip and she opened her mouth to him as he increased the pressure, becoming more demanding.

When his hand slid under her shirt to stroke her back, she shivered. His erection pressed between her thighs and she rocked slightly as his mouth left hers and moved to the hollow at her throat.

It took all of her willpower—which didn't seem to amount to much where he was concerned—to put her hands on his shoulders and lean back.

"Before we get carried away, do you happen to have a condom in your pocket?"

The corners of his mouth tilted up. "I keep them in my bedroom. It seems logical."

"I think we should move this to your bedroom, then. You know, the day I was rummaging through your closet, all I could think about was having sex in that bed."

"Really? You should have said something. I would have been more than happy to oblige." He kissed the side of her neck. "Assuming you were thinking about having sex in my bed with *me*."

She laughed and stood, hauling him to his feet. "Yes, with you."

"Oh, good. I'm very territorial about my bed."

She laughed until he slid an arm under her knees and lifted her, then she squealed and wrapped her arms around his neck. "What are you doing?"

"I always wanted to do this," he said, carrying her toward his bedroom. "I've just been waiting for a woman short and light enough to try it on."

MAX SET TORI DOWN on his bed and stood back to enjoy the view for a minute. He'd thought having Tori in her bed was the best night of his life, but seeing her on his bed triggered something primal in him. Something possessive.

She ran her hand over the comforter. "We need to mess up this bed."

"I've seen your bed. Mine may never be the same again."

"You know," she said, sitting up and scooting to the edge of the mattress. "You wore pants for far too long last night. We need to make sure that doesn't happen again."

He unbuttoned his fly, then sucked in a breath when she pushed his hands away. She lowered his zipper and slowly worked his jeans down while he tried to remember how to breathe.

When she tapped the back of his calf, he lifted each foot in turn so she could pull the jeans free, then the socks. Then she tucked her fingers into the waistband of his boxer briefs and pulled them down so he could step out of them.

"Luckily for you," she said, "I don't read passages over and over, savoring the words. I skip straight to the good parts."

When her lips closed over him, he buried his fingers in her hair and tried not to move. Her mouth was hot and wet and when she sucked gently, her fist following the path of her mouth up his shaft, his knees almost buckled.

"Tori." He needed her to stop because he wanted her in his arms. She flicked her tongue over the sensitive tip and he shuddered. "Get on the bed."

Her smile suggested she knew just how close he was as he took a condom out of his dresser drawer and ripped open the packet. Before she got on the bed, she pulled back the comforter and sheets, sending pillows flying.

He didn't waste any time today. He was barely hanging on as it was, so he lifted her ankles onto his shoulders and, after sliding in just enough to tease her, he thrust hard.

She gasped and the feel of her body and the sight of her fists clenching his sheets almost blew him apart. Fast and hard, he drove into her until she climaxed, her back arching off the bed. He dug his fingers into her hips, holding her as he thrust faster.

When she cried his name, he came, his body pulsing as the orgasm shook him. Once it faded, he reluctantly pulled free and slid down so he could bury his face against her neck.

"That was way better than *Thor*," she said, still slightly out of breath.

Chuckling, he remembered they'd left the movie paused downstairs. It didn't matter. The DVD player would turn off eventually or it wouldn't. And she was right. This was way better. "I like being friends with benefits."

"Me, too."

Once he'd caught his breath, he rolled away and went into the bathroom. After disposing of the condom, he looked at his reflection in the mirror. Colin had told him the most important thing was to get their friendship back on solid footing and, getting her into his bed so soon might have been a mistake, but he'd learned the hard way how they behaved now was important. He splashed some cold water on his face and then took his robe off the hook and slipped it on. Getting to the bathroom was one thing, but walking back out naked would make him feel awkward.

He was glad he did it. When he walked back into the bedroom, Tori was almost fully dressed. She pulled the shirt over her head and smiled when she saw him. "Do we have time to watch the end of the movie?"

It wasn't as if he'd made big plans for the night. "Sure."

She started toward him, or the door that was right behind him. "I'll make coffee."

"Decaf."

"Because it's after five." She stopped and reached her hand around his neck to pull him down for a kiss. "I know."

She kissed him like that again when the movie was over and it was time for her to leave. It was hard not to ask her to stay, but he had to be careful not to overstep the friends-with-benefits line. Casual, he told himself, like her good-night kiss.

Not yet ready to sleep, he picked up the remote and cycled through television channels, not landing on anything for longer than a minute. The action mimicked his thoughts, flipping through his mind without settling enough to let him focus.

It was hard enough to navigate relationships when they were clearly defined. Parents. Siblings. Girlfriend. Wife. But friends with benefits wasn't something he had any experience with and trying to take cues from her would wear on him eventually.

Tori wouldn't be asleep yet. Knowing her, she was probably at her computer, so he pulled her up on his phone before he could overthink it. I have a question. Still awake?

For a little while. Early morning, though.

That sounded like a hint. It can wait.

I'm not ready to sleep yet. What's your question?

So friends with benefits. Is this like insurance benefits? Maximum number of visits? Pre-approval? He smiled and hit Send.

There are forms that have to be filled out. In triplicate.

That made him laugh out loud. I'm already behind on paperwork?

We can fill it out together. When the mood strikes.

He pondered her words for a while, letting the subtext sink in. Casual and spontaneous. I'll make sure to have a pen handy.

As soon as he sent it, he realized that subtext might be too obscure, so he sent a follow-up text. By pen, I mean condom.

It felt like forever before she responded. You almost made me choke on my water.

I should let you go to bed. You have an early day tomorrow.

And a staff meeting. Whee.

He heard the sarcasm as clearly as if she'd said the words out loud. Good luck. And good night.

Good night, Max. xox

Kisses and hugs. It was a good start, and Max was smiling as he checked the locks on the doors, set the alarm system and went to bed. A very good start.

NINETEEN

THE STAFF MEETING was scheduled for ten, since it was squarely between breakfast and lunch. Tori had gone in for the early shift and was done, so she took off her apron and made herself a coffee before sitting at the counter with Liz, Ava, Carl and Gavin. Paige had Sarah on her hip, no doubt because Rose had shown up for the meeting, as well.

"I know you've all heard the great news. In a couple of weeks, Gavin's heading to Kennebunkport to wow the upper class with some of the Trailside Diner's best dinner specials." She paused while they all cheered, which made Gavin blush. "I'm so proud of you, Gavin, and I hope…"

Paige choked up and then they all got a little teary when Gavin walked around the counter to wrap his arms around her, baby and all. "I wouldn't have this chance without you."

"And you'd better make the most of it." She patted his back, and then laughed when Sarah gave him a good shove.

"To add to our joy," she continued once Gavin was seated again, "Liz's pregnancy has the distinction of being the worst-kept secret in the history of Whitford."

Tori caught Liz's smile through the corner of her eye, and the way she slid her hand over her belly. "I wonder who got the coupons for being the first to tell Fran."

"I told her myself," Rose said. "And, yes, I made her give me the coupons."

They all laughed, but then Paige's expression turned serious. "I've put an ad in some of the bigger newspapers and online. Needless to say, I'm hoping to hire a cook as soon as possible. Until then, we're going to try to make do by cutting back on the menu temporarily and keeping it simple."

"I think the worst of the morning sickness is behind me," Liz said. "I felt fine this morning, but it does kind of come and go."

"For now, I'm going to open. Then, ideally, I'd like Tori to come in midmorning and stay until Ava comes in at two. I'll come back in and cook for the dinner crowd, with Rose and Liz both stepping in when we need more hands on deck." She stopped and looked at Tori. "I know you're supposed to be *really* part-time, but if you could do the regular hours until we get a cook or Liz is over the hump, I'd really appreciate it."

Tori had been prepared for this and given it a lot of thought. On the one hand, she couldn't cut corners on her design work. It took years to build a reputation and no time flat to lose it. But these were her friends and, most importantly, Gavin wouldn't have this opportunity if not for Paige.

"I can do it," she said. "Honestly, it's easier for me to manage my work schedule if I know up front when I'm working rather than being called in at random times."

"Thank you, Tori."

She sipped her coffee while Paige went down the line, speaking to each of them about the schedule change and making sure everybody was on board. Not surprisingly, they were all willing to do whatever it took to keep the place going.

"I can still work for the two weeks," Gavin pointed out.

Paige shook her head. "You can help us streamline the menu so it's manageable and if we get in a bind, we might call you, but you have planning and packing to do. And you need a haircut, too, before you go."

They all laughed again, and the meeting was over. Liz was staying, so Tori was free to walk down to the market for some groceries and then head home.

When she unlocked her door, she almost tripped over a bag in the middle of the hallway. There was a book poking out the top and Hailey had a spare key, so she assumed it was a surprise visit from the library fairy.

Shifting both bags of groceries she'd picked up at the market after work to one hand, she picked up the bag and went upstairs. Since she wasn't on the waiting list for anything she could think of, curiosity got the better of her and she stuck the milk in the fridge, then dug into the bag of books.

The paperback on top looked like some kind of self-help book, and she frowned. There was a typical ILL slip stuck inside, with Hailey's lighthearted but serious warning of increased fines if the book was late. Hailey said it caused her professional embarrassment but Tori suspected she exaggerated how much in an effort to avoid the work of renewing through the lending library. And there was a sticky note on the front.

Even though I'm not single anymore, I'm still your best friend. I love you and I want you to be happy. Please don't be mad.

There were four books in the bag and they were all self-help books for dealing with divorce and toxic family relationships. Tori's hands shook and she dropped the books on her desk, glaring at them since the woman who'd left them in her hallway wasn't available to be glared at. She wasn't, however, out of reach.

Hailey answered on the second ring. "Please don't be mad."

"I feel like you're trying to tell me something."

"I'm trying to tell you what I wrote in the note. You're my best friend, I love you and I want you to be happy."

"I *am* happy."

There was a long pause. "I think you hope if you pretend you're happy long enough, it'll become the truth."

It sounded like Whitford's do-gooder librarian had been spending too much time in the self-help section. "If this is about Max—"

"It has nothing to do with Max. It's about *you,* I swear."

Tori wanted to be mad, but she knew Hailey's heart was in the right place. And she had to admit her current method of dealing with her parents—namely dodging their calls and avoiding going home—wasn't working. "Did you pick them by their titles?"

"No, I researched recommended books and then I researched the authors and I read a gazillion reviews." She heard Hailey sigh. "I wish we had a decent therapist nearby, but I know you'll come up with a million excuses not to make the minimum of a two-hour round trip to talk to somebody."

She couldn't deny it. "Did you highlight the important passages for me?"

"No! Bad things happen to people who write in library books, Tori. Very bad things. And the important passages will be the ones that speak to *you,* not to me."

Tori sighed and started putting away the rest of her groceries one-handed. "I thought putting some distance between me and my parents would help. It might have if that guy hadn't invented the telephone."

"It might have worked very short-term, but it's been two years. This crap show has become the normal and it's not going to change on its own."

She laughed. "I think you snuck a few peeks before you dropped these books off."

"I read some articles online. Like I said, I want you to be happy. And I don't even care if you're happy with a guy. I want you to be happy for *you.*"

"Fine, I won't be mad."

"Good. And since I know you're not mad, I have patrons and have to get back to work."

Since she'd grabbed a sandwich at the diner, Tori was free to get right to work. But first, bra off and yoga pants on. Then, as she waited for her computer to wake up, her cell phone rang. Her mother's number showed on the screen and Tori silenced it. She waited, but she didn't get a new voice mail notification, which meant her mom would try again.

Then, just as her email client coughed up her new messages, she heard the text chime. For a second, she was terrified her mom finally got a smart phone and learned to text, but it was Max.

Are you home?

Yes. Home from work and just sat down to work.

You know what they say about all work and no play.

She laughed. Are you trying to lure me out to play?

I wish. I'm working, too. Making steak & mushroom kebobs again tonight. Should I make enough for you?

Sighing, she considered her workload. She should eat at her desk, but those kebobs were so good. A couple of hours wouldn't hurt. Yes, but I can't stay for a movie.

A long time passed before his return message. Can you stay for a quarter of a movie?

Tori frowned at her phone. Why would I stay for a quarter of a movie?

The average movie is 2 hours so a quarter is 30 minutes. If you can stay 30 minutes, we can have sex instead because nobody wants to watch a quarter of a movie.

Who could resist that logic? I'll be there by six. Get some work done.

She took her own advice and focused on clearing the to-do list she'd written out that morning. There was a lot of tweaking—one author didn't like his title font, another wanted a more futuristic spaceship, which made Tori laugh, and one was thinking about redoing the covers of her entire series to boost sales. It was nitpicky, headache-inducing stuff, so after a while, she sat back in her chair to take a break.

The books next to her computer caught her eye and she grabbed the one on top. It promised a step-by-step plan for healing families split by divorce. By tilting her head, she saw from the spines Hailey had also sent books on being an adult child of divorce and coping with toxic relationships. They didn't sound nearly as fun as the novels sitting on the other end of the desk.

But Hailey had gone to a lot of work to choose these particular books, so she opened the one in her hand and scanned the table of contents. Then she flipped to the first chapter and started to read.

ARE YOU NAKED? Max hit the send button and waited patiently for Tori's response.

Why would I be naked?

A man can hope. It sounded more interesting than are you busy?

Of course she was busy. It had been almost two weeks since Tori's schedule at the diner had changed and they'd fallen into a routine of a lot of work, a lot of texting and the occasional exercising of their friendship's benefits.

I'm a little busy, but not crazy busy.

This Sunday's the bye week, so I was thinking we could go to dinner. Not at the diner.

What's a bye week?

He frowned at his phone screen. The Patriots don't play. They have a week off.

Why?

I can explain it to you, but that would probably tip over into actual telephone-call length.

Her reply came almost immediately. Dinner sounds good. Speaking of, tomorrow night we're having a goodbye party for Gavin at the diner. You should come.

A party? He wasn't sure about a party at the diner. He liked Gavin well enough, especially his cooking, but he didn't know him that well.

I'll let you walk me home after.

I'll be there, he responded so quickly he was surprised he didn't sprain his thumb. What time?

Eight. The dinner rush will be over and it limits the festivities to an hour.

I'll see you at eight, then.

Can't wait. xox

He'd figured out the xox was her way of ending a text conversation. Though he had no way of knowing if she ended all of her conversations that way, he liked to think those kisses and hugs were just for him. And he couldn't wait to see her, either.

Colin had called him earlier in the week to check up on him and see how the plan had worked. After Max explained the plan had gone south almost immediately, but that they were still friends with benefits, his brother had urged him to be patient and not push too hard, too soon. It wasn't easy, but he was managing not to tell her how he felt. Barely.

When eight o'clock rolled around the following night, he was confident enough he'd be walking her home, so he went ahead and parked in the back of the bank's lot and walked to the diner.

He'd been expecting the staff to be there, along with Gavin's family, so it was a surprise to find what looked like half the population of Whitford in the diner. It took him a while to find Tori, since she was shorter than most everybody else there, but he finally spotted her in the back corner with her aunt and uncle and started toward her.

Halfway there, he was hit by a sudden wave of anxiety. He knew Mike a bit, since he made it over for a few games now and then, but he didn't really know Jilly at all. Right now, she was the closest thing Tori had to a reliable mother figure and he had no idea how Jilly might feel about their relationship. Or how much she even knew.

"I told you you'd shake each other up."

Max looked down at Ava, who'd moved in next to him, and was confused until he remembered the advice she'd given him after his second and final date with Nola. But discretion seemed to be in order, or at least as much as was possible. "Tori and I are friends."

"Mmm-hmm. What is it the young folk call that nowadays? Friends with incentives?"

"Benefits. Friends with benefits." He told himself it was a correction, not an admission.

"Right. But you need to start thinking long-term. Like friends with retirement plans."

Max stared at the clock on the wall, wondering if the hands were even moving. An hour, she'd said. The festivities were limited to an hour by the diner closing, but did that mean Tori had to stay the entire hour?

Ava chuckled. "You're an odd duck, Max Crawford. I like you."

The way she said it, with amusement but also what sounded like affection, made him look at her. "I think I like you, too."

"I grow on people. It takes a while." She shook her finger at him. "But you take my advice and start working on that retirement plan."

She walked away and Max inwardly cringed when he realized Tori had spotted him at some point and was definitely within earshot. "A retirement plan?"

Max shrugged. "Ava was giving me some financial advice."

"Ava? Really?"

He didn't blame her for being skeptical and went for a change of subject. "I was on my way over to say hello. You were with your aunt and uncle."

"They're so excited for Gavin they can't stand still for more than two minutes. And he's just as bad. They're definitely moving targets tonight."

They moved around themselves, making small talk with different people as they went. Max was surprised by how well he managed. Between making the effort to get to know people over the last month and a half and having Tori at his side, he was comfortable in the crowd. Two parties in a row, he thought, where he hadn't made excuses to leave early.

Not that he was complaining when the cake had been eaten and the neon *open* sign shut off. There was still the walking home to look forward to, as soon as Tori was finished saying goodbye to her cousin.

While she had her arms wrapped around Gavin's neck, telling him how wonderfully he was going to do, Max shook Mike's hand and then Jilly's, congratulating them. Tori's aunt seemed nice as she talked about how proud she was of her son and how strange it was going to be not having him around. There were no sideways glances or speculative questions.

Once he'd gotten the chance to wish Gavin luck, it was finally time to head out. Once they were on the sidewalk, she slipped her hand in his and they walked silently in the cold night air.

TORI TOSSED HER KEYS onto her counter and took a deep breath. She'd lured Max into attending the party with the promise of walking her home, both of them knowing what that really meant.

But it had been a really crappy afternoon and, after the effort of putting her mood aside to enjoy the party, she just wanted to curl up in a ball and feel sorry for herself. Max's arms slid around her waist and she sighed.

He kissed the back of her neck. "You're very tense."

"I had a rough day, actually."

"Then sit down and I'll make you some hot cocoa."

"That sounds good. I'm going to change first, though." Comfortable sweats were a pretty universal *not in the mood* signal, but she wasn't sure if Max would pick up on it or not.

Her mug was already on the coffee table when she was done making herself less attractive, and he joined her on the couch when his was ready. He didn't seem to even register the sweats, but he left a little space between them.

"Do you want to talk about what's bothering you?" he asked. "Is it Gavin leaving?"

"No. My mom called earlier, about Thanksgiving." She sighed and leaned her head back against the couch. "And Hailey interlibrary loaned me some books about divorce and toxic relationships and stuff, and they've been weighing on my mind a lot."

"Do you think they're helping?"

"I tried explaining to Mom that it's hard to be around when she's angry, but then she tells me what my father did to make her angry. I told her that nobody wants to hear a litany of complaints over pumpkin pie and all she does is give me the whole list to prove it's valid." Tori shrugged one shoulder, rubbing her index finger over the edge of her thumbnail. "One of the chapters I read earlier—right after she called, actually—covered when a toxic person in your life isn't taking hints or redirection and has to be cut out of your life."

"If that concept's disturbing you, I take it you've reached that point with your parents?"

"Maybe my mom. Dad's not quite as bad and I have hope for him, eventually. But they'd have to hear what I say to get the hints. Maybe if the holidays weren't coming up, it wouldn't be so bad, but they're in a frenzy right now."

He put his arm around her and pulled her close, so she was snuggled against his chest. "Have Thanksgiving with me."

The words came out in a casual, almost throwaway tone, but alarm bells still went off in Tori's brain. Thanksgiving was a holiday. Spending holidays together was a big deal. A very big deal. "I was planning on going to Uncle Mike and Aunt Jilly's. My mom keeps threatening to show up, though. We might all come down with a case of the flu."

"If you tell her you're spending the day with a friend, she can't invite herself and, if you're not at their house, there's no reason for your aunt and uncle to have to pretend to be sick on a day dedicated to food. Besides, it would be fun."

Or it would be intimate. A couple spending Thanksgiving Day together. The familiar fear rose up in the back of her mind, but she did her best to shove it away. "It does sound fun. Friends can eat too much turkey together and then fall asleep on the couch watching movies."

"Or football."

"I'll definitely fall asleep on the couch. But aren't you supposed to go home to Connecticut?"

He shrugged, which she felt since she was pressed up against him. "With six adults and five kids, they'll barely notice. And I'll be going home for Christmas a month later, anyway. They won't mind. I promise. And it'll get you out of a tough spot with your parents."

Tears stung her eyes and she tried to blink them away. "Why can't I tell them to…I don't know, go jump off a cliff or something?"

"Because they're your parents."

"I don't want to end up hating them as much as they hate each other."

He kissed the top of her head. "I wish I knew what to tell you. But I can help you dodge Thanksgiving and maybe they'll start listening to you."

She doubted that part, but it would be nice to have a

reprieve from the marital warfare, even if it was a brief one. There was no doubt in her mind things would reach a fever pitch leading up to Christmas, just like previous years. One of the books, which she'd already read twice, had a recommended reading list and she made a mental note to ask Hailey to borrow a couple more.

"I'd like to have Thanksgiving with you," she said. "It'll be fun."

"We could try that thing where they shove a duck into a chicken and then shove the chicken into the turkey. Or maybe the chicken gets shoved into the duck. I guess it depends on which one's bigger."

She laughed, shoving away from him. "I'd rather go to my mother's."

He pulled her back, and she figured he'd make his move now. Maybe slide his hand up under her sweatshirt or start nibbling at her neck, but he only wrapped his arm around her again. "I think a plain turkey would be best. When you start shoving food inside other foods, it must be difficult to figure out the cooking time."

"Have you ever roasted a turkey?" She assumed, if he always went home to Connecticut, his mother probably did the honors.

"No, but they have directions on the wrapper. And there are YouTube video tutorials for everything."

She laughed, trying to imagine him watching videos on how to properly stuff a Thanksgiving turkey. "I usually just watch videos of people doing really stupid things."

"Speaking of videos, where's your TV remote?"

"Probably under the books on the table next to you," she said without bothering to lift her head to look. Her hot cocoa was getting cold, but Max was a great pillow.

A few seconds later, her TV came on and he started flipping through channels. "Stop me if you see something you want to watch."

When he landed on an episode of *Firefly,* she told him to stop. "You can't pass by an episode of *Firefly.*"

"This one's early in the season. If it's a marathon, we'll still be sitting here hours from now."

She snuggled deeper into his embrace. "Is that a problem?"

"No, it was a wish," he said, and rested his cheek on her hair.

TWENTY

MAX WORE THE blue sweater on Sunday. While he'd always known it suited him, because his sister-in-law had told him so when she gave it to him for Christmas a few years before, there was something about the way Tori looked at him when he was wearing it that made him wish he could wear it every day.

Unlike their first trip into the city for dinner, there were no awkward silences, even with the radio turned down low. They'd had some applicants for the cooking position at the diner, and Tori shared Paige's stories about some of the least qualified. It wasn't looking good for filling Gavin's shoes anytime soon, but at least they were all being entertained in the meantime.

They were almost halfway to the restaurant when Tori's cell phone rang. She pulled it out of her bag and he could tell by the sigh it was probably one of her parents. After the third ring, she hit the button to answer it.

"Hi, Dad." She was quiet then, and he could hear the faint rumble of a man's voice, though not the words. "I haven't looked for your fishing rod yet because I haven't been to Mom's house. I'm really busy and I don't know when I'll get a chance."

While her dad responded to that, Max reached over and put his hand on her thigh, trying to offer comfort. Or maybe strength. What he'd like to do was take her cell phone and throw it out the window, but that wouldn't do any good. She'd just get another one.

"Dad, I'm going to interrupt you because I'm actually on my way out to dinner. I live three hours away from you and Mom. If you want your fishing pole, you need to call your ex-wife and ask her for permission to look in the garage. Call your lawyer if you have to, or buy a new fishing pole, but this is not my problem."

Max squeezed her leg and she slid her free hand over his, her fingers curling around to squeeze back.

"I'm sorry, Dad, but I don't have your fishing pole, so those are your options. I have to go now, but I love you and I'll talk to you soon."

Once she'd hung up, she shook her head, as if trying to clear it. "Sorry. I should have sent him to voice mail instead of letting him into our date, but then I would have wondered about it. Now it's done."

"Are you okay?"

"Yeah, I guess." She didn't sound sure, but then she nodded. "Yes, I'm okay. I didn't tell him to take a flying leap or anything. I just told him getting his fishing pole is his responsibility and not mine. There's nothing wrong with that."

"No, there isn't." He squeezed her hand, knowing that, no matter what she said, it had been a big step for her. And she'd used the word *date,* which was quite the mood booster. "So you were telling me about the woman who asked Paige if she wanted a grilled cheese sandwich on toasted or plain bread…"

Tori laughed and fell back into the stories from the diner, though she didn't let go of Max's hand until he pulled into the restaurant's parking lot. He went around to make sure she didn't ding his door and to help her out, getting a kiss for the effort. This was definitely better than the mock date.

"You smell…nice." He kissed her again. "The good nice."

"Thank you. Did I tell you how nice you look tonight? Definitely the good nice."

"You didn't have to." He took her hand and started toward the door.

"What is that supposed to mean?"

"I see the way you look at me in this sweater." He stopped walking. "Maybe I should leave it in the car. This *is* a family restaurant."

She slapped his arm and nudged him forward. "I've created a monster."

"So, did Gavin settle into Kennebunkport okay?" he asked her once they'd ordered drinks and their meals.

"Yes, he did. He left yesterday morning and moved into the apartment they helped him find. I guess it's very small and on the third floor of some grand old mansion, but he can see the ocean and walk to the restaurant."

"Which is probably good, considering the condition of his truck."

When Tori laughed, Max was proud to notice more than one male head turned in her direction. "Aunt Jilly's driving the truck right now. She let him take her car until he saves enough to buy one of his own. So then she took *my* car to do her monthly grocery run because the truck burns too much gas. I really hope Gavin makes good money at that restaurant because we'll be playing hot potato with his truck until he gets rid of it."

She talked more about him and her work, but he lost his focus on her words. She was happy tonight, despite the call from her dad. Her eyes sparkled and she was quick with the smile that crinkled the corners of them. She could have been reciting weather forecasts and he would be mesmerized.

She tilted her head, narrowing her eyes. "Are you listening to me?"

"Of course." Kind of.

"What did I say?"

"You were telling me how amazing I look in this sweater."

She snorted. "Close. I asked if you'd started Christmas shopping for your family yet."

"Oh. I'm done, actually. I always order Christmas gifts the first week of November. Because I wrap them myself and bring them with me instead of having them delivered, I like to leave plenty of time. What about you?"

"I usually do one marathon shopping day, in actual stores, the Saturday before Christmas."

He frowned. "Between the depleted selection and the crowds, that doesn't sound very efficient."

"No, it's not. But it's a rush. Like my equivalent of rappelling down a mountain or bungee jumping off a bridge." She pointed her fork at him. "You know, even though you're done, you should go with me just to experience it."

"I've never experienced tequila shots, either. I can do one and then the other, and get both experiences out of the way at the same time."

"I'm not taking you drunk Christmas shopping with me." She leaned back in her chair and watched him over the rim of her glass as she drank her wine. "I might take you home with me tonight, though, and let you kiss me good-night. And good-morning."

"It's the sweater, isn't it?"

She smiled that smile from the photo on his phone, and his pulse raced. "It's a really *nice* sweater."

By Tuesday, Tori was ready for a day off. She'd found her rhythm, working the ten-to-two shift and doing her design work, as well as spending time with Max, but life at the Trailside Diner was turning into a sitcom. A bad one.

When Max walked in a little before two, she wasn't surprised when he stopped right inside the door, scowling. His nose wrinkled and he gave her a questioning look as he walked to his regular counter seat. "I may be a little on the straightlaced side, but I did go to college. Why does the diner smell like marijuana?"

Tori grimaced. "Another applicant bites the dust."

"At least he or she is probably pretty mellow about it."

"Uh, yeah. Unfortunately—or maybe fortunately, depending on your stress levels or general mood—she couldn't tell the difference between intake and exhaust in the HVAC system and was blowing smoke in the wrong one. Not that either was the right one for dispersing pot smoke on the job, but you know what I mean."

"What is Paige doing about it?"

"Rose is baking four batches of brownies. The first batch is cooling now if you'd like one."

"You're kidding."

His expression, which showed quite clearly he knew she wasn't kidding, made her laugh. "As soon as we could smell it, Paige left because she had Sarah in a playpen in the office. Drew came over, and Sam Jensen from the fire department, and they made sure all the exhaust fans were running. And I'm making signs to hang on the door so people can choose whether or not to come in."

"It's not very strong," he said. "Although I'm not sure if it's growing more faint, if I'm getting accustomed to it, or if I've stopped caring."

"I'll get you a brownie." She poured him a coffee and went out back to get two of Rose's perfectly baked, slightly gooey in the center brownies.

"Those look really rich," he said when she set the plate in front of him. "I was kidding about being high, you know. There's a trace odor."

"I know. But have you ever had one of Rosie's brownies?" He shook his head. "Then take advantage of the excuse and have two."

She hung the sign on the door, warning potential customers of the issue and noting that Sam Jensen had given the all-clear for them to remain open. Then she went through the checklist of things to do before Ava showed up, like checking sugar packet supplies and ketchup bottles. It seemed like forever before the clock hit two, and then she was free.

"Did you come to town for errands?" she asked Max once she'd left the diner behind her for the day.

"Yes, if having coffee and a slice of pie is an errand. Although the brownies were better. I also thought maybe I'd see if you wanted to hang out at my place. I'm making tacos for dinner."

"That's the best offer I've had all day." She tucked her arm through his as they walked down the sidewalk. "I'm going to take my car, though. I can't stay too late."

He bumped her with his hip. "How late?"

"Late enough," she said, and then she laughed when he gave her a suggestive raise of his eyebrows. "I want tacos first, though. I don't remember the last time I had tacos."

Since she was taking her own car, anyway, Tori took a few minutes to shower and change into non-diner clothes before heading over to Max's house. She probably should have declined the invitation, she thought as she drove, a country singer belting out a song about moonlight, sex and tailgates on the radio. It was a problem, her inability to hold Max at arm's length. Or, more accurately, her lack of desire to keep him at a slight distance.

She'd been excusing it to herself with the friends-with-benefits line. They hung out together a lot because they were friends. They had sex because that was the benefit. The truth—that they were together whenever possible because they liked being together and pretty much met the definition of a real couple—was like a sore tooth. Occasionally she'd gingerly poke at it until it hurt, and then she had to stop. But, also like a sore tooth, she was going to have to face it eventually.

But not tonight. She cranked the volume knob on her radio, letting the song drown out her thoughts. She'd already accepted his invitation and she didn't want to disappoint him. Plus, there would be tacos. As long as she kept telling herself she was in it for the food and the orgasms, she would be fine.

When she arrived, he took her down in the basement to show off an engine he'd just finished painting. She loved the way his eyes lit up when he talked about the train's history and she didn't have to feign interest when he pulled a huge, obviously old book off a shelf and showed her the picture of the real-life version he'd worked from.

They lingered in the basement for a while and then she sat at the kitchen island to watch him start prepping for dinner. She knew he preferred to eat at six, but he was making the tacos earlier than usual.

"I know you don't want to stay late," he said, pulling a variety of vegetables out of the fridge.

"Mmm-hmm." She'd told him she wanted tacos before sex, so he was trying to get them out of the way as quickly as he could get away with.

He talked about his family while he cooked. His mother had called earlier, so he had a lot of news from Connecticut. Though Tori didn't know any of them, she liked hearing him talk about his parents, his brothers and their families. Love and amused affection was strong in his voice and he was animated in a way he usually reserved for sports and trains.

"Did you tell your mom about me?" she asked when he paused for a moment.

He stopped chopping a strip of green pepper and looked at her, but his gaze returned to the pepper without really making eye contact. "I told her about you. I...I told her we're friends."

But not friends with benefits. It hurt somehow, that his family didn't know she was more than just a buddy who stopped by to watch ball games, but she was the one who'd made the rules. Throwing around cute phrases with his mom that were meant to elevate casual sex between friends wasn't anybody's style, really, but especially not Max's.

"Your mom sounds really awesome," she said. "Your whole family does, actually."

"Like any family, there are rough spots, but yes, I think they're pretty awesome."

Lucky guy, she thought.

An hour later, she'd had her fill of tacos and was ready to work them off. Because it was habit, Max went into the living room after they'd cleaned up and started looking for a movie for them to watch. She liked cuddling on the couch with him, but she'd been poking at that emotional sore tooth too much and she needed sex, not affection.

She went into his bedroom and stripped off her clothes. Then she took one of his crisp, white button shirts and pulled it on. It came almost to her knees and she had to roll the sleeves several times, but she liked the way it looked and she thought Max would, too.

Standing in front of the TV, he was flipping through the channels, so she leaned against the doorjamb. "Hey, Max."

"There's nothing worth watching on tonight. We might have to break out a DVD."

"Max."

He turned, his brow furrowed in annoyance. "I—"

The remote fell out of his hand as the annoyance magically disappeared from his features. She waited, but he didn't say anything. That intense gaze raked over her body and she felt the thrill of victory. There would be no cuddling in front of the television tonight.

"Now I know why I love long-sleeve button shirts so much," he said in a low voice. "I've been waiting to see you in one."

"Enjoy the view, because it won't be on long."

Giving her a naughty grin, he pulled his cell phone out of his pocket. "We should update your contact photo."

"Max!" She turned to retreat back to his room, but his legs were a lot longer than hers, so she actually had to run.

She didn't get the door closed in time and it hit the palm of his hand with a thud. "You are not taking pictures, Max."

His cell phone appeared in the gap and she plucked it out of his fingers. As soon as she had it, she backed up and he pushed the door open. "It's good to keep contact photos updated, you know."

She dropped the phone onto the thick braided rug and kicked it under the bed. "Nice try. There is no way in hell you're taking a picture of me wearing nothing but your shirt."

"I don't need a picture." He lifted her and set her on the edge of the bed, his thighs holding her knees apart. "I'll never forget the way you look right now."

MAX WAS A FAST LEARNER and, thanks to a wastebasket tucked discreetly under his nightstand, he didn't have to leave the bed after making love to Tori anymore. He was free to simply roll away for a second, then go right back to savoring the feel of her naked body under his.

"Tacos and orgasms," she mumbled. "You sure know how to make a lady happy."

"I should write a how-to book and make millions of dollars."

"I get half. Call me a research assistant."

"I don't think research assistants get half."

She chuckled and ran her fingernails up his back.

"I don't think most research assistants are as thorough as I am."

The shiver that tickled his spine was partly due to her touch, but also the rush of emotion that slipped the tight leash he'd been holding on to for dear life. This was what he wanted. Back on the first of October, when he'd made out his to-do list, he'd been looking for Tori. She wasn't just companionship and sex. She laughed with him and pushed his buttons and made him excited to see her, no matter how much time they spent together.

He pressed a kiss to his favorite spot—the soft skin at the base of her throat—and couldn't hold it back anymore. "I'm in love with you, Tori."

Her body went rigid, as if he'd physically shocked her, but he didn't regret saying the words. He'd tried to play along with the friends-with-benefits thing as long as he could, but he didn't have it in him to pretend anymore.

"Let me get up."

"Tori, I—" He was afraid if she got up, she wasn't going to listen.

"Let me get up. *Now*."

He rolled away and she slid off the bed. In the time it took him to pull a pair of sweats out of a drawer and pull them on, she'd managed to get dressed.

"That was a sucker punch, Max," she said, zipping up her jeans.

"I don't really have the ability to live a lie or pretend everything's okay when it's not. I've tried hiding how I feel about you and I can't do it anymore. I say what's on my mind—sometimes even when I shouldn't—and, if there's a problem, I fix it. You'll always know where you stand with me."

"And you knew where you stood with me."

"The difference is that I'm being honest with myself and you're not."

"Don't you dare." She pointed at him. "Don't you dare stand there and try to tell me what I feel."

She walked out of the bedroom and Max felt an insane urge to call his brother and ask him to talk to Tori for him. He knew he couldn't, but he also knew if Tori left angry, she might never talk to him again.

He caught her in the kitchen because she had to put her shoes on. "Please don't leave angry. I'm sorry I said you weren't being honest about your feelings for me."

"Max." She leaned against the island and put her face in her hands. "You don't understand."

"Then please explain it to me so I can."

"You and I want different things in life. You know that."

"I want somebody who understands me the way you do. I want somebody who laughs at my jokes like you do. Somebody who enjoys being with me and likes me the way I am. Like you do." He wished she'd look at him. "I made a new list to describe the kind of woman I'd fall in love with and it just said *Tori*."

"Stop. Stop saying you love me. You don't."

"If I don't get to tell you how you feel, you can't really tell me how I feel."

"You joked about practicing how to be friends with benefits, Max."

"I think we've been more than that for a while. And I was trying to convince myself I could settle for friends with benefits for now, and that maybe in time you'd trust that I wouldn't hurt you, but I can't hide how I feel about you."

It made sense to him, but he was afraid. The more he talked, the more Tori looked like a wild animal whose fight-or-flight instinct was kicking in. Maybe he should shut up, but if they didn't come to a resolution right now, in his kitchen, he was afraid they never would.

TWENTY-ONE

TORI'S HEART ACHED and all she wanted to do was run. If it had been some random guy, she would have. But this was Max and, if she didn't make him understand, he would blame himself.

It wasn't him. It was her.

"I didn't want you to love me," she said softly. "I've already hurt you, Max. I can see it on your face and that's the last thing I ever wanted to do. I knew you aren't really wired for casual sex, but I wanted you and I did it anyway."

"I'm a grown man, Tori. I might not be loud or assertive, but don't mistake that for weakness."

"I don't think you're weak. But you can be hurt and it kills me. It's killing me to hurt you now. Imagine being together for years and having children and doing…this."

"*This* is normal, Tori. This is a disagreement. An argument. Hell, call it a fight if you want to. But people do it. And you make peace and move on. Together."

Her heart felt as if it was going to explode in her chest. "I imagine saying the things to you my mother said to my father and you saying to me the words that came out of his mouth and it hurts. I can't…I just can't."

"Tori, I would never say something hurtful to you deliberately. I love—"

"So did they, Max!" She knew her voice was growing louder and higher pitched, but she couldn't seem to stop. "They loved each other. They vowed to love and respect each other forever and look where they ended up. They say there's a fine line between love and hate and it's true. I've seen just how fine a line it is and I'm not living my life walking that line."

"You're being unreasonable." Before she could give voice to the rage that toneless statement of logic filled her with, he held up his hands. "No. I'm sorry. That was the wrong thing to say."

"You think?"

"Tori. I didn't mean that your feelings are unreasonable. They're your feelings. But you're superimposing your parents' relationship over ours, and that's not fair. Not only is it not fair to me, but it's not fair to *you*."

"I'm messy, Max. Not physically. Emotionally. And you're not. You're orderly and logical and you can't understand how terrified I am that if I let myself love you, someday we'll turn on each other and inflict pain on each other. Or our children."

"You're right. I don't understand. I want to, but I just don't understand walking away from a chance to spend the rest of your life with somebody who loves you, messy or not, because your parents' marriage ended badly."

"I know how it sounds. It doesn't make sense, but there's logic and then there's feeling. And what I feel is fear. Every time I think about loving you—and I've done a lot of that—I see your face. The look in your eyes right now. It hurts me to think I'm causing you pain. But at least, right now, it can be a clean break. We're not married. Hell, we're barely a couple. We don't have children. I can just walk away and you'll find somebody who can love you the way you deserved to be loved."

"I'm not going to stop loving you because you go home and don't return my calls."

"You will. Maybe with me out of the picture you and Nola can give it another—" She broke off, unable to say it. Tears clogged her throat and she shook her head.

"I don't know how to make you trust me. How to trust *us*."

"You can't." She swiped at the tear that threatened to run over her cheek. "I'm going to leave now, but I want you to know this is my fault. It's nothing you did. It's nothing you said wrong."

"I love you, Tori."

"Except that."

She didn't look back. There was nothing left to say.

She made it halfway back to her apartment before she had to pull over because she couldn't see through the tears anymore. She cried hard, trying to purge enough emotion so she could drive.

But she couldn't stand the idea of going home. She didn't want to be alone. Even though it was late, she mopped at her face and drove to Hailey's house. The lights were still on downstairs, so she pulled in the driveway and shut her car off.

She hated being here. Hailey and Matt were probably snuggled on the couch, having some couple time and no guy wanted the hot-mess best friend showing up at all hours.

The outside light flashed and she looked up to see Hailey in the doorway, beckoning for her to come in. She got out and walked to the house, the tears already rising to the surface again.

"Hey, get in here."

Matt was sitting on the couch, but he took one look

at her and stood up. Tori wasn't surprised. She had to look awful and he'd want no part of what was coming.

"I'm going to take Bear for a walk. He loves being out at night and we haven't done it in a long time, so I'll probably be a while." He grabbed a coat that was hanging in the entryway to throw over his sweats. Then he shoved his feet in his shoes, grabbed the dog's leash and kissed Hailey's cheek. But he paused before he went out the door and looked at Tori. "There are two slices of Rosie's double chocolate cake left over in the fridge. You can have mine."

Tori's eyes welled up with tears and her throat tightened. When the door closed behind him, all she could do was look at Hailey and wave a hand in the direction he'd gone.

"I know," Hailey said. "Now you see how I could fall in love with a guy who needs his own shower in the garage. Now come on. Kitchen."

Hailey didn't break out the cake yet. Tori let herself be shoved into a kitchen chair and took several tissues out of the box Hailey set in front of her. A glass of water followed, and she drained half of it in one shot.

"What happened?"

"Max told me he loves me." Then she buried her face in the tissues and cried some more.

Hailey didn't push. She just waited until Tori was ready to talk again, about twelve tissues later. Tori told her everything, from the poorly timed I love you to her freaking out and leaving.

"He said we were just practicing being friends with benefits. And then, *boom*. He just said it."

"Anybody who saw you together could see he was crazy about you. And, to be honest, it looked mutual."

"I yelled at him and I could picture myself being my mother, yelling horrible things at him. He's sensitive, Hailey. I can't hurt him like that."

"Oh, Tori."

The way she said it, like a woman who knew her best friend was being crazy and couldn't figure out how to tell her, brought on a fresh bout of tears.

"Oh my God, I haven't cried in years," Tori said when it passed, looking at the mountain of crumpled tissues in front of her.

"Well, you're breaking his heart and your own heart and your parents are at the root of all it. Of course you're going to cry."

"I'm not having an emotional breakdown. It's a breakup. I know women cry during a breakup, but this much? We were barely even a couple, so this is ridiculous."

"Tori, you can't shut men out of your life because of your parents. Even if a marriage does end in divorce, it's painful, but most people don't act like that. They're destructive and you're letting them destroy your life along with theirs."

"Cake," she whispered.

Hailey took the two slices out and put them on paper plates. "I don't have any ice cream to go with them."

"Ugh. No ice cream."

The first bite of double chocolate didn't exactly soothe her soul, but at least it was almost impossible to burst into tears with a mouthful of cake. The second bite started the soothing process.

"Tell me why you're so worried about hurting Max."

Tori waved her fork in a gesture of despair. "Because I love him."

"This is progress."

"Not really. Like I told him, there's a fine line between love and hate and it's too easy for that line to be blurred. Nobody has the power to hurt you more than the person who loves you the most."

Hailey sighed. "I knew you were struggling with your parents' divorce and doing the cynical thing, but I honestly thought when you met the right man, you'd realize that the shit they've done doesn't define love and marriage."

"Have you ever looked Matt in the eye and hurt him?"

"Yes, I have. When he came to me, wanting to make everything better, and I sent him away. It ripped my heart out."

Tori used the edge of her fork to cut off another bite of cake. "Then you know how much love can hurt."

"I also know I wasn't cruel. And neither was he. And we got past it because we loved each other. I know love is amazing and wonderful and sometimes painful, but always worth it."

"I'm afraid I'd be cruel." Tori stared at the cake on her fork, trying to will away a fresh wave of tears.

"You're not a cruel person. You're just not. And, no, don't tell me your mother isn't either because, maybe you didn't see it, but she's been an unhappy person for a long time and that's why she's so miserable. You would never say the things your mother has said to *anybody,* never mind to Max."

"You're my best friend. You're supposed to take my side and make me feel better, so of course you're going to say that."

Hailey got up to refill their waters. "No, because I'm

your best friend, I'm telling you the truth. You're going to lose a great guy because you're a hot mess."

"I'd deny that if I wasn't sobbing in your kitchen, eating your husband's leftover cake because the man I love said he loves me."

"Wow." Hailey set the glass down. "When you put it like that, you're even more screwed up than I thought."

Tori made a sound that was almost a laugh, then drank some of the water. "I read the books you got for me. They made a lot of sense to me and they've really helped, but...I panicked. When he said he loved me, everything I'd read just flew out of my head. What am I going to do?"

"You're going to go home and go to bed. I can drive you if you want, and Matt and I can drop off your car tomorrow. Or you can stay here."

Tori finished off the last bite of cake and washed it down with more water. "I'm okay to drive now. I just didn't know what to do and I needed to talk. Although I was hoping for something more helpful than 'go home and go to bed.'"

Hailey shrugged. "Nobody can talk you out of this fear you have of ending up like your parents. We've tried. You have to trust yourself to have a relationship, or it's not going to work."

Tori shoved a couple of tissues in her pocket, just in case, and walked to the door. Hailey gave her a long, hard hug and then held her by the shoulders. "You need to let things settle and then think about what you really want."

"I blew it, Hailey."

"Not if he loves you. It doesn't just disappear like

that. He's hurt, maybe even angry, but he'll understand and he'll still love you. But you have to let him."

"I think you're right about going home and going to bed." She was so exhausted she could hardly think straight. Not that she wanted to. Not thinking would be preferable.

"Thank you." She hugged Hailey again. "And thank Matt for me. It's freezing out there. Hurry up and text him that it's safe to come home."

"Are you kidding? He and Bear live for this crap. Me? I'm going back to the couch. Call me tomorrow."

Tori had to mop her eyes a couple of times, but this time she made it all the way home and into her bed before the tears came again.

MAX WENT THROUGH the next few days on autopilot. He woke, worked, ate because it was a habit, and slept.

It didn't dull the pain of losing Tori, but he didn't think anything could. He just had to keep going through the motions until the routine became a comfort again and not a daily reminder that he'd almost had everything he wanted and blown it.

He'd run what had happened between them over and over in his mind until he'd almost driven himself mad. Every word. Every gesture. Every facial expression. Every moment of his last day with Tori was imprinted in his memory and he couldn't shake it.

He also couldn't figure out how to make it better.

Because he did nothing but work, he finished the Farmall tractor before he expected and sent an email to Josh that it was done. Josh responded that he'd swing by Thursday afternoon, and Max didn't bother trying to nail him down to a specific time. It didn't matter. He just told him to ring the doorbell instead of knocking, because it would chime in the basement.

When the doorbell sounded, a little after three, Max went upstairs and let Josh in. "Thanks for coming over. I would have delivered it, but I wasn't sure who else knew about it and there was no way Rose was going to let me deliver a box without questioning me about the contents. And I think I'd crack pretty quickly."

"I don't mind stopping by. And we all crack eventually."

Max led him down into the basement and went to the shelf where he'd set the Farmall. "I assume this is going to be on display, rather than played with, right?"

"It'll probably be on a shelf, but there's a good chance Sarah will get her hands on it at least once."

"It'll stand up to being run around the floor, but there's a weak spot in the paint, so it's best if it doesn't go outside too often. I did my best to blend the new paint and the old, and I put a protective clear coat over the entire bottom, but I wanted to preserve this."

Max took the tractor off the shelf and turned it upside down. When he pointed to the belly of the tractor, he watched Josh's expression change from one of curiosity to something like awe. Crudely scratched in the old paint, probably with a small pocketknife, were the initials FK.

"My dad," Josh said quietly. "Frank."

"I was using a wire brush to clear some of the crud away and once the corner of the F started showing, I went to a brush with softer bristles so I wouldn't damage the letters. By feathering out the edges of the old paint surrounding the initials, I was able to cover them with the new paint and then seal the whole thing, so it shouldn't lift."

He watched Josh run his thumb over his father's initials and stopped talking. The guy didn't care about the work process that had gone into it. He was thinking about a man he'd loved and lost.

After a minute, Josh blew out a breath and looked over the rest of the tractor. "This is amazing, Max. And not just the way you saved the initials. You do incredible work."

"Thank you."

"I bet it looked exactly like this when my dad played with it. It looks like a boy's tractor, but not one that was forgotten in a barn for decades."

"That's my specialty."

Josh pulled out his wallet. "How much do I owe you?"

"Fifty dollars."

"That's not enough, Max. I don't know what you make doing this, since it's not really my business, but all I have to do is look around and I know it's more than fifty dollars. You're an artist."

"I'm charging you fifty dollars because this is a gift from you to your brother and that requires some investment on your part. But doing that tractor was special to me. You guys are my friends and being able to do this is also my gift to you."

Josh pulled the money from his wallet and set it on the workbench, then tucked the wallet back in his pocket so he could shake Max's hand. "I appreciate it."

"I have a box for it here." Max took the tractor, wrapped it in thin bubble wrap and set it into the foam insert he'd cut to fit it earlier. Then he put the lid on the box and handed it back to Josh.

He hadn't been lying. Working on the Farmall *had* been a special experience for him. There was an underlying sense of history and nostalgia in model railroading—the capturing of a bygone day in HO scale—and quite often people modeled tableaus that meant something to them. The flag stop where the farmer's son had brought the milk to the train. A section of the B&O where a boy had chased trains with his grandfather.

But the Farmall was different. He knew Josh and Mitch, and they'd lost their dad. He still had his and he couldn't imagine losing him. So when he'd seen those initials crudely carved into the tractor's belly, it had become a mission to preserve them. Seeing the look on Josh's face had been worth it.

Once they were back upstairs, Josh didn't immediately head toward the door. "Do you want to talk, Max?"

"About what?" He closed the basement door and reset the alarm.

"Anything?"

"The last time you suggested we talk, you were trying to win a bet with Katie. I don't really have any more secrets."

"People are worried about you."

"Ah." Max interlaced his fingers, rubbing his left palm with his right thumb. "I guess everybody knows that Tori and I had a falling-out."

"It's not something that's being gossiped about over tea. But the people who care about you—about both of you—know. You haven't been into town or the diner. You're going back to being the mysterious recluse and we don't want to see that happen."

"I think it would be very hard for me to see Tori right now."

"You want to have a beer?"

Max frowned. "At three-thirty on a Thursday afternoon?"

"Why the hell not?"

"Okay. Why the hell not?"

They went into the kitchen and Max grabbed a couple of beers from the fridge. Josh set his box on the island and popped the tab on the can Max handed him.

"Are you going to let her go?" Josh asked him.

"Since everybody's finally figuring out I'm not really a serial killer, chaining her in my basement would be a bad move." The attempt at humor didn't make him feel any better.

"Have you talked to her since you…had a falling-out, as you put it?"

"No." Max shifted the Farmall box, lining it up precisely parallel to the edge of the counter. "She was very upset and I don't want to upset her again."

"Maybe she freaked out and now she's too proud or something to reach out to you."

Hope flamed through Max. "Do you know if that's the case?"

"No, I don't. Husbands and boyfriends are only given the bare minimum of details. But I do know she was wrecked. You're not the only one hurting." Josh took a long swig of beer. "All I'm saying is don't give up. Maybe don't push too hard, but don't give up."

"I'm trying to understand the way she thinks, but I'm lost."

"Buddy, we've *all* been there."

EVERY TIME HER phone rang for days, Tori's heart would leap in anticipation of it being Max. It never was.

She should call him. She knew he hadn't been in the diner since Sunday and she couldn't bear the thought of him going back to staying in his basement all the time because of her. But she was so afraid she'd make things worse, she never actually brought herself to make the call.

This time when the phone rang, it was her mother. Again. As tempting as it was to ignore the call again, they were coming more frequently now. She picked up the phone. "Hi, Mom."

"Hi, honey. I thought I was going to get your voice mail again. Do you ever check those?"

"I've been a little under the weather, Mom." She winced, realizing she couldn't use the flu excuse in case Jilly still planned to use it to save Thanksgiving. "I'm sorry."

"Do you have any idea what's going on with Jilly? She's not returning my calls. You do all realize Thanksgiving is next week, right?"

"Yes, we do. And I don't know about Aunt Jilly, Mom. I haven't seen her lately. She's probably busy and forgot to call you back. There's been a lot going on with Gav—"

"I don't think it's too much to ask for a person to return a phone call."

Tori sighed. If her mother didn't care what was happening in her daughter's life, it stood to reason she wasn't going to care about her nephew's, either. "If I see her, I'll give her a nudge."

"Thank you. It would be nice to have my sister's support in these trying times. Your father has a new girlfriend. Did I tell you that? I should feel sorry for her. It won't be long before she realizes what a sorry piece of—"

"Mom!" Tori felt something inside of her snap. "Do you realize that's my dad you're talking about?"

"Of course I know he's your father."

"He's my *dad*. It hurts me when you say awful things about him, just like it hurts me when he says things about you. You're my parents. Both of you. Still. You may have divorced each other, but you're not divorced from me."

"This isn't about you, Victoria. This is about—"

"You know what, Mom? I'm sorry you're unhappy. I'm sorry Dad's unhappy. But I'm not letting either of you make *me* unhappy anymore."

"Victoria Jean Burns!"

"When you call me, you can ask about me and you can tell me what's going on with you, but if you mention Dad, I will hang up on you. And I'm going to tell him the same thing and I mean it. I'm sick of your anger and the petty comments and…all of this."

"Of course I'm angry with your father. Do you know what he did? He—"

For the first time in her life, Tori hung up on a person. The fact it was her mother made her hands shake slightly, but she would do it again. And again and again until her parents got the message.

She was done giving their unhappiness power over her life.

Her parents were weak. It wasn't strength that had held their marriage together for so long. It was fear of walking away and starting over. So they'd stewed in resentment for years, hiding it from everybody because neither of them had the guts to end their misery, until it boiled over in a steaming heap of anger and hate they flung at each other, not caring that it burned their daughter in the process.

It wasn't love that turned her parents on each other. It was the *lack* of love and clinging to something that made them miserable and bitter because they were too afraid to go out and find what made them happy.

Tori wasn't weak. She was stronger than her parents. She was strong enough to take a chance on love and, if it didn't work out, she was strong enough to part ways before it got ugly.

She just needed to be strong enough to face the man she'd hurt figuring it out.

TWENTY-TWO

MAX WASN'T SURE how long he looked at the photo of Tori on his phone after Josh left, or how many times he had to tap it with his thumb to keep the screen from going dark.

He hadn't known when he took the photo that she'd be the woman he'd fall in love with. He only knew he'd been drawn to her friendly, funny nature and wanted to get to know her better.

But I do know she was wrecked.

He couldn't shake Josh's words. No matter how much it had hurt to watch her walk out the door without looking back, he couldn't stand the thought of her hurting, too.

Before he could talk himself out of it, he hit the button to call her. Then, drumming his fingers on the island counter, he waited. It rang three times and he was already wondering if he was about to get her voice mail because she was working or if she didn't want to talk to him when he heard her voice. "Hello, Max."

"Hi. I…" Now he had no idea what to say. Maybe he should have called Colin first. Or Josh. "I want to make sure you're okay."

"I'm okay. Not great. But I'm okay. Are you?"

"I miss you." He realized belatedly that could sound like pressure. "But I'm okay, too."

"I guess *okay* is going to replace *nice* in the 'words

we use to avoid saying what we really mean' category, huh?"

He realized at some point he'd stood and was pacing, and forced himself to sit down. "So you're not okay."

"I'm trying to be. I've been doing some thinking—some soul-searching—and trying to get my head on straight."

"I'm sorry I pushed, Tori. I knew you weren't ready, but I zeroed in on what I wanted, which was you. And I'm very direct. Too direct, I guess."

"You didn't do anything wrong. I never want you to hide how you feel about anything from me. Even if it's how you feel about me." She was quiet for a few seconds. "I'm glad you called. I've been thinking about calling you, but I wasn't sure if I should."

"You're still my friend, Tori. I didn't stop suddenly caring about you."

"You haven't been coming into town. I hate that you're isolating yourself again and it's my fault."

"As much as I like eating at the diner, that's your place of business. It would be wrong of me to show up there while you're working."

"I appreciate that. But you're still *my* friend, too. I guess I haven't been a very good one, but I mean it."

He wasn't sure what to say to that. It was nice to know they could still be friends, but he didn't think he was ready to walk into the diner and face her over a cup of coffee and half a turkey sandwich.

"I miss you, too, Max," she said quietly.

Fresh pain hit him like a fist and he swallowed hard. He wanted to tell her he'd stop into the diner or invite her over to watch another Marvel movie, but he couldn't get the words out.

"Maybe I'll call you tomorrow," he said, which was the best he could do.

"I hope so. I've missed the sound of your voice."

"I'm going to go now, but I'll talk to you soon."

"Bye, Max."

He hit the button to end the call and set the phone on the counter. He was conflicted—part of him happy that she sounded okay and wanted to remain friends, and another part angry that she was okay because he didn't want to be just friends.

Being conflicted made him anxious, so he rolled up his sleeves to do some cleaning. Anything to calm the jumpiness he'd been feeling since Josh had given him hope that all wasn't lost with Tori.

It wasn't until he went to take the garbage bag out of the can and saw the bulletin board on the fridge that he realized he hadn't made out his lists for November. He'd been too busy getting ready for the Halloween party.

Staring at October's lists, he looked at what he'd written over a month before.

Find a date.

He'd never even bothered to cross it off. Ripping the page off the bulletin board, he crumpled the paper in his fist and threw it across the room.

TORI WALKED OUT of her apartment not even five minutes after hanging up the phone. Now that she'd heard Max's voice, she needed to see him. She had things to say that weren't meant for cell phone conversations.

During the drive to his house, she tried to imagine what she might say to him, but it didn't matter. She knew as soon as he opened the door and she looked into those intense green eyes, she would forget anything she rehearsed anyway.

All she could do was hope that when the time came, she'd find the right words to say.

When she'd hung up on her mother, the tight and suffocating fear had started loosening its hold on her. Love hadn't poisoned her parents. They were, as Max had said that day in the grass, just simply assholes. Acknowledging it and cutting it out of her life had felt like cutting loose a cement block tied around her ankle, slowly dragging her under.

But it was seeing his name on her cell phone's screen, and his quiet voice asking her if she was okay that had pulled her to the surface.

She pulled into his driveway and took a deep breath before getting out of the car. Then, hoping she wouldn't get the same reaction she had the last time she showed up unexpectedly, she knocked on the door.

Max opened it, and his expression gave her nothing to go on. Somehow that was even worse than horror. His hair was tousled and his sleeves were rolled up, which was probably the most disheveled she'd ever seen him outside of bed.

Knowing he was probably trying to process the fact she was standing on his step rather than being rude by not saying anything, she smiled. "Can I come in?"

"Oh. Of course."

She followed him into the house and closed the door behind her. He leaned against the stove, his hands clasped.

"I'm sorry, Max. I'm sorry I let a relationship that had nothing to do with us torpedo ours."

"It didn't have *nothing* to do with us. They're your parents."

"I told her I didn't want to hear it anymore. I hung up on her."

"That was probably very hard. I'm sorry she made it come to that, but I think you'll be happier."

"I already am. I realized, afterward, that I'm not even *capable* of being like her. I could never behave like that to anybody. Especially you. And it was always about me and my fear of becoming my mother. I was afraid I'd hurt you, but I never believed you'd hurt me. I hope you know that."

"I know that sometimes things happen in life that cause fears that don't make sense to anybody else, but that doesn't make them any less real. I hope recognizing that what happened between your parents—and you—isn't normal helps."

"It did. But it was you. I freaked out and was totally unreasonable—and yes, I admit that—and I hurt you, but you still called to make sure I was okay. I trust you and you helped me trust myself.

"I love you, Max. I'm sorry I was too afraid to tell you that. I was so afraid to admit it to myself. But you are…amazing. There's nobody else I'd rather spend time with and you're not only my friend. You've become my best friend."

Finally, he moved toward her. Putting his finger under her chin, he tipped her face up and looked her in the eye. "I love you, too, Tori. I've waited my whole life to find you."

Relief flooded through her, making her knees weak.

Max was hers. Sweet, shy, sexy Max who hated the way she loaded his dishwasher but didn't say so because he was willing to make room for her in his regularly scheduled life.

"I guess *Operation—Makeover Max* is a qualified success," she said.

He winced. "It had a name?"

"Of course. Everything's more fun when it has a name."

"Why is it qualified?"

She grinned. "Well, I was supposed to make *you* over, not the other way around."

"I got a date to agree to let me take her home while I was wearing a Hannibal Lecter mask. I'm calling it a win."

Laughing, she threw her arms around his neck as he lifted her up to kiss her. Not until they needed to come up for air did he set her back on her feet.

He tucked a strand of hair behind her ear. "So, my fair lady, is this the part where I push you up against the wall, kiss you until you can't breathe and then bang you right here on the floor?"

"Let's get off this ceramic tile and you can ask me again."

* * * * *

Laura Caldwell

**Everyone knows it takes more than a darling
goldendoodle to save a marriage...**

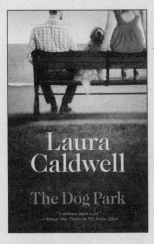

Stylist Jessica Champlin and
her ex-husband, investigative
journalist Sebastian Hess, had too
many differences for even their
beloved dog, Baxter, to reconcile.
So they've agreed to joint
custody, and life has settled into
a prickly normalcy.

But when Baxter heroically
rescues a child and the video goes
viral, life takes an unexpected
twist. Jess's new line of dogwear
becomes wildly successful, and
suddenly everyone is watching—
the press, the new guy she's
seeing, Sebastian and the past she
never imagined facing again. Soon there's only one person by her
side—and it's the person she least expected. Jess is willing to open
up to a new normal...as long as Baxter approves.

Available now, wherever books are sold!

New York Times Bestselling Author

MARIE FORCE

In book four of the *Fatal* series, a killer plays
a dangerous game…

Back from their honeymoon, Senator Nick Cappuano and D.C. Police
Lieutenant Sam Holland are ready for some normalcy. Until Sam discovers
wedding cards containing thinly veiled death threats.

Already on edge, a new series of baffling murders leave Sam feeling like she's
chasing her tail. With no obvious connection between the victims, she soon
suspects that she may be the ultimate prize in the killer's clever game. When
the danger starts to hit a little too close to home, she has two goals: find the
murderer, and live long enough to enjoy happily-ever-after.

FATAL FLAW
Available now, wherever books are sold.

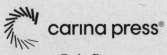

www.CarinaPress.com

shannon stacey

00228	TAKEN WITH YOU	___ $7.99 U.S.	___ $8.99 CAN.
00225	LOVE A LITTLE SIDEWAYS	___ $7.99 U.S.	___ $8.99 CAN.

(limited quantities available)

TOTAL AMOUNT	$ _____
POSTAGE & HANDLING	$ _____
($1.00 for 1 book, 50¢ for each additional)	
APPLICABLE TAXES*	$ _____
TOTAL PAYABLE	$ _____

(check or money order—please do not send cash)

To order, complete this form and send it, along with a check or money order for the total amount, payable to Carina Press, to: **In the U.S.:** 3010 Walden Avenue, P.O. Box 9077, Buffalo, NY 14269-9077; **In Canada:** P.O. Box 636, Fort Erie, Ontario, L2A 5X3.

Name: _____

Address: _____ City: _____

State/Prov.: _____ Zip/Postal Code: _____

Account Number (if applicable): _____

075 CSAS

*New York residents remit applicable sales taxes.
*Canadian residents remit applicable GST and provincial taxes.

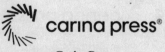

carina press®

www.CarinaPress.com

CARSS0814BL